Believe

a novel

by Geoffrey Visgilio

2nd Edition

ISBN-13: 978-1-7330709-0-4

This book is for Chrissy.

Prologue

There is a flash of white and I'm on the train.

I don't really remember how I got here, but I guess it doesn't matter. I follow the same colorless path I always do. I rise, perpetually surprised by the toll of the hangover from the night before. I shower, chug Advil from the bottle, and mentally prepare myself for a job that is meaningless to me. I select clothes bought from a thrift store and stuff a uniform I should really wash into a backpack that is weathered and fraying. I spend at least an hour debating the thing I shouldn't be debating until I force myself to choke it back down for another day. Maybe something will change. Maybe I'll change. But my faith in that is also fraying.

I've lived in New York, DC, Florida, California for a while, trying to outdistance myself from what's inside my head, but it always finds me. In AA, they call these "geographical cures". I go to meetings sometimes. I hate the

Jesus bullshit, and I'll never concede that I have a problem. No one is making me go either, though I suspect if I slide down this path much farther, that could happen. Sometimes I talk, mostly I listen. I find bizarre comfort in those meetings; anonymity is the grand equalizer. It doesn't matter if you're a lawyer, or a doctor, or a hotshot hedge-fund manager, when some sad bastard starts reading off the Preamble, everyone is equally pathetic.

I settled on Boston because New England is home. What did I expect to find here? Restoration? Rebirth? Catharsis, I suspect. Something. I've caused too much damage, burned too many bridges, been careless with too many trusting hearts to keep wandering. But I can't stop searching – that part of me never tires. So I came home, back to where it began. In the callow flourish of spring or in the desolate love song of winter, I suppose I've been trying to decipher the source of me. The root of it all. But there are only ghosts here, rattling at me with derisive glee from behind the wreckage of my past.

I know why I came. I won't admit it to you, anymore than I'll admit I have a problem with booze, or drugs, or depression, or self-loathing. You I'll lie to all day long, with a skillful cunning that would surprise you. I can even lie to myself, to some degree. When you've pretended a life as long as I have, the lines bleed and sometimes you can forget yourself. But I know. As the days wear on and nothing changes and I drag myself to wait for the train every afternoon, the truth becomes clearer and clearer.

I've come home to die.

Book One
BEFORE

"And what have you got?
At the end of the day?
What have you got, to take away?
A bottle of whiskey and a new set of lies.
Blinds on the windows
And a pain behind your eyes."

-Dire Straits

Chapter One

Dreams I've Had

I wasn't always like this. Once I knew love. Happiness. The warm gooshy center of my little life. That time has passed. But if we're really going to go back to the source of me, the decaying root of it all, then we need to go back to the beginning. To the place where it hurts the most.

***

It had been an odd summer, oppressive and humid, with rolling thunderstorms in the afternoons. The skies would darken and open as black storms lumbered past. The evenings that followed were wet and sticky, full of bugs and the thickening rustle of flora run riot. It was weather more suited to the Carolinas or to Florida than coastal New England. Even the sea breeze that would usually drive out the worst of the humidity was absent. The moisture of the sea melded with the hanging heat of the sky and a formidable blanket of soupy fog covered the coast from Maine down through Connecticut.

And our parents were spooked.

It's humbling for children to see their parents truly afraid. They are supposed to be superhuman protectors orbiting about you like ever-attentive satellites. The retinue of a child king. When your parents bow to fear, whether it's a small, sad sink of the shoulders or infectious panic, it stays. It takes root. It has the ability to rattle the sense of fearlessness that surrounds childhood, the unspoken promise of exploration without punishment. It makes kids understand that if their parents are afraid, there are things from which there can be no protection. Chinks in the armor.

It's worse when they try to hide it. They may smile and pedantically lecture you about one phantom danger or another, making you echo stern warnings back to them until they're satisfied it's sunk in. But there's uncertainty in their eyes that flares up when they look away, or when they share a knowing look with the other parent. It feels like it would only take the smallest of efforts to turn that thin line of panic into an ugly black smear.

That summer it was the missing kids and the dirty gray van. And there was no hiding it; our parents wanted us to see they were afraid. Four kids had been abducted on four separate occasions starting at the beginning of June. By the middle of July a body turned up that had been so brutalized, the fate of the other three kids looked equally grim. The only unifying facts in the case were that each of the kids was picked up in a dirty gray van and each was alone at the time.

Witnesses had described it as a dirty, dingy, unremarkable gray. That people couldn't be on the lookout for a van with a sinister color, like black or red, somehow made it worse. A dirty gray van could blend in with tourist traffic. No one paid attention to a grimy, beat up car in the summer. It prowled unseen, cloaked in dirt and dust, like it had passed through a dank place and bore the marks of its passing with pride. The absence of color, the permeability of evil, had developed an almost talismanic power over us kids.

But our parents were all about the isolation factor. The kidnappers could have been driving a lurid red El Dorado; it didn't matter. The kids were alone. Alone meant the game was up. So we all got a big sit-down about the rules that summer.

Always tell us where you're going and who's with you. Call if you're going to be late. Call if you need a ride. This is money for a taxi-this is not money for candy or comic books. Don't be afraid to go up to a policeman or an adult if you're afraid. Don't go in anyone's house. Don't get into anyone's car. Always keep track of your group. Don't wander off. Trust your gut. And never, never go anywhere alone.

This was Rhode Island in the eighties. I was ten. Nothing like this had ever happened in the state; people were horrified. But it didn't take long for the shock to evolve into a grim, community-wide call for vigilance. There was an understanding among local restaurants, train stations, and bus depots that kids had unrestricted access to the phone. Taxis offered free rides and the cops had a special number you could call if you were stuck or saw something out of place.

My dad was all about strategy. He pulled me aside and gave me the lowdown on how a swift kick to the crotch or sand thrown in someone's eyes could give me time to run away and get help. My mother and I went with him up to Boston for a weekend conference and at the hotel he instructed me to always walk in the center of the hallway, no matter what. If I hugged one side of the hall, someone watching through a peephole could throw open the door and snatch me inside the room, locking the door behind them. They could kill me while he screamed for help and hammered at the door.

"Don't make their job any easier," he would say. "I can't get to you if they get you behind the door."

Fear is an astonishing teacher of children. My imagination would spin horrifying visions of what could happen to me on the other side of a hotel room door. Not only would I always walk in the center of the hallway, I did it in every hallway.

I do it to this day.

***

My mother was much more practical, if a little less rational, about dealing with potential kidnappings. She simply kept me with her at all times. If I fell out of her line of site, I wasn't following the rules. She followed this doctrine to the extreme. Imagine a ten year old kid in a public men's restroom at the mall, trying to pee and shout out numbers so she can hear that he's not being abducted behind the door. All the while other men and boys are looking at him like he's gone insane.

1…2…3…4-

(*I don't hear counting!*)

-5...6...7...8...

But we were carefree that afternoon. The two of us. In the middle of August, a cold snap with a brisk wind had risen and swatted the gloomy wetness off the coast. We woke to streaming sunshine and clear blue skies. Tufts and strands of white darted the blue and the air was dry and hot. The breeze that sighed off the ocean beckoned us to play at the foot of lapping waves in the soft, crumbling sand.

We were in the kitchen and I was cleaning up plates after breakfast. My mother made sandwiches, packing them into our little Igloo beach cooler with some Caprisun and those flat, blue cooler packs that never seem to keep anything very cold for long. She promised a quick stop at J.C. Penney to look for something to wear outside before we headed down to East beach.

That the trip to J.C. Penney would be quick, there was no question. My mother was known about town as a bit of a lead foot. She would tear around in her little brown Datsun hatchback at breakneck speeds on even the smallest errand. The police knew her by name and the kids at school had nicknamed her the Brown Baron. Or sometimes just, the Baron. But while the Baron would get us there in a flash, time would halt inside the store and I would have to work to get her out if we were going to see any time at the beach.

I loved this time with her. She would sing Karen Carpenter songs to me among the clothes.

We've only just begun — to live.

She would toss on boas or wrap scarves around her head like Jackie-O. We would make faces at each other and I would hover near her while she would try things on in the three-way mirrors, climbing into the racks of clothes and losing myself among them. I found, if I worked my way through clothes on the circular racks, I'd find myself alone in the center with a fort of wool, cloth, and linen surrounding me. A secret spot. I would always pretend I was pushing through the clothes to find another world like the little girl in *The Lion, the Witch, and the Wardrobe.*

White lace and promises.

When I was smaller, she would take me in the dressing room with her. She would chat and gossip with me like I was one of her girlfriends. She would check herself in the mirror from every conceivable angle and try various poses with assorted faces, turning to me for final approval when she'd narrowed down her favorites. The small room would resonate with her high, infectious laughter, the papery sound of clothing moving against skin, and the tender soar of her voice.

A kiss for luck and we're on our way.

But I had lost interest playing games among the racks, and at ten, I was too old to accompany my mother into the dressing room. When I asked her why, she pursed her lips a bit and her eyes fluttered, color reddening her cheeks.

"Because I'm a *lady*, Jared. And you're getting older."

All this meant to me was that I would be sequestered to some uncomfortable chair outside a dressing room, likely shouting out numbers as she frowned her way through an enormous pile of clothing. She was my whole world at ten. Even on a day like that Friday, I would indulge her. But not for long. Not with that tidal pull to the outside, tugging us to come out into the beaming caress of the sun.

That day was one-in-a-million.

I put on board shorts and a semi-clean Hobie shirt and I was poking around my room, looking for my flip-flops. She came in with the cooler in one arm and towels tucked under the other, my flip-flops dangling from the end of her finger. She had on these Jaclyn Smith bellbottom jeans and a faded yellow shirt tied at her belly. Her fall of brown hair was up in a bandanna and she had on these big, fish-eye sunglasses that covered most of her face.

"Ready, Freddy?"

"Ready, Betty."

She grinned and waggled her finger at me. I retrieved my flip-flops and followed her out to the garage. We loaded up the umbrella into the hatch and we were off, windows open, The Supremes pouring out from the radio into the lush morning. My mother's laugh was giddy as her little brown Datsun revved down our street and out onto East Avenue with a spirited chirp of screeching tires.

***

Outside the dressing room at J.C. Penney, I was swinging my heels in an uncomfortable chair, talking with my mother while she was trying on clothes. It had already been twenty minutes. It's easier to forget about evil when the sun is shining, but when you're a parent, you never all-the-way forget. There's always that burning ember of rote habit if nothing else.

"Do I have to count?" I had asked.

My face was serious, eyes frowning. She let loose a girlish gale. She shook her head, smiling.

"No, but the floor is hot lava."

I rolled my eyes at her. "Are you serious?"

"Lake of fire."

She made a long, loopy figure-eight motion around the room with her finger.

"But mom, that's so gay-"

She took off the sunglasses and the smile was replaced with steel.

"Excuse me, Buster Brown?"

I groaned and settled into the chair. "Fine. Are you happy?"

"Just talk to me," she said. "Is that so bad? Talking to your mother?"

I shook my head, sullen, and she ducked into the changing room.

"What do you want to talk about?" I called after her.

She was humming to herself and I didn't think she'd even heard me when she called back.

"Tell me about camp."

I had one of the new kids ask me if I wanted to touch his dick in the changing stalls by the beach. The older kids had tipped the outhouse on Butch Kennedy earlier in the week and he had flipped out, screaming, running around the main camp, covered in shit, crying until three of the counselors hosed him down and called his parents. I had tried a cigarette out on the lake in a sailboat. We had all watched in stunned silence as one of the counselors slapped a kid to the ground for mouthing off during the morning Pledge of Allegiance, kicking him in the ass until he was facedown in the dirt. And there was a girl. Angela Nova. Exploring, wandered off, we found this hidden blackberry grove and she kissed me there. None of this was the sort of thing I could tell my mother.

"Camp is boring."

My mother, who knew that camp was in fact, not boring, had found a folded note from Angela in the back pocket of my swim trunks. She pressed the issue.

"No sunshine," she mused. "You guys have been all cooped up. What sort of stuff do you do when it rains?"

The note, passed from Angela as our boats came alongside each other in a race, said simply: *meet me at the place after you furl your boat.* Signed: *Angie.*

"We play board games in the barn. Do arts and crafts mostly. Sometimes we explore."

My mother suspected what kind of exploring was going on and it didn't set well with her. It probably involved furling, whatever that was, and with some loose girl named Angie. She knew the song.

Angie, Angie, when will those clouds all disappear?

"Exploring sounds fun," she said, more a question than an opinion.

"It doesn't suck," I said noncommittally.

"Angie better not suck either," she said under her breath.

"What did you say, Mom?" I asked.

"Nothing," she called out. "Nothing. I said nothing."

I heard something crash against the inner wall of her dressing stall, a surprised *Oooh*, and she was laughing in great, heaving belly laughs. I shook my head and frowned like my father did when my mother had done something loud or picked a fight with someone or cracked herself up at an inappropriate time.

She's my wife, folks, he would say. *You can't have her.*

While my mother tried to get herself under control, I was thinking about how Angela stopping to tie her shoelace had started the whole thing. The group moved on without us and she spotted the wall, hidden way back off the trail, almost completely covered by trees and vines. Up and over, protected by a stone-wall on two sides and a copse of thick trees surrounding it, was a tiny, run-wild grove of blackberry bushes.

Later, laid back against the wall, sated after we'd eaten our fill, knowing people were looking for us and not caring, I noticed she'd stained her camp shirt with blackberry juice just under her chin. And when I pointed to it her hands were on my face, her mouth at mine, and the ripe tang of blackberries hit me at the moment I closed my eyes. Wasn't there a song my dad liked?

Oh Angie, don't you weep, all your kisses still taste sweet.

"So who do you go exploring with?" came my mother's voice, composed, calm, questing. We were back to fishing.

"Just the gang, mom," I said.

The gang consisted of a pair of blonde twin boys who had grown up with me, a tomboy from down the street who always had dirty knees, and a brother and sister pair who were inseparable since their parents divorced. A few other kids wandered in and out of the scene from time to time, but this was the core group of kids I spent most of my summers with. My mother saw no immediate threat in this gaggle of usual suspects, but she was willing to bet that a loose fish was swimming just below the surface. She'd seen us cover up for each other in the past. So the game continued.

"These are the kids that you do that hunt around the camp every week with, right?" she asked.

"The scavenger hunts. Yeah, our team always wins," I said.

"Did you win this week?" she asked, baiting me. "I'll bet you did."

We had, by a very narrow margin. The other four teams had younger kids on them and no one had the guts to try and get a live horseshoe crab. That's what put us over the top. We came running back into base camp cheering and hooting with a stunned and harmless horseshoe crab in Tucker's metal pail.

"We won because we brought back a live horseshoe crab," I told her, brimming with self-satisfaction.

"That's gross, Jared," she said.

"They can't hurt you, mom," I told her. "But they are kind of gross."

"Were you scared?" she asked.

"No way. Tucker was freaked out. And Angela was scared. But only a little."

"Angela?"

She tricked me.

"Shit," I said aloud.

"What was that, honey?" she asked, and while her tone was sweet, the satisfaction underneath told me she knew damn well what I had said.

"Nothing, mom," I said, hoping that now we all knew there was an elephant in the room, maybe we didn't have to talk about it.

"So who's Angela?"

Not a chance.

"Shit," I said again, but with no voice behind it.

I sank deeper into the chair and brought my legs up so I could hug my knees.

"She's just this girl who hangs around us. Jeez."

"Do I know her?"

"I don't *know*, mom. Do you know her?"

She was quick on the rebound.

"Watch that mouth, Jared," she said, with no trace of sweetness.

"Sorry," I moaned and corrected myself. "No. I don't think you know her."

"What do her parents do?" she asked.

"Her dad's a veterinarian. They have a bunch of dogs."

My mother loved all dogs. We had a scruffy medium poodle and she made him wear these awful reindeer antlers that tied under his chin during the holidays. She would knit him these embarrassing sweaters with snowmen on them. And once she had the groomers shave him to actually look like a poodle and he shit the bed, specifically her side. So whether all dogs returned my mother's love remained in question. But you could do a lot worse than a vet's kid.

"And what about her mother?"

"Her mom died."

Angie, you're beautiful, but ain't it time we said goodbye.

"Is Angela nice?" she called, her voice a bit uneven.

"Yeah, she's cool."

She was a lot more than cool, actually. She was twelve and she swore all the time and talked back to adults. She smoked cigarettes. She punched one of the bigger kids in the nose three times before he hit the ground when he called her "Tits" during free swim. She could do a bang-up impression of counselor Betty (the Backside) Croy's monotone, nasal voice. She was a great sailor and good with knots. She could keep secrets. She liked to wander off. But most of all, she was-

"Is she pretty?"

Mindreader, I thought and I almost got a fundamental understanding of the nature of women right there, but I was too young and it was too big. And so I lost it for almost twenty-five years.

"Mom, she's just a girl okay?"

"Okay, okay," she said and finally dropped it.

But she was humming to herself in the dressing stall.

***

Ten minutes later, this older, heavyset man who looked like a stockboy came awkwardly foraging through the summer sundresses with a jar of Dum-Dum lollipops tucked under one arm like a football.

"Are you lost?" he asked.

His nose was running and he was pale, a few beads of sweat at his brow. He looked like he'd caught a bad spell of cold.

"Allergies," he chuffed, reading my expression. "Are you lost?"

I shook my head slowly and thumbed behind me to the dressing room.

"My mom's trying on half the store," I said.

"What did you say, Jared?" came my mother's voice, but she wasn't really listening.

"Nothing, mom," I smiled and shrugged my shoulders.

He recognized the gesture and responded in a perfect imitation.

Whaddya gonna do?

Man-to-man. This is how it is. He held out the jar to me. It was so primitive, such a simple way of communicating. We have something in common, we are well met, let me see what I have to share. The costumes and the customs have changed a bit, but we still act off those dim basic constants of human interaction.

"Want a pop?" he asked and shook the jar at me.

He was harmless, this guy. One good breeze would have blown him over. Kids have a keener sense of danger than adults give them credit for. He was not a psycho. A bit ungainly, maybe, but not a threat. Still, I could see an episode with the Baron, some heinous scene that would end with a broken jar and lollipops sprinkled throughout the women's sundresses.

"No thanks," I said and waved him away.

He frowned, tugged at his chin with his free hand, and took a few steps closer. It was as if he was doing complicated theorems in his mind. Kid plus lollipop equals happiness. Does not compute. I noticed as he stepped in that he smelled faintly of Vicks Vaporub and he was positively cracked on cold medication. He held the jar out again. Back to square one.

"You sure?" he asked, foggy puzzlement punctuating the question.

I nodded and thumbed to the dressing room again.

"She's crazy," I mouthed, making a little pinwheel with my finger to the side of my head.

He made a wan smile and nodded, that universal recognition again. But understanding didn't dawn in his face and he tried one more time to seal the deal.

"They're good," he attempted.

"Look," I said. "I'm not supposed to talk to strangers."

"You're God damned right you're not," my mother shouted and we both jumped.

She had chosen fervor over decorum and stormed out of the dressing room in her jeans and her bra and nothing else. A fussy firestorm with her hands on her hips like a commanding wartime general, she whacked me once on the shoulder, arm out and back to her hip in a flash.

"Who's this guy?"

"He works here."

"You work here?"

He nodded, tightening his hold over the Dum-Dums, tucking them into his chest like a pro footballer, as if anticipating an attack on the jar.

"What was he doing?" she asked me.

A quick snap of the hand, out and back.

"He was giving me a lollipop and-"

She cut me off and ran with it.

"What's with the lollipops, guy?"

"I thought-" he began, rolling his free hand in a tight orbit around his wrist, trying to goad the words.

"I thought he was lost," he said in a rush of air.

She put her hand up to him, palm out, waving it at him. *You stay put, buddy.* She ducked back into the dressing room and came out with her pocketbook, her sandals, and sunglasses. Still sans blouse. When she popped back out, it was go time.

"You go around giving little lost alone kids lollipops? What are you, some kind of a sicko?"

He was flummoxed and didn't know what to say, so he took a long, healthy look at the swell of her breasts. It was a look that I didn't fully understand at the time, but my mother got it just fine.

"Eyes front, soldier," she said and his head snapped up like a whip-crack.

She screwed up her face and gave him a once-over, no longer concerned that he was a threat of any kind. Now she was just driving it home.

"You got a name?" she asked, waving her hand impatiently at me to get up.

"Harold," he said without much enthusiasm.

"Listen here, Harris-" she started.

"Harold," he tried.

"You look like a Harris."

"It's Harold."

"Right. Listen. You're sweaty. And you're sick. Have your momma make you chicken soup when you get home."

"How do you know-"

"I know, Harris," she said and grabbed my hand. "Come on, let's go."

Harold looked after us, forlorn. I waved at him and shrugged my shoulders again.

We're still pals, right?

Harold waved his free hand out at me like he was swatting flies and nodded his head.

Hey, it's nothing, buddy.

I waved again and followed my half-naked mother out of J.C. Penney and into the August afternoon.

***

"I'll have to come back and get my blouse," she said, muttering under her breath.

"Why do you always embarrass me like that?" I accused her, angry.

"Oh come on," she teased, snapping the straps of her bra at me as if they were a pair of suspenders. "That was pretty funny."

"It's not funny!" I shouted, suddenly close to tears and not knowing why. "You always *do* this."

It *was* funny. Most of it. My mother was a character. We would tease her about it and she'd made enough good scenes in public that the town had things to talk about over the cabana walls during the summer. But this wasn't overreacting or some spunky, quirky kink my mom had adopted. It was a hovering, almost birdlike way of watching over me that carried such an-

(*adult*)

-awful intensity behind it.

I hated its scrutiny. It made her seem crazy, like she was checking me over for wounds, checking to make sure I was still there. Sometimes she'd look at me when she thought I couldn't see her. I'd watch her stare at me with a mix of greed and terror, fearful or maybe jealous that I was outgrowing her. It came out at odd moments and if she caught me looking, she'd flush. If I were close, she'd touch me somehow, brushing away lint or fiddling with a collar. She'd beam and her face would lift and her eyes would smile. But that haunting concern would never leave her fully. She wore it like a shroud.

Those looks always made me feel so small, like I couldn't take care of myself. I was a helpless baby bird that needed to be constantly minded lest it fall from the nest and into the world too soon. It felt like she was keeping something from me, some horrible truth that we just didn't talk about. What could be that bad? What could be bad enough that you look at your kid like you're not sure when you're going to see him again? It wasn't dirty gray vans. Not that many times, not for that long. Not when she got quiet for a while.

The question came, rising up over me like an ominous shadow peeking into the window late at night.

What is she so afraid of?

"I just get scared sometimes, Jared," she said and sighed deeply, her whole body sagging in the car seat.

Mindreader. It came again and I almost touched that tenuous ecstasy of understanding, but then it slipped away.

"I know, mom," I said, humoring her.

"No Jared," she snapped, red-faced. "You don't know. You don't know what it's like."

She tried to put the key in the ignition, but her hand was shaking. When I moved to help her, she slapped my hand away and dropped the keys, rubbing her forehead and screwing up her brow.

"I just need to sit. For a minute, Jared. Okay?" she said and sunk deeper into her seat.

"Okay, mom. Okay," I said, just going along with what she needed. "Let's open the windows, we'll get a breeze."

I rolled mine down and she was sort of gyrating in her seat and mumbling to herself. It was like she went from supercharged to worn-out in the space of a few minutes. She made no move to roll down her window and I climbed over her lap, turning the lever with my hand balanced on the steering wheel. I passed over her and I smelled-

(*sickness*)

-sweat and sunscreen and a faint hint of her perfume.

"Thank you, Jared," she said when the window was down and she patted me on the back absently like a drunk. "You're a good boy."

I settled back into my seat and soaked up the calming cross-breeze that passed through the open windows of the Datsun. My mother reached a hand out and found mine and held it to her leg, squeezing gently. The car was filled with the sound of her ragged breathing and the dusky sigh of the wind. I sat with her like this for almost an hour, thinking of blackberries and longevity with equal severity. When the key finally turned in the ignition, I knew we were going home.

"We're not going to the beach." I told her – it was not a question.

"I'm sorry, Jared. I've got a headache. I need to lie down," she said and I suddenly feared for the months ahead.

I nodded and she put a finger under my chin and brought my face up so she could look at me.

"We could stop for Del's lemonade on the way home?" she offered and smiled at me, some of the old sparkle returning to her eyes.

"Del's sounds great, mom."

She grinned and jerked the car out of the parking space like it was a little rocket ship.

"You're a good boy," she said quietly, but she didn't touch me again.

To do that would be too much. Her fears would erupt in a tide she could not stem.

***

She perked up once we got moving and by the time we got Del's she was back to her usual laughing self. Once we got our lemonade, she drove us up to this turnabout that overlooks a stream with some docks, a twist of pines, and a covered bridge crossing it at its deepest point. We sat on the hood of the Datsun, listening to the pops and ticks as the engine cooled, towels placed under our butts for protection. I had dug up a shirt for my mom in the hatch and she had let me tune the radio to Live-105 out of Providence. The latest summer "it" tune slipped out of the windows and into the day as we sat side-by-side in companionable silence, lazily working through our frozen lemonades.

Ninety-nine dreams I've had.

But she'd only take small sips from her lemonade and by the time we left for home, she had thrown away almost a full cup. The cold aggravated her headache and she'd be cursing that she even stopped by the time my father got home from the college. He'd put a warm compress on her head and close the door to their room so she could have quiet. At about ten o'clock or so, he'd go in and make her take one of the blue pills her doctor prescribed for her headaches. She'd fight him, because she didn't like the way they made her feel, but he'd make her take one anyway. Unhindered by pain, she would drift.

And every one a red balloon.

"Mom?"

She turned.

"Are you okay?"

She laughed and leaned over, nudging me in the shoulder with her side. But when she looked away I caught that rising panic behind her eyes.

Floating in the summer sky.

"I'm fine, baby," she whispered.

But she wasn't fine. Two days after that Friday she would back into the side of the garage pulling the car out. Two weeks later, into the school year, she would collapse on her way to pick me up from art class. Shortly after that the docs would find something on her brain that wasn't supposed to be there. Less than two years later, Angela Nova and I would have something in common.

I would discover that the most awful sound in my short childhood was not the glaring shriek of a sliding van door, but the gritty scrape of a coffin being lowered into the ground. And every single thing that has followed from that point on has been dulled, lacking the saturation of color and the depth of joy that one moment with her produced.

Ninety-nine red balloons go by.

Chapter Two

Damage Control

The dream dissolves. Chasing her down a dark hallway. A flash of white out of the corner of my eye. *White lace and promises*. No. Please don't leave me. And laughter. Dissolves. Dissolving. The phone is ringing, pulling me out. My eyes are wet and I have a choky spasm in my stomach. As I return to my body, I am aware of cool tile under my cheek and a rumpled feeling. I'm still in last night's clothes. Someone's thrown a blanket over me in the night, but didn't try to move me.

Paige.

My shoes are off and there was a pillow, but it's since been shoved under the feet of the clawfoot tub in favor of cool tile on my face. A two-thirds empty bottle of gin comes into focus and a revolted groan escapes from some wounded place deep in my belly. My stomach clenches and I begin to sit up, arms thrust out to either side like support struts. Then comes the merciless slap of the headache and

I'm over, curled into a ball on the floor of the bathroom, moaning softly. The sour reek of juniper berries is like a hothouse garden in my mouth and the phone is still ringing.

What time is it?

The machine picks up with the same pithy, disinterested message I've used since college. *This is Jared, leave a message.* I don't tell you if I'll call you back. I tell you to get what you need to say off your chest and we'll go from there. I screen. I'm one of those people. I'm afraid of the phone. I can't explain it, I'm just fearful of bad news. I've become flaky about the phone as I get older. Sometimes I just don't have the empathy to interact with others. I shirk my social obligation.

Click. A dial-tone.

No message this morning. It *is* morning. I can tell by the light outside the bathroom window and the pre-dawn chorus of birds. The tiny, inner clock in my head puts it at about 5:30, but I can't be sure. The clock is competing with the Hendrick's wrecking crew and the booming pulse of my heartbeat, which seems to come from everywhere, throbbing down to the tips of my fingers.

I hear a meow from the kitchen. It's her favorite *Well, Since You're Up* cry. She adds just a spin of whine into the meow that really makes it hurt. And she's crafty. She'll wait until you just start to ignore her and then she'll cry again, longer and more desperate. It goes right through you, like getting your fingernails dug into a bar of soap in the shower. You can't get the soap out and you feel somehow violated. Another volley will kill me and I couldn't get up if she was on fire, so I call to her.

"Cora," I groan. "Help me."

She makes a half-meow and I hear her padding across the living room and down the hallway to the bathroom. She stops at the edge of the door, assessing the damage with cool green eyes. A poofy black cat with a white face and tufted white paws, question mark tail tucked around her neat front feet. She makes an inquisitive meow. *What the hell happened to you?*

"I'm dying, baby."

She bows her head and comes trotting over, rubbing her nose over my face, bumping the top of my head with hers. I manage to wiggle some fingers and she turns, pushing her whole face into my clammy hand, purring like a little motor. She sticks her raccoon tail right in my nose and I roll off with a moan of disgust.

"God dammit, cat."

I wrap my hands around my head as if protecting myself from a beating and she comes around the other side, poking her head into the crevice between my elbows. The phone starts to ring again and the first real sensation of the sour cellar that is my mouth hits. I will have eye-watering burps all day and my voice will be scratchy well into the evening. The headache has localized its forces to the soft place at the back of my head where my skull meets my spine. If I lie still, it only hurts in the back of my head. But if I move, it shoots sideways around my temples and crackles like lightning bolts across my eyeballs.

The phone keeps ringing and my head is killing me, so I start rolling around on the tile on my back, Cora butting at my shoulders. This makes me nauseous enough to retch and I sit up. Quick. It's like someone slapped a mace into the side of my head and I cry out, spooking the cat. I throw open the toilet lid and grasp the sides like I'm holding down a wild animal. Cora bolts out of the room and the machine picks up.

I lay my head on one of my arms and time slows down. I concentrate on keeping my breath even and my diaphragm from revolting. I break out in a cold sweat and my mouth starts producing saliva that I swallow frantically to force the upchuck reflex back down. My hands are moist and shaking. My whole body is rubbery and weak.

A click and a dial-tone.

Please. Please, don't let me puke. Pleasepleasepleaseplease…

I hug the toilet like a life preserver, breathing raggedly, forcing calm into chaos. I wait for the next barrage of phone calls in a pure Zen Buddhist moment, completely present and immersed in my surroundings. I fall asleep this way, hugging the toilet, crumpled against it, exhausted. Sometime later I find my way to bed and sleep through the rest of the morning, adrift in the hum of air conditioning.

There is no guilt. It's my thirty-fifth birthday. The bitch about thirty-five is that I'm a grownup and I should know better. The beauty of thirty-five is that I'm a grownup and I'll do whatever I damn well please.

***

I've been having the dream two or three times a week. It began as an errant thing, a dream that made me feel bizarre and unsteady for a few days after. But it seemed an isolated incident, one of those moments where a channel opens straight from your subconscious. Visions from the inner oracle. In the beginning, I thought the dream was about timing. Now I fear it is about being left behind. Trapped between spaces.

In my dream, the train moves through the underground. Between stations the world beyond the windows is black. Murky. The inner dark of subterranean tunnels. The clack of steel wheels on the tracks and the steady rush of air past the cars produce a droning white noise below the rustle of newspapers, shuffling commuters, and spots of conversation.

I'm on the B Line, the Boston College line, heading into the city's heart. This is my daily commute. I'm in one of the new bulky, lumbering trains, towards the front by the conductor. I have a seat against a sidewall, facing an opposite row of seats and windows across a narrow, claustrophobic aisle. People usually fill the aisles, all the way down into the belly of the train, packed in tightly, jockeying for a spot that isn't in the way of the doors. But the normal crowd of college kids and commuters is thin today, some of the seats are empty, and I have an unobstructed view of the other riders.

The train slows with a hiss of air brakes and a lighted oasis comes into view. The usual, cheerfully indifferent mechanical voice that calls out the station names is absent. Instead comes the weary, gruff voice of the conductor.

"Arlington Station. Arlington."

Only it doesn't come out exactly like that. It comes out in that dropped R, elongated vowel, New England drawl.

Ahhlingtun Station. Ahhlingtun.

There's some movement, bags and papers. A few people shuffle on, a few wander off, clumped together like moths in the light and activity between the dark spaces. A slim, tallish woman gets on wearing a short, pleated skirt and a tight cardigan sweater. She has on this great red fedora hat over dark hair that curves over the top of her head like a parasol, obscuring her eyes. I can only see a thin line of red lips curled into the faintest ghost of a smile.

She takes a seat by the doors, folding her hands neatly over the clutch bag in her lap. I pass a look over her, curious, complementary, but the hat cuts off her gaze, leaving me with only that strange, merry widow's smile. She has great legs and shapely feet squeezed into pumps with little bows on them. The skirt hikes up enough so I can slide my gaze over the curve of her thighs. But it's her lips that captivate me. The twisting mirth of her mouth. Some secret satisfaction. With her hidden eyes and extravagant hat, she is thick with mystery. I am always drawn to the woman who looks like she might lead me away on some illicit, dangerous adventure. The one who will devour me when I catch her.

"Boylston Station. Boylston."

Boilstun Station. Boilstun.

No one comes on or gets off, but it feels like something is happening. The lights on the train dim and the air compressor winds down with a sputtering sigh. The doors stay open too long. It's like the conductor is waiting, holding the doors open until the last possible moment, in hopes of-

(*her*)

-a late arrival. But the longer they stay open, the stranger it feels, like something unseen is gathering.

The lights on the train dim more and the woman in the red hat looks up, eyes luminous and shining brown, boring into the hanging, empty space between the sliding doors. In the dim, there are shimmers. I can see them only out of the corner of my eyes. When I turn my head to look at them, I see only empty space. But I know something is there. More than trusting my eyes, I trust my inner sense. I can feel tingling down the back of my neck and my arms break out in gooseflesh. Somehow, with that dream surety, I know a passenger is boarding the train.

It is unseen. Invisible. Whether a ghost or entity, I do not know. But it fills the car with its presence, with an indelible sense of *intent*. The woman with the obsidian eyes looks at me, expectant. I nod at her-

(*I see it too.*)

-now aware of the click of heels, coming fast. A woman on the run. The doors begin to close and the click becomes a gallop. The train starts to pull away as hands slap against the door. A woman's voice comes, loud, frustrated. Frantic.

"Wait! *Wait!*"

But the train pulls away. As it does, that invisible presence leaks out of the car like air from a balloon. There is a great sigh, tension released. The woman slaps an angry hand against the side of the train in fury and the lights come back up. Just like that. The presence is gone. I look around the car in a stupor, trying to get my mind around what just happened. The woman in the red hat turns to me.

"The spirit always moves ahead of the body. But the two cannot be separated."

She points.

"Except in your case," she says and lowers her head once more.

I don't know what to say. Her voice is calm. Familiar. My head is spinning and that half-smile is impenetrable. Her obligation is finished. We made contact and she passed her message. The tether is broken. Again she is a stranger to me. A nameless connection on the subway.

"Park Street Station. Park Street."

Pahhk Street Station. Pahhk Street.

The doors open and the woman gets off with a few passengers, vanishing into the throngs of people. Now a man is striding through the crowd. I notice his gait first: confident, arrogant, sure-footed. Then his shoes. With buckles instead of laces. Monk strap shoes. I have a pair that's almost identical. I move my eyes up and take in his dress. Gray wool, flat-front slacks, a black dress shirt, an overcoat. Then his build. Short. Trim. Broad through the chest and shoulders. I am cataloging these similarities when I see his face and breath catches in my throat. He looks like me. Exactly like me. Down to the glasses, the goatee, the wild black hair.

A feeling of vertigo threatens me and I have to clutch the side of my seat to keep from reeling. There's a feeling of doubling, detaching from myself. Stepping outside of my skin. I feel at once naked and fragile. My hands begin to shake and a panicked sweat breaks out down my back. My vision blurs and I think I'm going to faint, but it passes and there he is, walking right onto the train. He stops at the threshold between the sliding doors. He's like some kind of vampire, transfixed outside, awaiting invitation. He looks at me, with my own eyes. But they are vacant. He is an empty vessel. Hollow.

"Who are you?" he asks, challenging me in my voice.

I try to stand, but that vertigo, that unreality, slaps me back down. I can only shake my head at him, at me-

(*at it*)

-trying to speak as the doors slide closed and the train lurches forward into the swallowing dark. His combative force follows me into the tunnel, demanding an answer to his question. A question of identity.

"Who are you?" comes the voice like phantom fingers at my neck.

And then my own, in rote repetition.

Who am I? Who am I? Who am I? Who-

The lights on the train go out and I am only a voice in the blackness.

***

I wash up onto the shores of semi-consciousness after noon. Cora is tucked up under my shoulder, curled into a ball with her tail wrapped around her body. Wind from the AC vents rustles over her fur in rhythmic waves as the fan blows across one side of the room, pauses, and then sweeps back across. Beyond the chilled hum of the bedroom, I hear the heavy equipment of a street crew chewing up pavement down the road and the heady regalia of kids with idle summer time. The damned phone is ringing again and I begin the re-entry process into my skin.

The nausea and queasiness have passed to some degree. And the headache has become more of a chewing in my head than an angry bite. The thirst however, is appalling. The aftertaste of gin has encrusted my mouth like barnacles. Gummy, sap-like residue has collected at the sides of my lips and my tongue has sunk to the bottom of my jaw, shriveled like a salted slug. I make a gagging sound and roll up onto one elbow, blinking bleary-eyed at the alarm clock.

12:53.

Cora thrusts her paws out in front of her and yawns, arching her back, shaking her whole body with delight. She blinks at me and starts cleaning herself with the rough, pink pad of her tongue. I roll over to the side of the big, messy bed and throw my feet over, resting them on the side rails. I put my elbows on my knees and sit this way, half-propped, half-sunk into the mattress, for a good ten minutes.

I have huge, thick drapes drawn on all the windows, so not even a sliver of sunlight gets in. There is instead the diffused glow against them from the outside, throwing the room into sleepy shadows, like an Arab bazaar tent in the desert. The AC passes cool air over my back and it feels good to sit in the dry half-light, summoning the will to move as the phone messages begin to roll in.

This is Jared. Leave a message.

"Jared, are you there? Hello?" It's her authoritative voice – everybody out of the pool. "Are you screening? I hate it when you screen me. Are you there? Are you sleeping? It's Harriet."

Hi, Harry.

Harriet is Eddie's fiancé. Eddie's been my friend since our college days; we're thick as thieves and twice as nimble. Harriet adopted me shortly after they started dating. It started with straightening ties and slicking down cowlicks, that sort of thing. It grew, pervasively, into this sometimes hennish mother, sometimes pestering older sister relationship that Eddie shakes his head over all the time. But despite bickering, taunting, and a generally antagonistic relationship, she's the one phone call I would make if I got into the kind of trouble where you only get one phone call.

Please go away, Harry.

"Are you alone? Are you even home? Well listen, dinner's at nine o'clock. Eddie is going to come to your place to pick you up. He said he was going to go early so you guys can do whatever it is ya'll do when it's boytime. I'll see you at the restaurant. And your chippie is *not* invited. Happy birthday."

There's a click and a beep.

Harriet is a pivotal gateway for me. She's my strongest link to the world of women. She can cut me down or talk me onto a pedestal at a moment's notice with equal enthusiasm. The choice is always hers to make. She translates girlspeak for me, helps me with dinner party and gift etiquette, and occasionally tosses me tidbits on the whimsical wrecking ball of feminine psychology. In return for the inside track, I go shopping with her, indulge her madcap theories on men and dating, and endure those awful moments when she offers me too much information on her and Eddie's sex life.

She is fiercely protective and possessive of me. She screens potential dating candidates with severity, giving them the same detached scrutiny I use to screen phone calls. Harriet is from Texas. You don't mess with Texas, I've learned. She chooses impatience over restraint, bluntness over tact, and she's not shy about voicing her opinions at volume the moment they shoot into her mind. Texas doesn't cultivate the "hold your tongue" option in conversation, it would seem. She'll be polite to potentials, eerily so at first – there's that Southern hospitality thing. But she doesn't try all that hard if she doesn't like the girl and she doesn't much care if this ruffles said girl's feathers or not.

Paige (the chippie) was carefully hidden from Harriet through Eddie's and my combined finagling. Knowing she would try to chew her up and spit her out, great pains were taken to ensure their paths would never cross. But I tend to hide out from the group when I have a new interest, and Harriet started sniffing bullshit in the air. She got Eddie drunk one night and steadily wore him down until he spilled it. She finally caught us one day, sitting outside having lunch on Newbury Street, and came waltzing over with a big, shiteating grin on her face.

Paige is a twenty-three year old punk chick from Hull who looks a lot like Parker Posey. Combat boots, tats, a tongue ring, jet black hair, shaved on one side. She's petulant, surly, and frequently drunk. She's sharply intelligent, an avid book geek, and constantly on the lookout for weaker people to use as chew toys. As one of Harriet's cubs, you can imagine my terror over the idea of these two coming together.

I think Harriet expected to sit down, give me a bit of shit for hiding this from her, and then wait to deconstruct her in proper MLA format when we were in private. I'm sure she didn't expect Paige to shoot a warning shot across her bow. And the look on her face, despite the aftermath, was priceless.

"She's very pretty, Jared," she had said, talking about her as if she wasn't there.

Then, as if realizing her rudeness, she had turned on Paige with a patronizing look, patting her on the hand. "You're very pretty."

"Thanks!" Paige bubbled, and her lips broke apart, exposing a grin that was all teeth. "I hope it lasts when I get to be your age."

The sides of Harriet's mouth pinched and her lips drew into a thin line of ill will. She arched one eyebrow high and her nostrils flared. The waiter who had been walking over to our table with the dessert menu stopped, turned smartly around like he was in a military parade, and strode away in the direction he'd come without a look back.

I cleared my throat and slid my chair back away from the table. I was anticipating the crashing, rolling dust cloud of flailing limbs, stars, and exclamation points you see in the cartoons. But Harriet just laughed shrilly, clutching her hands over her chest like Paige had just said the funniest thing on earth, and kicked me savagely under the table.

From then on, it was war. If Paige turned out to be the love of my life, Harriet would never buckle. If the two of us were to get married, she would boycott. If she were to slip under the wheels of a city bus, Harriet would see providence where others saw tragedy. She refused to address Paige by name and she would punish me until her shine wore off and I finally cut her loose. To bring her to my birthday dinner this evening would be a bit like tossing a Christian into a pit of starving lions.

The phone is ringing again and-

(*This is Jared. Leave a message.*)

-speaking of chippies.

"Jared. Are you alive?" She talks quickly, every sentence spoken like a threat or a challenge. "Are you screening? Jared? Fine. You were a real prick last night."

She pauses. I hear Lana Del Rey in the background-

(Choose your last words, this is the last time.)

-and I know she's chewing her lip, debating the next words out of her mouth.

"But I hope you're okay. You were really wasted. I have a present for you. You don't deserve it and I know I'm not invited to your little fucking Stepford party tonight. But I want to give it to you. Come over after the bars close."

Another pause. I cradle my head in my hands and rock back and forth.

Don't say it, Paige, please don't say it-

"Happy birthday and all that."

A click and a beep.

She didn't say it. But I'm not as relieved as I'd hoped. She's right, I don't deserve a present.

***

Eddie calls while I lean against the open door of the fridge, power chugging orange Gatorade with a gratitude that borders on ecstasy. Despite it being the middle of August, it's cool today and a steady breeze moves around the apartment. The combination of chilly refrigerator air and gusts passing through the open windows is delicious. But it pales in comparison to the rejuvenating powers of the liquid pouring down my throat, spreading out to my roots, bringing moisture to the arid nooks and crannies.

"Hey dipshit, you made it. The big three five." He's totally enjoying himself, the bastard. "All these years you've been training and putting in the extra hours and you finally made it. Congratulations, you're a dirty old man. I'll be at your place at seven. Later."

I feed Cora and roll a couple of joints at the kitchen table while she daintily works her way through a can of wet food. Some people check in from the restaurant with well-wishes and to give me shit about taking the weekend off. I make some sandwiches and pack them into a beach cooler. Though it seems revolting at the moment, I know I'll want food later. I toss in a couple cans of Pepsi and a big bottle of Poland Spring and hunt around the living room for the radio.

In the bathroom, I take a good look at my face to see what thirty-five looks like. I'm holding together fairly well, but I'm no longer good at drinking. It's starting to show when I overdo it. The skin around my eyes is puffy and I have this loose, haggard look about me like I've been doped up on Haldol. I brush my teeth, down some Advil, and run cold water over my face until I feel half-human again.

From the cave of my room, I retrieve my keys and cell phone, still in the pockets of my jeans from last night, tossed unceremoniously to the floor. I throw on some shorts and sandals and turn off the AC on my way out. I'm expecting a call from my dad in Florida later in the day. He'll be antsy if he can't get in touch with me to wish me a happy birthday. I'm also hoping Celine will be free for a couple of hours in the late afternoon.

Celine doesn't call me at home. We only talk on cell phones. There's an arrangement. Code-words, dummy e-mail accounts, blackout dates. All this cloak-and-dagger nonsense is so her absentee husband won't catch on. But the hush-hush running around we do is more out of her desire for drama than her husband's suspicions. I've met him; he's one of those pompous, corporate, conquering jackass types. He doesn't give a rat's ass what she does. He's likely got an assistant who services him in the copy room after everyone's gone home for the day. Whether said assistant is a young woman or a young man is up for debate.

She's one of these Backbay idle rich who got into real estate as a hobby and got a taste for it. We hook up for frenzied sex when she shows houses or for longer interludes when the husband is out of town. I met her at a Museum of Fine Arts fundraiser and she spotted me long before. We have a complicated history. She is forty-two and may be the closest thing to pure evil I have ever known. But Celine fucks likes it's her last day on earth.

And she never calls me at home.

***

I've stuffed all my supplies for an afternoon safari into the seat of a folded butterfly chair. I pocket the joints and enter the hallway that leads out to the back stairs and up to the roof. The phone is ringing. It's always ringing. I pause at the back door, straining to hear for a message.

Click. A dial tone.

Déjà vu.

I shake my head, annoyed, dismiss it, and head out into the stairwell, closing the door behind me with a dusty thud. It's like an Egyptian tomb back here. Light trickles down in rays from the skylight at the top of the stairs, revealing sheets of slow-moving dust while the rest of the stairs are cast in shadow. The air is dry and hot, the absence of breeze, stifling. Heavy plank stairs lead up to the roof or down to the basement of the building. Sound is muffled and the progression up the stairs to the outside takes on the feeling of an archeological expedition.

I trudge up to the top of the old brick building and three steps from the landing on the roof, she's there. In my head. Sarah. I feel her. She slips around the inside of my skull like syrup, settling over my consciousness with a downy caress. I laugh uncontrollably, as if being tickled. I'm suddenly light-headed, like I'm floating, and I have to sit down on the landing. I prop up the chair against the wall on one of the steps and lie down on the dingy floor of the landing.

Just behind me is the massive metal door that leads to the roof outside. Beyond the skylight above me, clouds hang, lazy and massive, sailing across bright blue sky on a slow course. The heat is violent in the stairwell and only the smallest wick of a breeze teases through my hair from the crack under the heavy door.

But time has slowed down. Her shuffling in my head has settled and become a cool, breaking wave, reaching deep into my mind like tendrils to solidify the channel between us. The dust rays dance in swelling, undulating sheets. The clouds move as you imagine great starships to travel across the black vacuum. Each breeze is a gale. Outside I can feel the green stretching of summer growth, the buzz of insects. My heart is slow and even in my chest. The spot just above and between my eyebrows tingles and she's speaking in my mind as if she were standing next to me.

Do you remember what you said to me last night?

Her voice blows away some of the drunken haze from the evening. I have a flash of being on the roof, under the moon, drunk and railing at her about something while Paige waited impatiently downstairs. No, that's not right. It wasn't just something. It was *the* something. The something we didn't talk about. The same way we didn't talk about the spooky telepathy thing we could do. I remember. And I tell her so.

It's all bullshit.

There is a satisfied opening of the unseen umbilicus between us, like a sigh of relief. Or resignation.

You do remember.

Not much of it. But enough to know the cat's out of the bag. This is why she was calling at 5:30 in the morning. It was only 2:30 in California. She'd had a good couple hours to let it stew before she decided she was going to be furious about it. She'd also likely been well drunk herself at the time and cruising for a fight. A clean slate at thirty-five. That's what I wanted. Jesus, this is going to be a bitch of a first day.

I conjure the image of a cell phone and send it to her across the open channel. There is a rustling in my head like wind passing over a hill of tropical grass. Then her voice, loud in my mind:

HALF AN HOUR.

It's like the voice of God. The channel narrows and her presence, like a receding wave, pulls away from my head and back into a great churning sea, leaving me exposed and alone. Time snaps back and cloying heat is everywhere. My guts flop like beached, struggling sea creatures and I sit up, eyeballs bulging, sweat popping out across my brow. I force myself to stand and stagger down a step to grab the butterfly chair. I drag it up to the landing and kick open the big metal door.

Light, breeze, and the smell of leafy growth break across me and I blink, raising an arm up against the sun. I take a deep inhale of fresh air through my nose and my gut settles. Cobwebs clear from my head. The afternoon is gorgeous, splendid and beaming. The sky is buoyant with clouds. The sun is a cleansing fire on my skin, burning away the last damp puddles of my hangover.

I bring the chair out to the middle of the roof and unfold it just outside of the circle of shade made from overhanging branches of trees. Mine is the tallest building on the block at tree level. The walls that surround the roof are chest height, like castle turrets, and no can see up here. With tree branches filled out with leaves, spilling over the walls, it's like a secret rooftop garden. A sanctuary. I spend as much of my free time up here as I can. Memories of this place keep me sane during winter. It's my restoration.

I take out the bottle of water and put the cooler down into the circle of shade, setting the radio beside it. I place my phone and keys, the two joints, and a BIC lighter on a towel over the cooler. I rub on some sunscreen and take a healthy pull from the water. I stash the bottle at the foot of the cooler and settle into the butterfly chair with the great, satisfied sigh that follows exertion.

I bake under the sun, watching clouds go by in great, rolling flotillas. The air is that urban oasis of sunscreen, skin, and sweat mixed with grit, sap, and overripe berries. Brick walls, roof tar, and creeping vines. The smell of barbecue wafts over with exhaust and the steamy, oily tang of the city's buses and trains. Firecrackers, the running screams of adventuring kids, bugs, and planes droning overhead replace the sleepy sighs of the shorefront. People pass under the roof and their conversations drift up and out into the day, joining radios blasting raucous summer tunes.

I light one of the joints and take a long pull, sucking the drug deep into my lungs. I hold my breath and the leaves on the trees shimmer and come into sharp focus. I let my breath out like a dragon breathing fire and a plume of white smoke rises and comes apart, whipping away into the sky. The second hit brings the sounds of the outside alive and my mouth tastes sweet. This is one of my favorite times to smoke a cigarette, but I don't do that anymore, so I suck down a third hit, bigger than the first two, going for the good stuff.

I hold my breath and replay her voice in my head.

Do you remember what you said to me last night?

It is so clear in my imagination, it's like she's back in my mind. I exhale and a barrage of possible ways this conversation can go comes forth. I begin to clinically examine all the ways she can feel, cut apart her probable reactions to things I could say, gauging the severity of what's passed between us in the last twelve hours. But even in that first bit of digging for damage control, I know there's no way out. It's time to face the music.

This is the spot where we duel, out in the open, under the sun. Here on the main street with our bootheels planted and our hands at our guns. I have about twenty minutes to prepare myself before we settle. With a tranquility that astonishes me, I watch faces and creatures form in the clouds and keep my mind silent, save for one fragment over and over. A protective mantra.

It's all bullshit.

It's not quite telepathy between us. It's more like synchronization. She's my equal and opposite force. Sometimes I'm a little ahead and she's a bit behind, other times it's reversed, but we're always on similar, parallel tracks. Now and then our paths come into alignment and we are open to each other in a way that isn't rational and shouldn't be possible. But *is*. I can't explain it, but we exist at the same frequency. It is a protective feeling, knowing she is there, knowing we share a secret. It is a feeling that comforts me in way that nothing has in years. One I fear I may lose today forever. I watch clouds in silence, counting down minutes in my head.

It's all bullshit, Sarah.

Waiting for the phone to ring.

Chapter Three

Kine

Sarah and I met like storybook lovers. Locked eyes across a crowded room, a penetrating gaze that made everything else dim, the fugue-like feeling of falling into her. The only thing that stopped me from kissing her was the presence of so many other people on the floor. In retrospect, as I've played that first encounter back in my head, I've wondered if she would have stopped me.

I've wondered if things would have turned out differently between us. If I had just stepped up and been a man, both that night and later, where would we be now? Would the outcome be the same? Would three thousand miles divide us? Would I be so calm waiting for the phone to ring? Does how we get to a place matter as much as actually getting there?

Do the rules matter if the outcome is predetermined?

***

Every man has incidents where he wakes up in the morning and smacks himself because he did something stupid. Or he does it at the instant, gets trashed, crashes, wakes, remembers, and smacks himself again. If there are witnesses to the incident, he will try to wait it out or live it down. If no one sees, it will be privately agonized over, even years later. When a man has one of these incidents involving a woman, they are never forgotten. They live on to become some of the great *What If* laments of his life.

Miami, Florida. New Year's Eve. My early twenties. Eddie and I had gone out to our favorite bar for the night. We had gotten friendly with these two blondes and we were chatting them up, waiting for the ball to drop. I got up to get drinks and this little brunette cocktail waitress threw a boa around my neck, shaking her hips at me in slow circles. She was fishnets and spiked heels. Tan and drunk. Willing and looking. We'd been eyeing each other shamelessly for weeks. But I was with the blondes and Eddie and it looked like we had a shot at them. I walked away. The blondes took off shortly after to find men who had cocaine and Eddie and I went home alone. And I know that brunette dragged some boy home and fucked the everliving shit out of him. We went in the next day. She'd been fired. Drunk on the job. I never even got her name.

Washington, DC. Fall. Post-college. Tristan Sebonne. We were at this bar in Adams Morgan shooting pool in the back with friends. Me and a buddy came in hot, running the table for hours. Two girls wanted to play partners and I met Tristan. She was French. Paris, French. Visiting for eleven days. Blue-black hair. Willowy. Huge blue eyes. A perfect pink curve of mouth. Her voice and accent dripped sex. French women are a marvel. She told me to take her home with me. She whispered to me in French: *Je veux mettre votre quéquette dans ma bouche.* But I let her go. Because I was in crazy love with the bartender, who didn't care one way or the other if I lived or died. All I got from Tristan that night was the name of her perfume: *Cabotine*, by Grace. It still drives me crazy. I had the smell of it in my clothes for days.

Very little shames a man more than missing a cue for sex. We can be more stupid about this than you'd think. There are moments when sex is blatantly staring us in the face and we have no idea. Maybe it seems too easy, too good to be true, or we're pining for one lost love or another. We're so caught up in our own egos that we miss clearly marked road-signs and wind up floundering and facedown in a ditch. The universe gave a window of opportunity for the kind of sex we dream about and we shoved it out of the way in pursuit of loftier goals. It's like watching a jackass try to be a horse. Woulda. Coulda. Shoulda.

Gone.

Boston, Massachusetts. Gayle. Spring. College. Senior year. Upstairs in a bathroom of the student annex during a ska band show. Free beer. Armbands. Dancing. It was ending and we slipped up and locked the door. Her skirt hiked up, leaning over the sink, shaking her ass and watching me through the mirror. I went to her and as I put my hands on the slide of her hips, someone pounded on the door. We said nothing, but he pounded again, now adding voice. *Come on,* she whispered, *he'll go away.* But I couldn't. I didn't want to. I almost recognized the voice on the other side of the door. A bad feeling came over me and I had to stop. We waited, silently dressing, until the pounding ceased and the person went away. Then we crept out like thieves just as people were leaving and merged into the crowd, off to a party. Chasing the buzz.

We fucked all over campus; it was our thing. Our secret. But our thing was ending and both of us knew it. Later that night we had angry, tangled drunk sex, but it wasn't the same. Something had changed. So many other things were wrong by then and it's crazy, but I always thought if I had just fucked her, it would have been okay. If I could have connected with her, at that one moment in time, maybe we could have saved it. That was a last gasp moment, a turning point. A point where I was weak. Gayle and I stopped fucking in public.

Things began to collapse shortly after.

***

There are, by contrast, near-perfect moments that balance out the incidents. These are shining moments at a party, a date, a job interview. Critical junctures. These are periods where you are at your best, untouchable, possessed of impeccable timing and balance. These are memories that sweeten with time, warmed by the hazy embers of nostalgia, wept over in old age.

San Francisco, California. Sarah. Spring. I was twenty-five. I came into the restaurant on my way to a jazz club in North Beach. I had stopped in to grab my paycheck and my manager, Felix, pulled me aside, asking me to come meet the new floor manager. I rounded the corner, past the big ovens and the hostess area, and she was seated at the bar, turned away from me. She was in a sleek suit with a long black spill of hair tied into a loose ponytail with a red ribbon. Her heels were tucked over the back rails of her barstool. She was straight-backed, poised and alert, like she was ready to deal cards.

She must have felt me because she turned and our eyes locked. Time seemed to slow and stretch. My arms felt heavy, but my shoulders were loose, my stride solid. She drew me to her and I could feel the pull like denseness in the air, the force of our combined gravity radiating out around us. I moved up to the bar and the bussers and servers parted silently for me, not even realizing they were doing it. All eyes were on us as the moment lengthened and I drew within three feet of her.

"Hi," I said, absorbed, unblinking.

"Hello," she said and rose slowly, making to get off her stool.

When she put weight on her foot, her heel slipped off the rung and she pitched forward, arms pinwheeling. I jumped as her body began to turn and I caught her out of the air, landing hard, one arm around her shoulders, the other tucked up behind her knees. She looked up at me, both of us breathless, staring at one another, entranced, until Felix coughed politely from behind me.

She flushed and shook her head. Her face cleared and she smiled at me, both of us moving in concert to get her to her feet as expediently as possible. She smoothed the front of her skirt and pulled at the bottom hem of her blazer to straighten it. Felix nodded at her, disinterested.

"You two are going to be working together on the Calazzo Affair. I thought you should get acquainted."

I rolled my eyes.

"Is it as bad as I've heard?" she asked.

"It's much worse," I answered.

"Oh, I'm sure you two will figure out *some*thing, being creative types and all," Felix said and made an about-face, sashaying over to the busboys to bitch about their napkin folding.

She stuck her hand out.

"I'm Sarah."

I took her hand.

"I'm Jared November."

I held it longer than I should have. Held it until she flushed again and laughed nervously, free hand rising to cover her mouth. She pulled the other one away and crossed them both over her breasts, holding her heart. Protective. Then she reached out and smoothed my tie, fingers lingering at my chest.

"Thank you for catching me, Jared," she said.

"You'll fall for me again," I said. "I'm sure of it."

Before she could respond, I turned and walked away. There were no *What Ifs* in that moment. Those would come later. And with great force.

What if she finds out?

What if I lose control of it?

What if it happens again?

***

We survived the Calazzo Affair, a catered mafia wedding in Pacific Heights. The father of the bride, Alberto Calazzo, was known to his family and the FBI as *il Martello* –

the Hammer. We were patted down at the main gate of the estate for weapons. Our van was checked over by bomb dogs before we were directed to servant's quarters at the back of the property. Sarah and I slipped into eerie synchronization once we stepped out of the truck. We gave the staff their marching orders and made the rounds, finding out who the VIPs were, who to take special care of, and where we might run into trouble. I was in charge of the bar; Sarah had the floor.

It was black tie and tails, wine stewards with white gloves. It was perfect to the guests, while we ran our asses off behind the scenes to avert calamity at every turn. By the time we plated dinner, I could look at her and know what she wanted. She'd point and nod and we'd pass elaborate hand signals to each other like pitching coaches across the field. At the last song, she crept behind the bar to join me, rested her head into my shoulder, exhausted, and finally let herself rest.

The Calazzo family praised us. *Grazi. Grazi. Il due di lei è la magia.* Alberto Calazzo paid for the job with a fat white envelope stuffed with cash and slipped us each a rolled wad of bills for our trouble. It was like a drug deal. Since then Felix put us together for all the big jobs. But events like the Calazzo Affair were a rarity. Most of the things we catered were much smaller. Large parties at the restaurant itself were orchestrated so carefully and went through so many channels, handling them was really just a matter of knowing the layout of the place.

I hardly spoke to Sarah outside of these campaigns. She would walk the floor, correcting and marshaling, and I would work behind the bar, stalking around my enclosure like a caged animal. She would rarely come out with the rest of us after work, and if she did, she would spend those evenings aloof, like an outsider. Or she would disappear, running off early without telling anyone.

Even when we had breathing room at functions, she remained cool. Ever since I caught her, she'd shut it down, blocked something off, and refused to acknowledge it. When she was tired and punchy, we'd kid around, but she never let me in. Outside of that one moment when she nestled her head into my shoulder and the world smelled of Chanel *Chance*, she was closed to me. Most of what passed between us was silent, the core of our bond unspoken. Smoldering gazes said what we could not, a frenzy of longing thinly masked by protocol.

That summer was the itchy madness of being so close to her and being locked out. Passing her on the crowded floor, I would breathe in her scent until I was drunk with the force of it. I was unable to keep from staring when she would stop to catch her breath, placing a hand on her hip and the other, palm up, flared over her brow. She would cock her hip forward, making a line from the bottom of her heel up the arch of her back that I would follow with reverent eyes until she caught me looking. And she would look away.

By the time Halloween came, I was frustrated and pissy with her, exhausted by the hot and cold depths of her. I did a juvenile about-face, becoming professional to the point of being an asshole, and I would fight her on everything. I went out of my way to avoid her and our discussions remained cursory, devoid of humor. I'd started sleeping with one of the hostesses as an outlet for my impotence with Sarah. It was a shameless, sophomoric ploy to incite jealousy behind the castle walls. I didn't want to go to the restaurant's party. I wanted to be lost in the parade at the Castro. I went because the hostess wouldn't shut up about it and perhaps I could spark some envy in Sarah. I was resigned to the state of affairs.

But she came as Holly Golightly. I take full responsibility for all that followed. If it didn't happen that night, it would have happened eventually. It was only a matter of time. That night was so strange and she was so beautiful. I was weak. Her costume was the killing blow.

***

I was trapped in an interminable conversation with Felix and his activist boyfriend, Hector. They were defending the behavior of the Critical Mass cyclists and the surge of anger that was growing throughout the city over the event. It was supposed to be a parade of bicycles, celebrating the freedom of cycling, promoting the betterment of the environment through awareness. But like every movement in San Francisco, it had degenerated into a misguided, self-righteous display of bad manners and anarchy.

"We can't even ride in traffic anymore," Hector said, in a tone of outraged superiority that was growing wearisome.

"You're not supposed to ride in traffic, Hector-"

"We have *rights* to be in the road," he said. "And they better watch out for us. We're going to make them listen."

"Cyclists are starting fights with motorists, you know. They're clogging the roads on *purpose-*"

"That's not true," Felix chimed in, but I held my hand up to him.

"People just trying to get home after a shitty day don't care about your message."

"You have no idea what it's like to be a cyclist in this city," Hector said, inflated and indignant.

"I bike to work, Hector. I bike all over the city."

"But you don't see how big corporate America is everywhere…"

I'd had enough.

"Bleed for what you want, but it's my right to ignore you. If you push your cause in my face, you deserve everything you get back."

He snorted at me with distaste.

"I'll bet you're a Republican,"

Felix sucked in breath and the conversations around us hushed as the R-word came out. I grinned at Hector, showing my teeth.

"And I'll bet you're not half the fuck his last boyfriend was."

Hector made a face like he'd just stepped in dogshit. Felix reddened and I turned on him.

"Whatever happened to Juan Carlo, Felix?"

He wagged a finger at me like a headmaster at a boy's school, his face crimson.

"Juan Carrrlo," I said, rolling the R, taunting them.

"We're done here. You're a penis, Jared," Felix said.

He took Hector's hand, passed me a disparaging look, and dragged him off into the crowd like a ragdoll. I stood there for a moment, chuckling to myself, clinking the ice cubes in the bottom of my glass. Costumed co-workers, a fairy, a geisha, a witch, a dominatrix, swam around me like a school of colored fish. Someone dressed as the purple

Teletubbie tucked a cigar into the breast pocket of my suit, patted me on the back, and whirled off to rejoin the other fish. I was at once aware of the bass from the DJ thumping in my chest and I felt a tickle like a feather across the back of my neck.

Turn around.

I whipped around. I thought someone had snuck up behind me and whispered in my ear. When I realized no one was there, I looked out in front of me, searching. She was about ten feet away, in a pool of light at the foot of the stairs. The costume was perfect, down to the gloves, the length of pearls, and the long cigarette holder. She'd swept her hair up, framing her face, exposing her neck and shoulders. The dress showed how petite she was; slim through the hips and back. She watched my reaction with a grin at her lips.

"Close your mouth, Jared," she said.

I was paralyzed.

"What are you supposed to be anyway?"

I couldn't speak or draw breath. The blood was pounding in my head and my ears were burning. I got a tickle again, this time at the point between my eyebrows.

You like it, don't you?

I took a deep, steadying breath in a big draw through my nose.

"I love it," I said, the words spilling out in a rush. "You look beautiful."

Her brow furrowed like she wasn't sure if she'd left the iron on at home and she cocked her head.

"Thank you. Did I-" She stopped herself and shook her head. "Never mind. What are you supposed to be?"

I grinned at her, exposing sharp ceramic fangs at my canines.

"Why am I not surprised?"

I shrugged at her and looked off into the crowd on the dance floor.

You're dangerous. Aren't you?

I turned to look at her and she flashed a quick, nervous smile to me. The kind children give when they don't want you to know they're up to something.

"How am I dangerous?" I asked.

She recoiled, shocked. I stepped in, pressing past her comfort zone, grinning.

"How am I dangerous, Sarah?"

She put her hands up to my chest to ward me off.

"Jared, *stop.*"

I stopped, bowed my head, and put my hands up like I was surrendering to the authorities.

"You *heard* that?" she asked, fingers floating at my lapels.

"Of course I heard it, you're standing right in front of-"

"Because I didn't say it out loud."

I brought my teeth together with a click and looked at her, shrewd, like she was putting me on. She was trembling lightly and goosebumps had broken out down the length of her arms. I remembered the tickle like a feather at the back of my-

(*turn around*)

-neck.

"Do it again," I told her.

Her face clouded and she crossed her arms over her chest.

"I'm not a light switch, Jared. I can't just flip on and off."

"Come on, try," I insisted.

She scrunched up her face, exasperated.

"What the hell! This isn't funny, you-"

"Come on, *Sarah*," I said and her cheeks bloomed with color. "Just something off the top of your head."

She raised her eyes and passed me a combative look that carried with it-

(*GO FUCK YOURSELF!*)

-an arrow of words that came through between my eyes and lodged itself in the back of my brain.

I pressed the heel of my palm to my forehead, reeling a bit.

"There," she said, clearly flustered. "Are you happy now?"

I nodded at her, rubbing at the point of impact absently.

"You don't even know what I said," she spat. "Quit acting like an-"

"Go fuck yourself."

She charged me, hands covering my mouth, her body pressing into me. Her face moved inches from mine as she made panicked sssshhhh faces. I put my arms around her, laughing, my hands finding the small of her back. She looked up at me.

Please, don't hurt me.

I leaned down to kiss her, but she turned her head.

"I can't," she said, pulling away from me.

"You *won't*," I said, releasing her.

"No," she said, taking steps back away from me, out into the crowd. "I won't."

She turned and dove into the throng of dancers.

Woulda. Coulda. Shoulda.

Gone.

***

I found her in the alley next to the restaurant, leaned up against the brick entrance, smoking a cigarette.

"Go fuck myself, huh?" I asked.

She made a face.

"You said off the top of my head," she accused. "You're an ass, Jared."

"Everyone's calling me names tonight."

She rubbed her hands over her shoulders.

"What?" she asked.

"Nothing," I said, waving at her. "Are you cold?"

She smiled, sheepish.

"A little."

I removed my blazer and handed it to her. She pulled the jacket on, wrapping it around her shoulders, tucking herself into it.

"It smells like you," she said.

"Booze and cigarettes. It's my signature scent."

"No," she said. "It's different."

I stepped in to close the gap between us. People on their way to the parade passed by the mouth of the alley in a train like a traveling circus. The sounds of regalia and shouting seemed far away, muffled, somewhere worlds away from the two of us.

"I have a boyfriend," she said and I stopped. "I love him."

"Who are you trying to convince of that, Sarah?"

"Don't do that. It's not fair."

I turned and walked off a few feet, digging for a cigarette of my own. After I'd lit it and had a few drags I felt more composed and together. When I returned to her I was already aware that it was going to happen again.

"Fair?" I asked. "You wanna talk about fair?"

"Don't start-"

"Let's talk about fair. You've been acting nuts since I met you. You're nice one day and cold the next. We're buddies when we're in the shit, but once we get back to base it's like you don't even know me. You flirt with me one day and then ignore me for a week. You didn't even tell me about this boyfriend until tonight. Oh, and apparently, you can shout your fucking thoughts at me. Does that sound fair to you?"

She lit another cigarette off the embers of the old one and laughed sarcastically. It was a shrill sound, loud in the alley.

"I do *not* flirt with you."

"I think you're missing the larger picture here, Sarah."

"And that would be?"

"I don't know, maybe you can enlighten me. How about telling me why I'm so dangerous? Let's start with that?"

She flung her arms out at me like she was pushing off a sloppy dog that had jumped up.

"You can't badger me about something I didn't even say out loud!"

"Will you listen to yourself?"

"No, Jared-"

"Because you sound like a crazy person-"

"I'M NOT CRAZY!" she shouted and threw her cigarette against the brick.

It landed in a splash of sparks.

"I'm scared of you," she said at last, very softly.

I reached up, put my hands around my head, and looked up at her. Helpless.

"Why?"

"You make me feel safe," she whispered.

"That's a bad thing?" I asked, incredulous.

"It is for me."

"I don't understand you."

"I know you, Jared. The girls warned me, but I knew the moment I met you. You're a fuck and run guy. A smooth talker with a string of them running after you. But you never pick one. One's never enough. Isn't that about right?"

"You don't know anything about me," I said, mean.

"I know enough to keep my clothes on around you," she said, biting back.

"Oh come on," I yelled, kicking at the crumbling brick. "That's such BULLSHIT!"

Please don't yell at me.

Soft in my head, like a child. It drained the frustration from me in an instant. Anger fell away. Music for savage beasts.

"I'm sorry," I said.

A silence rose between us and we drifted off into the deep forest of our private thoughts. Something flashed through my head, but I only got a snatch of it.

-but for how long-

Then she was speaking aloud.

"You're not on anyone's side but your own, Jared. That's why you're dangerous. I shouldn't trust you at all."

"Sarah-"

"I mean you're like a train wreck."

"Thanks," I quipped.

"But I do. I know you'd protect me. And I have a hard time trusting men."

"What happened to you?" I asked.

There was a long pause, long enough to make me think she wasn't going to say anything, and then, painfully, earnestly, it came.

"I was molested when I was little..."

She started spilling, telling me the story, her voice breaking. I came forward and put my arms around her and she let go, sobbing into my shoulder in great, heaving gasps. I held her, swaying gently, watching the parade goers pass the alley. Jugglers. Men on stilts. Sequined showgirls. After a time, her breathing slowed and she broke my embrace.

Her tears had made runny lines of mascara down her cheeks. I reached a hand up to wipe them away and then I was cupping her face, bringing it up to mine, meeting her with my lips. She put her hands up behind my jaw and into my hair and for a moment, began to relent. Then she caught herself and backed away, covering her mouth with her hand, looking off. When she turned her head back to me, her eyes were bright with rage.

"*God*," she said. "You don't even *care*."

I felt the threads of my tie to her coming apart, knots slipping loose. The slide of rope connecting us was unraveling.

"Why did you do that?"

I couldn't tell her the truth. That she was right. I didn't care. I didn't want her friendship or her trust. All I really wanted was my hands on her, her body pressed into mine, lost in the taste of her. I wanted her with an urgency that frightened me. She was so vulnerable and open to me and perfect in that moment that I couldn't control myself. Everything was wanting her.

No, I couldn't tell her the truth. There was only one answer to her question, an answer she dared to hope for and one that would buy me time. Time to befriend her, learn her, know her. Turn her. Over to my side. Away from this other man, the boyfriend. Who was loved. This is the dilemma of impossible questions. If I tell you the truth, you will be crushed and disappointed. If I tell you a lie, I am deceiving you and the truth looms in my silences.

Does the truth matter if you feel good with the lie? If the lie makes you feel safe? If it gives you a place to turn and trust? To hide? Do you really want the answer? Or do you want the answer that allays the fear that forced the question?

I offered her the only thing I could offer in the situation. Commonality. Knowledge that she was not alone. Any other answer would have been wrong. Any other answer would have let her down. Her eyes were shining, accusatory. One right answer. A password. One thing to say to keep it all together. The lie was effortless, falling from my lips like the careless flight of autumn leaves.

"I was molested too."

The lies have always been effortless for me.

***

I never expected to make a friend.

Sarah would come to surprise me in many ways over the coming months, but that surprise was the most profound. I had never really become friends with a woman. I'd used and been used, manipulated or been manipulated, or adopted the quasi-relationship familiarity that comes from sleeping with someone for a while. But never for long, and never with any real depth or vulnerability.

I'd tell you that when you can read someone else's thoughts or talk without speaking that intimacy is a given. But that's too easy – it gives too much credence to otherworldly powers and detracts from the very real and very earthly bond that Sarah and I cultivated during our time together. Yes, the telepathy thing was bizarre and added a level of interconnectedness that I have never experienced before or since, but so much more of it was just *her*.

Since my false confession, she had made a complete turnaround. Something huge changed inside her after that night. She brightened, opened, and threw herself into creating a partnership for us. From that moment forward, we were a team. I understood her, I could relate to why she was the way she was. I had been there too. Hadn't I? She carved a space for me in her world, giving me access to a part of her that had been closed, not only to me, but to everyone for more years than she could remember.

Because I had lied to her, I felt compelled to be honest in other areas, letting her into dark corridors of my life that were normally reserved for private agony. We talked about my mother, my childhood, my walls, the mutable nature of the mask I wore to protect myself. I found, ironically, that if the single lie anchored me, I could be almost shamelessly honest about damn near everything else.

As the weeks passed it became starkly clear that, despite my careful plotting and diligent efforts, we weren't going to sleep together. In the beginning, this drove me near insane. The wanting was enormous, and she was so close, so free around me, so welcoming now that we shared a common enemy – it was slow, terrible torture. My normal response would be to turn on her, hate her, dismiss her through insults and coldness, but she was so kind to me – so wholly new – that my frustrations would shrink and wither, embarrassed, scurrying away from the light of her smile.

After a while, the frantic nature of my longing softened and the baser desires started to fall away. The more I saw of her, the more I was able to see *around* the wanting and glimpse a side of her that was carefully hidden from the rest of the world. Once the sexual compulsion was dealt with, I noticed an exhilarating freedom growing inside me. I didn't have to resort to games or romantic misdirection with her, I didn't have to be slick or cool or sharp, I didn't have to keep up the exhausting pretense of pretending to be something I wasn't. With Sarah, for the first time in my life, it was okay to be myself. Or at least, to begin trying.

But the lie grew, crawling and stretching ever outwards like weeds in an abandoned lot. It pervaded everything, like a cancer, lurking just behind every phone call, every walk, every lunch, and every trusting glance. At first, my silence was okay, it was allowable. After all, who's really going to press someone for details about such painful trauma?

But the more she confessed, the more my silence seemed obstinate and the scales between us appeared unbalanced. So I started peppering the lie with details – the when, the who, the scars. More bullshit. Deeper and deeper, I lay down lies like bricks in a shameful edifice that was spinning further and further out my control.

No, I never expected to make a friend. But deep down, in the places even Sarah couldn't see, I never really expected to keep one either.

***

I only met the boyfriend once. He came into the restaurant one night to pick her up after her shift. He was a tall European guy, in his late thirties, sharply dressed, with an air of cruelty about him that turned me off immediately. He stalked up to the bar, gratuitously eyeing the hostess and the other female servers, immensely self-important. I knew who he was. I'd seen him waiting in his BMW for her in the valet spot enough times to place the face.

He rapped his knuckles loudly on the bar to get my attention. It was late and the place was practically deserted with only a few customers still dawdling at the bar. But I lingered at the wine cooler, ignoring him, rearranging bottles without really looking at them. I wanted to make him wait, for him to see that his alpha male bullshit meant nothing to me, but I knew it wouldn't matter to him one way or the other. I found myself seething, gripping the bottles too tightly, clanking them violently against each other. Why did it have to be *this* guy? Of all the people in the city, she had chosen the worst kind of Euro trash. Over me.

But was I really any better? Lying to her, insidiously trying to worm my way into her life because I didn't have the stones to face my feelings for her outright? Who was I to judge anyone else? My inner struggle was coming to a boiling point when he rapped again. I took a deep breath, turned on him with a perfect fake service-industry smile, and walked over to where he was sitting.

"What'll it be tonight?" I asked.

He was silent, assessing me with an insolent smirk that made me want to hit him.

"You're the Jared Sarah's been talking about," he said.

There was no overt confrontation in his voice or his manner, but I instantly knew that he didn't waltz in here randomly. He was here to check me out and size up what had apparently made it into conversation between the two of them.

"In the flesh," I said.

His smirk hitched upward.

"I thought you'd be bigger," he said, dismissive.

My server's smile widened to hide the murder behind my eyes and I tapped the side of my forehead.

"I'm bigger on the inside."

He locked eyes with me and I finally sensed genuine menace hiding just underneath his perfectly pressed exterior.

"We'll see," he said.

I broke his gaze first, more out of loathing than intimidation, but hating myself for it nonetheless. When I turned back to face him, he was grinning openly, satisfied that I was no longer a threat to his superiority. He pointed absently to the bottles on the top shelf of the back bar, now content to boss around an underling rather than face down a potential rival.

"Make me a Belvedere martini," he commanded. "Dry. Three olives."

Steaming, I grabbed the bottle and the shakers and went to scoop ice out of the sink. Standing over it, I could feel his smugness boring into my back and I debated for a much longer time than I should have whether a broken bottle to the face would wipe that grin off for good. When I couldn't stand it any longer, I dumped the half made drink down the drain and turned to the well bottles underneath the bar. I found a cheap bourbon in a plastic bottle and poured three fingers into a rocks glass with no ice. I set it front of him with contempt.

"Drink up," I said. "It's on the house."

He looked at me with a mixture of surprise and irritation that turned my smile genuine for a welcome moment.

"This isn't what I ordered," he snapped.

"I know," I said and placed the Belvedere bottle back on the shelf.

I tossed my towel and my apron on the bar and I left the restaurant. The boyfriend made a stink to management and Felix read me the riot act the next day for ditching in the middle of my shift. I'm pretty sure Sarah came to my rescue behind the scenes because Felix kept reminding me that he ought to fire me and I was lucky I had people looking out for me in the wings.

Sarah never said a word about what happened, but she knew what it meant. We both did. Walking home that night, swearing under my breath, chain smoking, shouting out snarky remarks in a fake fight with this guy in my mind, I finally understood that my feelings for Sarah ran far deeper than sex. Far deeper than friendship. They ran into a place inside that terrified me, that made me irrational and hugely unsteady.

I had crossed a gulf with Sarah from wanting her to needing her, and that gulf, once crossed, was impossible to take back. I knew that night that I had fallen for her, but that to stay with her, to surrender to that hugeness, would slowly, steadily, and surely destroy us both.

***

Ten whirlwind months after that first Halloween, we were sitting on a blanket under a sky filled with kites in the Presidio. It was my last day in San Francisco. The city had knocked down a few of the older military barracks out in the Presidio district. They planted grass where there were old parade grounds and put in walking paths. There was a grassy field and a small beach, waves lapping at the shore, and a view of the city and the Golden Gate Bridge. They opened the park up to the public that weekend with a kite festival. We didn't even know about it. We were heading down to Golden Gate Park when we got caught up in the crowd and diverted to the water's edge.

Laid back in the tall grass, a bottle of malbec between us, we began to talk about *it*. The daylight was waning and the shadows were growing long. We'd been walking on eggshells all day, trading barbs and passive-aggressive remarks over stupid, forgettable things. We fought like a couple that knows their relationship is collapsing, but are too co-dependent to talk about it.

"You could stay," she had said.

"You could leave," I had said.

We'd called a weary truce after the first bottle of wine and began to talk about the link between us. We talked about things like if it would work from 3000 miles away or if we may have been spoiled by our proximity over the last year. We talked about it to cover up the truth in the silences. That maybe it wasn't a bad thing if the link did evaporate for a bit. That she was too close for me to think clearly anymore. That our friendship was tottering on a rude foundation of lies. That maybe some time away from her was what I needed the most.

"What do we call this?" I said at the end.

She looked up at the sky, hands folded in her lap, eyes half-closed. Serene. Sarah needed to name. Personalize. She had her own nicknames for all sorts of things, a carryover from childhood. Teepy, for example, was a dangerous mixture of tipsy and sleepy. She needed to give feelings and odd states of mind life and ownership, to label them and catalogue them so she didn't forget.

"Kine," she said at last.

She turned and looked at me, taking me in, as if for the first time.

"Kine," she repeated. "We're like these kites, floating around in each other's heads. Just string holding us to the here and now. That's half of it."

I looked up at the sky, to box kites, bats, stunt kites, and ornate, swooping dragons.

"And the other half?" I asked.

She touched my face, stroking down the side of my jaw in a tender sweep.

"I am yours and you are mine."

The moment slowed, floating. I should have told her then, tried to explain, tried to make her understand how wanting her had made me do it. How morality had been banished in an effort to be close to her. But she wasn't mine. Not really. Not when possession was nine-tenths of the law. I suddenly felt helpless. Hollow. Bottomed out.

"Will you come to the party?" I asked, trying to keep the helpless feeling out of my voice.

"I can't," she said, making a move to touch me, then stopping. "I'm sorry."

I nodded and rose from the blanket, brushing myself, clearing my throat, trying for more time. I made my hands into fists and stuffed them into the pockets of my jeans.

"I'll call you when my plane gets in."

She nodded and her eyes filled up.

"I'm going to miss you, Jared."

I couldn't watch her cry. I couldn't bear it. It was killing me. To stay would unravel my lies one right after the other, like pulling a loose string on an old sweater. I couldn't comfort her. If I touched her I would stay. The apartment was rented, my life was on a truck on its way to Boston, and I had tickets in my bag. But if I touched her I would stay. So I took a snapshot of that afternoon in my mind and I walked away, tucking the memory into the same, safe place where my mother still bakes cookies and my dog still chases tennis balls across the back yard. This snapshot is smooth and lovingly dog-eared from looking at it. I have kept it with me for almost nine years.

Until today.

I am yours and you are-

Kine.

The sound of the phone ringing is like the fall of the executioner's blade.

***

"You're sick, Jared."

"I know."

"I'm not kidding."

"I know."

"Like you should be examined by someone-

(*I know.*)

"-or hospitalized."

I see a perfect dinosaur in the clouds.

"Are you done?"

There is an indignant breath on the other end of the phone.

"Am I done? You're an asshole. I haven't even started."

"So we're going to do this all day?"

"Jared, I'm going to do this until I'm God damned good and ready to stop."

Cold, so cold.

"Because I had a rough night last night and I'm really not in the-"

"You're a fucking prick!"

Blinding rage from 3000 miles away.

"Sarah-"

"You're a fucking prick if you think you can make me feel sorry for you about a *thing-*"

I close my eyes.

"-how *dare* you."

There is a laugh at the crest of that, a caesura for breath, and then she dives in.

"How dare you fucking sit on the other end of that phone while I-"

"STOP YELLING AT ME!"

There is silence. The dinosaur in the clouds breaks apart into white whorls as tall as skyscrapers. An airplane cuts across the drifting puffs of its flank on the final pass into Logan. The sounds of the outside are magnified by the heat. Everything feels bigger in the summer. Open.

"I'm sorry," she says.

It is small, fragile. The last word dips into a sob.

"I had to tell you before today."

"No. I'm *sorry*." Her voice is firm again. "I can't do this anymore."

"Can we talk about this?"

"All you are is talk."

Cold again.

"You're the Great Pretender."

"It's not like that-"

"Don't ever call me again."

"Sarah-"

"Not ever, Jared."

Jet engines pass overhead, sweeping out the day with the scream of turbines. Clouds consume the sun. In the cool from the shade, the trees sigh.

And she's gone.

Chapter Four

The Great Pretender

A boy's first love is his mother. Every woman who comes after will be held to that standard. An impossible standard. Of course, this is all very Freudian and subconscious, but a man will look for qualities that made him feel most safe and secure as a child, those small, indefinable things we long for. Need.

The difficulty for men who were especially close to their mothers comes once the current woman starts showing the selfish, needy, or irrational characteristics of any young person. It breaks down the illusion of her being a perfect, wondrous goddess archetype. The man begins to see her for what she really is and not what he made her out to be, or worse, what he was trying to turn her into. Women do this all the time too; I suppose it's not restricted to one gender. *People* only see what they want to see, never what's really there.

Usually by the time they finally do, it's already too late.

***

I'm typical in that I blame everyone else for my problems and not myself. I steal, I cheat, I take. Especially, I lie. I destroy everything around me. I possess an abhorrent devotion to entropy. To say that all this sprang solely from my mother's death would be hyperbole, but it was the catalyst. I can't blame anyone around me for that – the blame solely lies with God for that one. But I can blame people from that point on because no one told me *No*.

You walk a delicate line as a victim of tragedy. You're fucked up in your own right just by living through it, and people are willing to accommodate the emotional roller coaster that invariably follows. You get space, time, distance, a tacit understanding that a member of the tribe is going to go berserk for a while. People rush in at the same time to fill the void with whatever they have, offering comfort in any fashion they can. Food comes, cards, flowers, photos, stories. Collective memories and moments. But you discover early on that these things they bring are not what you need the most. This discovery, when learned hard, is nearly impossible to let go.

Along the razor's edge is a tortuous place of empty longing. You are torn between blinding gratitude and insidious resentment. You are grateful to these people for doing whatever it takes to keep you fed, clothed, and moving. Moving on. But you hate them, just the same, because they get to leave, go home, and move back to their own placid, meandering lives. Everyone has limits to their kindness before their own lives must intrude. They give what they can and then leave you to the bitter work of reconstruction. When the bedroom door closes at night and all the food and flowers and awkward platitudes are left behind, you are alone. Your insides are a cavernous hall of echoes.

As you age, you discover you are different. You carry with you a sense of the raw, a resilience of will, a sense of self-entitlement surrounding a simmering cauldron of rage. People do what you want. They attach obligation to you. They feel compelled to include your well-being in with their own. And that resentment of them grows, deepens. Your empathy towards them withers. You feel the need to prove to them and the rest of the world that you need no one, that you are a self-sufficient engine. You are an island. Their pity disgusts you.

If no one resists you, you never learn the proper parameters of what is socially acceptable. If no one stands up to you, you never learn to be humble or subtle. Instead you forge an unjustified arrogance and weaponize yourself-awareness. You take what you want, you bat your eyes when you need help, and you take the lid off that bottomless well of fury when someone stands in your way.

If it continues into adulthood, your sense of self-preservation will ensure you learn the finer arts of diplomacy and decorum so you don't go too far and take obvious advantage of others. But that hollow is always there, yawning, hungry, reaching out for the one thing no one has. It doesn't matter what they give you or what you take from them. As before, so again, it is never enough.

If you can't find a way to stop, you will wipe out every person who tries to get close to you.

***

I'd like to say that losing Sarah will rip me up. I'd like to tell you that it will kill me a little inside. That I will spend the first few weeks of thirty-five in mourning, realizing the full scope of what I've done to her. I'd love to feel like this has finally cleansed me. No more lies. No more manipulations. No more games. Absolution. But I only feel a bland sadness and a sliver of guilt. I have become a creature of appetite. I have surrendered to the vortex. After thirty-five years, I am no longer trying to pull myself back, a holdout at the edge of the maelstrom. I am sinking into it. Losing *myself*. Falling into surging oblivion.

I'd like to say that losing Sarah will rip me up. But it won't. Not when my whole life has been about losing women. I expect them to leave. Whether I drive them away or they leave me on their own, it's all familiar. It's all been done before. Women are to be loved and lost, worshipped *in absentia*. It is their nature to leave, to wander off. It is my destiny to chase and wait. Always wait.

Anticipating this ending keeps me from ever getting too close. It keeps me from getting hurt. I don't even cry, not since Gayle. She was the last, the most heartfelt because she was the only one who ever came close to pulling me back. All the others have been merely shadows.

I have no tears left for what I have become.

***

Celine calls around three-thirty.

"Where are you?"

She purrs when she talks to me.

"On my roof," I tell her.

"I'm showing a house up the road from you at four." She pauses. "I have time."

"When can I expect you?"

"Five."

"I'll be waiting."

"Jared?"

"Yes?"

"I shaved."

She clicks off and I feel a hot surge of blood swell down into my cock. Celine has this throaty, low voice with a trace of deep Louisiana running through it. The trace comes out after a few glasses of wine, if she's angry, and when she fucks. She isn't loud in bed. She's a talker. I tend to prefer louder women –the screams, the guttural shouts, a bit of pain in the ecstasy. But Celine offers these little whimpers and low moans that lead into luscious filth. She will pull me to her, lips at my ear, biting and gasping, spouting obscenity in a Deep South drawl.

You make me feel like a slut. A little wet slut.

Celine is my first talker. I have experienced the chipmunk squeaks of cute girls, the canned moans of beaded, dirt-smelling hippies, the rapid barks of club chicks tweaked out on coke. And I always loved Gayle's cries from the bottom of her belly, like she was fighting back great sorrow. I used to tell her I wanted her from the moment I saw her because she looked like a girl who would cry when you fucked her.

Their face softens. Their eyes fill. Their mouths open into a wide, perfect O. Their foreheads scrunch up with effort, lines across their brows. Their eyebrows raise and peak at the center. Their eyes half close as they writhe, moaning at something larger than both of us. They cry out like they're hurting. Like it's too much.

I don't actively seek to make women cry. I don't feed on sorrow. Morbid women are compelling, intriguing, but end up proving selfish and sheltered in the end. They are birds caged too long, made delicate and bored through captivity, too weak to handle real emotion, real work. Their negativity sucks away at you. It makes you want to prove them right, that it's all true. Life is only a series of disappointments.

But I like the idea that a woman can cross those wires. The most satisfying reaction is the one where you lose control. When you can't make it stop. There is release, a freedom from responsibility when you can't stop, when it spills out of you. You are powerless, at the mercy of raw, biting emotion. You are naked. Your scars show. Your vulnerability is open, like a diary left carelessly by the bedside or a telling photograph peeking from the pages of an old book. You become someone else.

I love those moments. Rapture. A woman over the edge of reason. I find females to be hugely emotional creatures, prone to whimsy and indecision. They try to exhibit outward control. They micromanage, nitpick, force themselves along the path of custom. There is etiquette, role playing. But underneath, they swirl, formless rivers of passion and longing. I love to break that down, the veneer, get inside that frenetic calm. I want a woman to be a woman, to surrender to her fundamental nature. Cry or moan, demand or beg, just give me the knowledge, the satisfaction, that I did this to you. I made you short-circuit. *I touched the raw.*

Celine has this perfect Southern gentility about her. She is a lady, crisp, cultivated, smooth in her sweetness. She never yells, never bickers, and she doesn't argue. She is disarming with flattery and gracious around power. She remembers little details, wielding control with subtle nudges and a slow hand. Sweet enough to rot your teeth. But that pleasantry is cold. She keeps people at a distance with a detached show of manners. Everything is agreeable. You can't see beneath her. When she exhibits emotion, it is private, violent, and short-lived.

Her word is never questioned, her actions never scrutinized. No one challenges her because she has power. Her will is indomitable. Young women flock to her as a role model, the perfect matriarch, though she has no children of her own. The older women defer to her, despite being barren, because her coldness frightens them. It means she is free in ways they are not. No one tells Celine *No* either.

But when the door is closed and she leaves it all outside, she is alone with her hunger and a life built on the surface of things, with no passion behind it. It is a theater backdrop with only timbers and tossed-together frames holding it up. Celine once told me her greatest agony is that she is not her own woman. She was raised to be a perfect lady, a gracious hostess, queen on the arm of the king. But the kingdom does not belong to her, the subjects do not love her, she is only powerful because she belongs to the king.

When she comes to me and she slips out of her clothes, her role, her pretending, she remains a queen. Only her body betrays her as a woman. She speaks to me of longing.

Her voice carries a litany of outrages, a catalogue of little hurts. Little wants. Desires a lady cannot utter in public. *Need me. Want me. Fill me. Hurt me. Fuck me. Make me feel. Something.*

The sound of her voice makes me shake.

***

I polish off the second joint and a couple sandwiches and debate calling Sarah two or three times. Each time something stops me. But I don't know what that something is and it's giving me a headache. She can't be mad at me for long, she can't *stay* mad at me. Not with what we have, not when we're so close we're in each other's heads. Not when we kine. Isn't disbelief the first of the seven stages of grief?

I'm starting to get that baked hot weariness in my joints and my eyes are fried from the haze and bright. I want a cigarette and I start to feel twitchy for a bit, my fingertips dancing. I put it away by promising to take it out on Celine when she comes and I begin packing up my things. When everything is tucked into the safe pocket of the butterfly chair, I pull a quarter out of my pocket.

"If it's heads, I call her. If it's tails, I let it go."

I flip the coin into the air and let it drop to the tarred surface of the roof. Tails.

"Two out of three."

I pick it up and toss it again. Tails.

"No," I say in disgust. "That's not right."

I pick up the coin and toss it another fifteen times. Each time it's tails and my headache is getting worse.

Stage two is denial.

***

Stage three is bargaining. It's where deals are made. I have a feeling most of the Devil's contracts for souls come about in this stage. A man who believes he has nothing to lose is free to offer anything as currency. What does your body mean when you're hollow? What does pain mean when you've already bled so much? What is a soul? Thinner than paper, lighter than air, the monkey on an ape's back. You want this thing? You want this flapping, floating banner of my despair? What'll you give me in trade?

It's all about us in the end, selfish fucks that we are. Even the Mother Theresa types give because it inflates them. Self-aggrandizing fucks that we are. I. I. I. I'll barter. I'll trade. I'll make deals all my life. Everything is a bargain, a negotiation. How much can I get? Can I stay up later? Can I have another? Can I put it in?

There's a joke. A guy says to this babe on the subway: "If I give you a million dollars, will you go to bed with me?"

"Sure thing, daddy," says the babe.

"How about if I give you a hundred dollars?"

"Get lost," says the babe, "what sort of girl do you think I am?"

"We already established that", says the guy, "now we're just negotiating price."

Ba dum bum. Women never laugh at that joke. It's too close to the mark, the human mark. What's your price? How bad do you want it? What are you like when it gets to a place where you no longer care what other people think? What will you sign away to give your self-aggrandizing prick of a being one more moment of happiness? No one is selfless. No one bargains with Gods and Devils to save little kids and mothers from the volcano or the drunken surgeon, the out-of-control city bus, the guy who just walked into the First Class cabin with a hand grenade.

No one bargains for others, not when it counts. No matter what we ask for, we are bargaining for time for ourselves. To keep our loved ones, smite our enemies, have witness to our suffering, people to humiliate for our shame. Humans can't let go. They cannot accept the finite.

I'll change, God. I know I can change. I can stop doing it. I can just be myself and let things happen the way they're supposed to happen. I don't have to manipulate. I don't have to feed on control. I can stop the games. The lies. The way I feel so empty inside. I can learn. I can grow. There's still a chance. I am a thinking animal. My soul can still learn. Please, I don't have much time. Just let her call me. Let her still love me. Just a little longer. Just for today. *Please*.

My father has a saying: Every man finds God when he's late.

When he's run out of time.

***

I met a woman on the trains about six months ago. When there was still snow on the ground. You start seeing the same people if you commute long enough. You find people running similar paths to you. They become fixtures. Most of them only have nicknames. There's Toupee Guy. Fratercrombie Boy. Skater Chick. Trust-fund Tramp. Some of them you have customary greetings with: a head nod, a wave hello, idle banter about the weather, the Red Sox, the goddamned trains.

Others you befriend. Some shared observation leads to laughter, softening, opening. A train buddy to make the commute go faster. Rail pals sharing some dirt over steaming cups of Dunkin' Donuts. These friends are low-key, low maintenance, easy because you know them, but you don't have to *know* them. Your time together is always limited, structured, like kids at recess. You don't follow them home. It's all the benefits of a friendship with none of the responsibility. Bonded but not bound.

I met this woman, Amanda, waiting in the screaming wind for the morning B-Line, ankle deep in snow. Irritable. One train lumbered in, packed full with commuters, stopping, comically, to let one or two out and try and stuff a few more in. She rolled her eyes and went into a rant about the trains, the annoying warm bodies pressed up against the glass inside, and the cold. We didn't even try to get on, both of us knew better.

We started laughing, watching the eager younger kids push their way into the teaming masses of bundled flesh, bags and arms akimbo. It was like watching stage divers. Somehow our chat turned to our jobs, hers something in finance. Her suit and heels, the leather portfolio, roughing at the corners. By the time we caught the next train, we were pals. By the time we debarked at Government Center, we were trusted friends, having shared gossip, jokes, and companionable chit-chat in the metal womb of the train.

I saw the ring, but I said nothing. I wasn't concerned about that sort of thing. Not then. Not until she began to show the river underneath. She was just a woman I vaguely knew on the commute. This was strictly a first name relationship. But each time I saw her she was more nervous, more disheveled, more erratic. Her moods would vary from somber and serious to elated and giddy, sometimes in one train ride. Other days I know she would see me, but she would ignore me and I wouldn't push. Something was eating at her, it was evident. Evident to anyone who took the time to look. But no one ever looks. That's why I don't feel guilty.

After a month of this and her escalating, percolating inner pressure, I confronted her. Trouble at work? Trouble at home? *Are you all right, Amanda?* And she gushed, like a dam burst open, telling me troubles, listing her stresses, expunging her demons. She was getting married. The wedding was in two months. So much was left unfinished. Caterers. Florists. Band versus DJ. Chicken or fish. Her parents were driving her crazy and her husband-to-be had detached himself from the preparations, clean as a surgeon's cut.

Did I know what stationary cost? How expensive it was to dye shoes for the bridesmaids? How tricky a prospect it was seating a room full of people who hated each other? That her fiancé had cheated on her, just once, back when they were in grad school?

I absorbed her fervor. I took it into myself, deflected the worst of it, turned it into fluff and jokes. I made her laugh. I made her calm. I made her breathe. She came back into herself, a little at a time, a few days here and there. I became her confidante, the guy on the train she could confess to because he wasn't involved. An outsider. A perfect stranger. I gave her my e-mail and she wrote. I gave her my number and she called. Every day we deepened. Each week she opened more. Petals of a stretching flower.

Two weeks before the wedding, I caught her at the station on her way home. She looked lost, confused. Overwhelmed. I touched her arm and when she looked up at me her eyes were bright with tears. *Oh Jared.* She cried out, sunk into my arms, whole body heaving with the force of her sobs. I held her to me for six or seven stops, people looking at me with curiosity or derision. Breakup? The Big Fight? Cheater? Everyone blames the man she's with when a woman is crying.

When Amanda finally got under control, she told me she'd gotten in a terrible, mean-spirited fight with her mother and with everything looming over her, she just lost it. Cold feet. She wanted to call the whole thing off. She was scared. Alone. I comforted her. I stuffed her full of platitudes and ego boosters. I wiped tears away from her eyes. I asked an old Chinese lady for some tissue. I put Amanda back together again.

This is my stop. Her voice was shaky, still hiccupy from crying. *No*, I told her, taking her arm, *let's get a drink*. The *I can't, I can't.* Excuses. Reasons. All of them valid, none of them good enough. So we drank. We laughed. We forgot what was around us. We fell into our own safe little world. Partners in crime. Two people on the same team. She drank. She giggled. She flirted. She opened wider.

Last call. It was snowing outside. So late in the season for snow. *I'll walk you home.* The smile. *I'd like that.* And the kiss. Outside on her stoop. The kiss. Her lips at mine with an eagerness, a tenderness I didn't quite understand. I put my hands around the curve of her waist and she melted, like child's clay, into my arms. Then I understood. I knew how she needed to be touched. Fiancé was away. Always away. On business. Important business. Expense reports and flight vouchers. Hotel shampoo in little bottles. Roving eyes in the dim of the lobby bar. I understood everything.

She ate me, absorbed me, pushed me inside her. She forced herself against my hips with astonishing strength, bucking at me, holding to me like she was drowning. Begging. Fill her. Use her. Her nails like claws at my back, legs wrapped tight around my hips, dripping honey. The room swam with the scent of her, the heat of her. No radio, no television, only the hard, slapping wetness of bodies in motion, slick with sweat. The music of her screams. Opening. Opening. Bottomless.

In the morning she was tender. Soft. Adoring. We cooked breakfast in her kitchen. Ate eggs at her table. Grinning like accomplices after the crime. We showered together and dressed for work. Her in another of a long line of tailored suits. Me in the same clothes from the day before. We waited for the train at her stop in comfortable silence, warmed in the afterglow, fingers of our gloves touching lightly, her fingers tracing over the insides of my palm. The snow was already melting. The day was bright. Amanda was ready to be married. *Thank you, Jared. Really. Thank you.*

I got home and found a wedding invitation stuffed into the pocket of my blazer. *For Jared.* No last names. Am I wrong for what I did? I knew it would happen. I knew it in the first week I met her. When I took a sip of my coffee and she looked at me, held my eyes a second too long, and then fell silent, I knew. I knew what she wanted, what hid beneath the surface, the swelling tide of her. Am I wrong because I led her into the events that followed? Guided her to what she really wanted? Needed? Some women say men are dogs, that we only think with our pricks. This may be true to some degree, but the woman always decides. She lets us in. She opens. There are no unwilling victims of seduction.

I didn't go to the wedding. No last names. Perfect strangers.

That's why I don't feel guilty.

***

I feel the fourth stage rising on the heels of the third and I head to the kitchen to choke it back down with Scotch. Guilt. You get to a point where you've gone so far and seen so much, you can't be bothered with guilt. It's insulting. It wastes time. It eats at you, slows you down, keeps you awake. It gnaws, like a rat gnaws, like the Tell-Tale Heart beating under the floorboards. Almost all the world's problems could be handled if people surrendered guilt for resolve.

When the plans are big, when the stakes are high, you don't have time to stop for guilt. Reactions and behavior should be studied, losses analyzed and reverse engineered so the next move is stronger. Strategy should outweigh emotion. Control over oneself is paramount. Playing with people's emotions is like playing chess.

Both are a science of entrapment.

***

Back in the bathroom, I'm grooming myself. I shed my clothes and hop in the shower, washing off the oily grime of the afternoon. I do Kegels while I'm washing my hair and tug myself half hard, relaxed in hot steam, thinking about-

(*little wet slut*)

-the voice that enslaves me. I turn around and bow my head, letting the hot jet of water pound the back of my neck. The last of my headache, the dregs of my hangover, sluice down the drain of the battered clawfoot tub.

I towel off and wipe a patch of fog off the mirror at the sink. My face is puffy from the shower, my skin tight. The razor cuts through my stubble, whisking down my face with a satisfying scrape, careful around the chin and mouth. I wash off shaving cream and pat my face with my towel. I brush and floss, gargle mouthwash, washing out Scotch and pot smoke. Finally I put in my contact lenses and study my face, tugging at my goatee.

I meet my eyes in the glass. Dark, fierce orbs.

"I hope you're happy," I say.

Hope you're happy.

A perfect mimic from lips across the gap. I smile. The lips smile back.

"You're the Great Pretender."

The smile widens. But it doesn't touch the eyes.

***

In the ninth grade, I had Ms. Johnstone for Freshman English and Composition. She was an effete, bitter woman whose husband had traded her in for a much younger model in the secretary pool at his office. They were in Reno. She was here, running Freshman English like a death camp. Her humorless grunts as she acknowledged our raised hands for questions punctuated the stuffy room like gunfire. When she did speak, it was a haughty, patronizing thing, cultivated at some baby Ivy school that wasn't good enough to get her a job at a college. And she never used our names.

But she knew my name. Master November, she called me. I hated it. I hated her. Deep down in my well of ill will, there was room for her. I was a smart little bastard in school. I had A's in everything. My mom was two years in the ground and everyone had backed away from me. I was bored and clever, chewing through teachers like it was my job. *Issues with authority. Exhibits ringleader behavior. Leads by defiance. Corrects and questions unmercifully. A disruptive classroom element.* Blah. Blah. Blah.

But Lauralie Johnstone was ready for me. She was equally smart, tough, and she took less than one sentence of my bullshit and I got suspended for a week. After five days of suspension, I wanted a taste. So I played by her rules. I read, I studied, I learned. I pushed myself. I *applied* myself. And we began trading barbs and insults behind heated discussions over the material. Class was my daily dose of chess. She just kept winning.

The breaking point came when we were assigned to write a short story about things you didn't see every day. I decided I wanted to write a story about drug dealers. I raised my hand. I knew very little about drugs at that point; alcohol was still my faithful golden ticket. She grunted to acknowledge my hand.

"Are we allowed to use basic profanity if it's used in dialect?"

"No."

"It paints a picture-"

"We will have no profanity of any kind."

For all my limited knowledge of drug dealers, I was fairly certain they didn't say *Aw Schucks* when a deal went bad. I went home and addressed my father with the quandary. He was still a professor at Brown, just then starting to debate teaching in Florida. Away from spirits. He taught history, elitist and stern about his education and the education of his children. He'd been to enough parent-teacher conferences to know the players and the rules.

"You could write what you feel and hope it stands by the writing," he told me. "Or you can burn her and write a story where the situation is so ridiculous, the absence of profanity seems absurd. The first is noble, but she'll flunk you for breaking her rule. She won't get past the first swear. And she may very well flunk you if you burn her. But it's the smarter of the two."

"Why is that?" I had asked.

"It shows she's a poor teacher."

So I wrote a story about a man who ran off on his wife with a young pretty thing from his office pool. I was vague on the details of the wife. You just got an idea that she was humorless and frumpy. The climax of the story was the fight between hubby and wife, the ugly *why*. There were a lot of *aw shucks* and even a *cotton pickin'* at one point. It was baseless, ridiculous, and petty. But it was otherwise well-written and it proved the point.

She failed me. I was furious. My father saw red.

She WHAT!

Haunted by my mother's ghost, godlike in his fury, my father stormed into the high school and screamed Lauralie Johnstone into the ground. Swinging his PhD around like a mace, he demanded justice all the way up to the Superintendent. Professor Stuart November, a lion on the march. He wears brimmed hats and flip-flops now. He teaches two or three days a week at U Miami and he has pink flamingos on his lawn. He goes to commencements in shorts. And he never remarried.

When it was over, everyone went on their best behavior for a while. I got a C on the story, and that must have killed her. But I'll hand it to her, she wouldn't cough up an A for me if they tortured her. And I don't blame her. We settled and life went on. I got her good, just once. That's all I wanted, to prove I was the better survivor.

When the school year ended, I caught her out by her car. It was packed with what looked like all her stuff. She was on the hood, smoking a cigarette.

"Go easy on your teachers next year," she said.

"I'll try," I said and grinned at her.

Her face was stone.

"You're smart, Jared, but you're a prick of a kid."

"It hasn't been easy, you know?"

"Spare me," she almost shouted, rising up off the hood of her car.

"What's the matter with you?" I asked, sincere. Just so.

"Drop the act," she said, stamping out her cigarette.

She was a thin, bony slip of a woman who was once beautiful.

"You don't like me very much, do you?"

She grunted at me in affirmation, as if my hand were raised.

"Does it matter to you what people think?" she asked.

"I'd like to know what you think," I replied.

She opened her mouth and shook her head.

"I think you'll be fine," she said, devoid of feeling. "You've got them all fooled."

"What are you talking about?" I demanded, feeling heavy in the pit of my gut.

She looked at me like she saw something far away.

"You're the Great Pretender."

The words rang through my head like a sucker punch. The playground noises, school kids, teens revving cars, the fanfare, it faded out. Tunnel vision. She saw. *Me.* She got me good, just once. That was all she wanted, to rattle the cage. She got in her car and drove away and she didn't come back to teach the next year. Last I heard she died a few years back after a long battle with Emphysema and lung cancer.

Serves you right. Way to make a kid instantly self-aware. Way to make a kid feel like a serial killer. Make him question his motives. See himself as he fears others really see him. You were on to me and it serves you right, Lauralie, for putting those goddamned words in my head. You cunting catalyst, you don't know what I paid. You don't know.

My mother would have known it was a from a Platters song. But she had wandered off by then, and I didn't dare tell my father. I never told anyone. I never thought to look it up and it wasn't until Gayle that I even heard it. Dancing in her mother's garden, against the trellis, stealing a kiss.

I didn't know. I just heard those words and they wasted time in my head. They ate at me. Slowed me down. Kept me awake. Like a rat gnaws. She's one of the ones I've blamed along the way.

Two weeks after she left I started smoking.

***

It isn't until I see that I'm gripping the sides of the sink tight enough to turn my hands into white wires of sinew. It isn't until I look up and see my face drawn back into a rictus of disgust. It's then I realize that I'm fully immersed in stage five. Anger.

"Fuck you, bitch," I say into the mirror.

You bitch.

Echoes. Teeth. Fury.

My anger dulls, dissipates. But I leave the bathroom unsettled, unsure if I was yelling at the ghost of my old teacher or across the miles. To Sarah. The buzzer scatters my thoughts, loud like a churchbell, and I'm at the door, grinning in a towel.

Right on time, Celine.

I want a cigarette when I see her coming round, up the bend in the stairs, legs stretching up the landing. A flash of thigh under a short skirt, toned by personal trainers and Bikram yoga. A flash of jewelry worth more than a year of college. Jet black hair tucked up around her head with Japanese sticks. Sleeveless blouse, silk, with frog buttons and an Asian hem. A cloud of *Calyx* perfume. Blue eyes. Slingbacks.

Depression is the sixth stage of grief. I know a thing or two about depression. I've been pretty manic for over twenty years. Some days it's bad, most days it's worse. A lot of the time it's a low hum. Even keel. But it's always there.

Knowing that I will return to it, no matter what I do, allows me to never grow up. It allows me to take the pleasure of things in the moment, at face value. When I'm up, I'm really up. When it's Celine, I'm as up as up can get. I'll be depressed. I am depressed. But I'm enough of an opportunist to push it aside when I sense pleasure. I am made of flesh. Sex is therapy. It helps me cope.

For a little while longer.

***

In the pantry. It's sweltering hot. The door is shut. Cora is outside, crying. I'm fucking her again. Celine. Again. Smooth and dripping. Glistening. I want it to be hot. I want to feel like I'm choking. Both of us are naked. Slippery. I'm fucking her bent over Cora's litter box, her arms knocking over cans of tomatoes and soup. Our feet are gritty with cat litter. Hot. *I want to feel you. On me. Inside. Harder.* She's pulling at shelves. Her mouth is a stream of curses.

You make my cunt hurt.

Playing with her clit, palm against smooth, buttery soft skin. Biting the back of her neck. Hand around her throat. Goading her to talk. She comes. Shakes. Shudders in the heat. Backing herself into me. Thrusting her ass back at me. Writhing. Gasping. I feel myself building. Strained. Painful. She pulls herself off and turns around, sliding to her knees, one hand around my ass, devouring me, the other hand working at the smooth patch between her legs. Frenetic. She releases me for a moment and looks up, dripping, face a sheen of sweat.

I want to come with your cock in my mouth.

Then I'm lost in her, in blinding heat. Exploding. Screaming. Blind.

There is a great white silence.

And I am someone else.

***

When she leaves, I go into my room and take the gun out. I sit in my chair with it, hefting the weight of it, the severity. Naked in the sweaty stink of sex and *Calyx*, I rest it in on my thighs, watching it, fearing its intent. It is nothing without me. I make it work. It needs me to function. And shells.

I rake the action and check the barrel. Empty. Just as it was when I checked it last. The action is smooth. I oiled it again. I pick it up, stock against my shoulder. I pull the trigger and there's a dull click. You're not supposed to dry fire a gun. It's bad for the firing pins. It stresses them and they can shear. A gun is not a toy.

If you can't find a way to stop, you will wipe out every person who tries to get close to you. But I know how to stop. I've known for a while now. Even when I bought the gun outside of Miami four years ago. When I bought fresh shells last week. I had to tell her before today. I couldn't let her go on and think horrible things. Such thoughts. I came clean because I love her and I can't stop. Pretending. She is the last. Sarah. Sarah who was.

I put the shotgun back into the closet, wrapping it in a blanket, tucking it behind boxes and shoes. I sigh and go over to my bookcase. There, hidden back behind a Riverside Shakespeare is an almost full pack of Marlboro Lights and a silver Zippo. The inscription on it says *Petit Mort*. A gift from Gayle, for graduation, before I left. I stand in the bedroom, naked, and light a cigarette. Smoking it, I begin to cry. It's a long time before I stop. But I do stop.

The final stage is acceptance.

Chapter Five

Brothers in Arms

I dream about the end of the world.

My dreams are vivid and alive, tactile and overwhelming. They are superior in detail. When I have dreams where I am flying, I can feel the wind, the tears at the corners of my eyes, open wide to the passing clouds. When I have nightmares, they are indistinguishable from reality. The monsters are real. The torture is real. The exposure is real. The bottom of my mind is like an abattoir. I believe a person can go insane from a dream, that our minds can betray us. I believe sanity is merely a curtain, a coping mechanism covering heaving chaos.

These end-of-the-world dreams are always nuclear. No aliens, no wrath of God, no disaster movies. It's always war. In the way we all fear war can end. And I always have them when I've lied to someone I care about and I've been caught in it. I don't know if it's a warning or a manifestation of my inner guilt and shame. I don't know if it's some metaphor about my own world coming to an end. I'm not sure about any of it. But when it's done, when the lie is out and I'm exposed, there is always a mushroom cloud.

And the release of being utterly obliterated.

***

Boston. Middle of August. The heat is maddening. Traffic has been backed up on the Zakim Bridge and into the tunnel for so long people are out of their cars walking around. Some guy in a big, green Chevy Suburban has thrown down his tailgate and is grilling up burgers on a Walmart hibachi ten cars up. The afternoon smells of cooking meat and that muggy, wet city smell coming up out of the tarmac, seeping from the rivets of the suspension cables, saturating the air as it wafts in slow desert ripples in the distance.

The sun is a screaming white inferno and the sky is pale blue. The Budweiser billboard on the Garden says 102, but it's got to be five degrees hotter on the bridge. People started turning their cars off after an hour or so, fearful of running out of gas. The muttering and bitching went on for a surprisingly short time and now people are out and exploring, trying to find out why everything has stopped dead.

This guy with the hibachi is trying to make the best of it, handing cold beers around, and sending his chubby redheaded kids out to other stranded cars with hotdogs, chalk-white zinc oxide spackled on their freckled noses. Some Brazilian teenagers have cranked up their stereo and are dancing on their cars, waving hotdogs around, grinning with mustard smeared all over their lips. And this shoeless guy in a spotless seersucker suit is sitting on top of his DeSoto, smoking a joint. Wisps of smoke rise lazily up into the eaves of the bridge.

But it's been almost two hours since we stopped moving and all we can hear are sirens. There's no smoke and no fire, but it sounds like everything they've got is heading downtown. We can't see anything from where we're stuck, but some people in the cars next to us are talking about walking down into the tunnel to try and see what's going on. A while ago we heard helicopters, but we didn't see anything.

There's a lady going around asking for a water collection and trying to find a doctor. A ragtag group of guys who said they were a mix of off-duty cops, firemen, and EMTs were looking for people to open up mini-vans and SUV tailgates for people with heatstroke. A woman in a Volvo station wagon ahead of us is handing out soft, silver Caprisun packs to any kids nearby from out of the back of the car.

This big lady with pendulous breasts mops her brow and stalks up and down alongside her car, asking all the right questions, telling it like it is.

"This is bullshit! This is crazy. How come no one's told us anything? How come we're just sittin' here? How come they closed the bridge down? How long are we going to be sittin' here? People are going to start dyin' if this keeps up. Gonna run out of gas - cooked where you stand. And why won't my radio work?"

She's been carrying on like this for the better part of an hour and it's amazing she still has the energy. She's wearing a black church dress with great pink and red roses printed on it. Sweat is pouring down the front of her face in sheets as she raves up and down on the burning pavement in tiny pink heels. All that's left of her makeup is an angry slash of candy apple red lipstick like Amazon war paint on her huge, furious lips.

This beautiful Siberian husky with perfect markings and bombardier blue eyes is pacing in nervous circles around the bed of his owner's pickup truck. The owner has the same eyes. He is a hardcase in a chambray work shirt, faded blues, and a cowboy hat. His boots have spurs on them and they're dusty. He didn't want the dog to swelter in the cab, so he let it into the back. He put water down, but the dog doesn't want it. It's throwing nervous barks out into the day, tail tucked between its legs. Its eyes are blazing. Fear is bright in them, broadcast to the huge mass of sweating flesh on the bridge. They are pleading eyes. Human.

It knows the same thing that I know, the thing the others still won't let themselves feel. The thing they're all still in denial about, but which their primal, animal selves feel in every pore and crevice. That prickling sense of impending force. A mounting fear of coming danger. It's a crackle like the air before a thunderstorm or that eerie green calm that comes over a field before a twister touches down. It is this thing, this crowning inevitability that somehow, from when I was a small child, I knew I would one day see. Something huge is about to happen.

The sound of rotors comes from overhead and a heavy-bellied helicopter passes over the bridge, flying low. It's gleaming in the sun like a metal insect and its rotors look like great, buzzing wings. It banks and hovers next to us.

People are crossing lanes and coming to the edge of the bridge, peeking out from tailgates or out of sunroofs. The dog woofs three times and the hardcase cowboy comes out of the cab, taking off his hat and holding it to his chest, squinting to get a good look at the chopper.

Men in suits and dark sunglasses peer out from its belly, peeking out at us like swimming fish in a bowl. We wait, expectant, eager for news. Was there an accident? A disaster of some kind? A spill or a leak? A terrorist attack? More and more people are crossing over to the side to get a look at the helicopter, a wave of expectation running through the crowd. Smatterings of conversation drift down the length of the bridge.

Why is it just sitting there?
Why don't they say anything?
What's going on?
Why won't they talk to us?
Something's wrong.

The helicopter banks away from the bridge and takes off fast, its silver underbelly reflecting sunlight in a bright flash. Rustles and sighs of consternation and anger ripple through the crowd now. Some people throw things after it. There is a stream of bottles and cans, shoes, even a lawn chair and a plastic paddle from a kayak, light enough to seem to be floating down, falling end-over-end to the water below.

Four jets streak past at impossible speed, close enough to read the call numbers off their cockpits. They shake the cables of the bridge, shrieking past the crowd to cries of dismay, and finally, terror. The panic infects the people, spreads from the side of the bridge closest to the city, and blooms. A small trickle turns to a wave and soon people are rushing past us, abandoning their cars, some overloaded with possessions or burdened with screaming, badly frightened children. They are running from *it*, that unknown and unseen vibrating force coming from somewhere deep in the middle of the city. They don't know what it is, only that it means death.

I catch eyes with the big lady. She brings a hand up over her mouth and looks at me with solemn, liquid eyes.

"Oh, Lordy," she says. "It's the end."

She waves her hands in front of her like she's trying to shake water off them, turning and craning her head to try and see every direction at once. She starts to spin in tight circles like a top on her tiny pink heels, her eyes growing wider and wider as more and more people run past. Finally, she breaks for the mob, joining their ranks, diving into the stampede. After a short time, she disappears among them, lost in a sea of panic.

"They can't run."

The voice startles me out of my freeze of indecision to stay or flee. It brings me back to where I am and I look up to the voice and meet the hard eyes of the cowboy. He continues on as if it doesn't matter whether I'm there or not, like he's just speaking aloud to himself. But the intensity of his eyes pin me where I stand.

"The blast radius will balloon out at least thirty miles. We're standing at ground zero."

He sets his hat back on top of his head and looks out across the water into Boston's heart. He looks otherworldly, out of place with his getup and the day. He is so easy in his skin, completely unruffled, calm like he's been waiting for this all his life. His dog makes a low whine, lies down in the bed, and tucks its head under its paws. The cowboy passes a hand over the dog's magnificent fur and it raises its head, snuffing at his hand with its snout. It whines again, with a heartrending loyalty for its master. The dog too, it seems, is resigned to its fate.

"You're not supposed to be here, are you?" I ask him, finding my voice at last.

"No," he says and turns on me with those gunslinger's eyes again. "And neither are you, kid."

The guy in the seersucker suit waves his joint at us and winks. He hasn't moved. He is serene, smoking, watching the city. There are others, beyond the running masses, who have climbed atop their cars or leaned against the bridge cables, staring out at the city or looking skyward, as if anticipating fireworks.

"A word of advice," the cowboy says, fingers still deep in the dog's rich fur.

There is a pressure change and my ears pop. A breeze crosses the bridge and it feels like all the air is being sucked into the tunnel. A low hum starts and my chest feels thick and heavy. The cowboy's eyes sparkle like chips of ice from under the brim of his hat. I nod at him. He nods back.

"Don't look at the flash," he says. "You'll go blind."

There is a scream of wind, like a tornado. Then there is a sound like the ripping of titanic fabric, like a great sheet across the sky being torn in two. The cowboy reaches into the bed of the pickup and wraps his arms around his dog, burying his face deep in the dog's coat. I close my eyes. The world becomes a white flash and a deep rumble rattles the bridge, shaking it like a child's jump rope. I hear metal strain and squeal, feel cables snap, and the bellowing cacophony of the explosion.

I open my eyes. I open my eyes and see.

Blooming like a great, dazzling flower, a dome of fire grows over the city, rising higher and higher and mushrooming out and over the skyscrapers. The shockwave comes barreling over the bridge, spreading across it like a massive ocean wave, obliterating everything in its wake. It comes closer, devouring anything and everything that stands in its path, cutting a swath across the lanes, rending even the cohesion of atoms apart in its wake. Like a scythe it comes, reaping merciless death across bridge. The air grows unbearable, the heat merciless. Screaming can be heard, horrid wails over the roaring rush of the shockwave.

My skin begins to blacken and burn, falling off my bones in flakes like old paint. There is agony, a pain unlike any other, a pain of coming apart on the deepest of levels, of having even death taken in the raving storm cloud of nullity, nothing, and fire. The sound of the blast is deafening, even to my already disintegrating ears.

I cry out in ecstasy.

And my body explodes into pieces.

***

Bang.

Banging. Someone's banging. I open my eyes. Someone's banging on my front door. I groan and sit up, shaking my head, looking at the clock.

7:37.

Jesus.

More banging. I leap out of bed and grab the nearest pair of shorts hanging off an armchair. I manage to put one leg through and somehow get the other stuck. Hopping around on one foot, I reach out for the dresser to steady myself and miss, collapsing to the floor in a tangled, graceless heap. Eddie's hammering on the door now like an angry husband. I'm about to yell at him to hold the fuck on and then-

How do you know that it's Eddie?

The thought snaps my mouth shut and I feel a chill of panic rise and tighten around my chest.

What if it's-

"Come on, dick! I know you're in there. Open up!"

The breath I'd been holding escapes in a rush with a nervous bark of laughter. I half jog to the door and throw it open. Eddie grins at me, sharp in his dark suit, arms up in pretend consternation.

"What the fuck happened to you? You look like shit."

"Thanks. I fell asleep. Come on in."

He crosses the threshold and wrinkles his nose at me.

"And you *stink*."

"Sorry," I say, meeting his eyes sheepishly. "I had company."

He passes me, poking his head down the hallway and then heading over to my room, peeking into the darkness.

"Who was it? Paige?"

"No," I say.

He wags a finger at me.

"Was it the MILF?"

"Shut up."

"Was it?"

"She's not a MILF, Ed."

"Like hell she's not," he says.

"In order to be a MILF, you have to be someone's mother," I tell him. "She doesn't have kids."

He waves his hand at me and makes an annoyed face.

"Pfft…semantics. Whatever. Even better. No stretch marks. No cavernous pussy. Mmm…mmm. Good for you."

"I do it just for you, Ed."

"I know you do," he says, turning on the light in my room. "Is she still here?"

Is the gun still out? Are there shells on the dresser? What about-

I step in and shoo him out of the room before he can get a good look. I feel like a mother turning her kids out to play so they'll stop bugging her and leave her alone.

"She left a couple hours ago. I had to crash."

He raises an eyebrow.

"So the MILF tuckered you out, huh?"

"You never stop, do you?"

"Not yet," he says.

"How does Harriet even put up with you?"

He shrugs his shoulders.

"Fuck 'em right the first time and they'll do anything you want."

"Nice," I groan.

He shrugs again.

"What times is dinner?" I ask.

"Nine," he says. "We'll get there before ten. Build the suspense. Give Harriet some time to run around and micromanage everything. Make everyone insane."

"What is this place anyway?"

He shakes his head.

"Some little place in the North End. I've got the directions on me. This is all Harriet's doing. I'm just supposed to escort you there."

I nod, trying to decide if I can handle a roomful of all my friends and copious drinking for-

(*one last hurrah*)

-a second night in a row. Eddie seems to read my mood, like he always does.

"Don't sweat it, we've got time. We'll hang out. It's just a birthday, man. Just another number. It's not like we're going to a fucking funeral, right?"

A chill reaches down my neck and slides all the way down my spine.

"Right," I say weakly.

I can't meet his eyes so I turn from him and walk into the living room.

"Bong is in the bookshelf. Stuff is in the cigar box."

"Good man," he says.

He opens the glass doors to the bookcase and pulls out the drugs and accoutrements. He sits himself down in front of the coffee table and starts packing a bowl with careful scrutiny, like a scientist huddled over a microscope or a row of beakers. An alchemist on the brink of a transmutation.

The chill won't go away and I'm afraid I'm going to start shivering any minute.

"I gotta throw on a shirt, I'll come back and join you in a minute."

He turns up his nose again and looks at me with joking disgust.

"Dude, take a shower first," he says. "You smell like a Tijuana sideshow."

We both laugh and the chill is replaced by a sickening feeling of guilt in the pit of my stomach.

Oh, Eddie.

His teeth are perfect. His eyes sparkle. His laugh reaches down into his belly, filling the room with mirth. Effortless joy. Easy camaraderie. Eddie being Eddie. It's dazzling. Blinding.

(Don't look at the flash.)

My eyes well up and a hard, bitter lump rises in my throat.

(You'll go blind.)

I have to leave the room before my nightmare comes true. Before Eddie's simple, stupid, unquestioning love kills me where I stand.

***

Eddie is an asshole. There is no need to mince words. I speak the truth and Eddie won't deny it. The two of us have a long and sordid history of escapades and incidents and our friendship is forged out of deep respect and admiration for each other. At its simplest, we are stronger together than we are apart. Our combined force is insurmountable. Indomitable. Enormous. Our crew of friends has always stood out. We have always been notorious. But Eddie and I are the core. We are the brain and the heart of our collective. The head of the snake.

There are jokes among our inner circle, about Eddie and me. The humor is that Eddie and I, for all intents and purposes, should be natural enemies in the wild. We should be at odds, at each other's throats. We are two proud, territorial predators who defend their turf to the death. His manner is almost polar opposite to mine, his demeanor disharmonious to my own. But through a mix of tragedy and fate, we found ourselves on the same side, united against a common foe. We were bound by another we swore to protect, one less fortunate than ourselves. But that is another story.

I strive for harmony. Balance. I use charm, flattery, lies, and an almost psychic power of empathy to relate to others and put them at ease. I unite myself, align myself, to what other people are feeling. I need a degree of inclusion, validation, in the lives of others. I need to be, if not the center of attention, then at least a provider of some kind. Whether it is providing advice, entertainment, or counsel, as long as I am looked upon as a source of energy – nourishment – for others, I am happy.

Eddie has no such needs. He does what he pleases with a stubborn resolve that is, at best, maddening, at worst, bullheaded and obnoxious. He doesn't bother himself with flattery or anything beyond basic manners. He has no need to pull his punches. Eddie is, at his heart, a pragmatist. He finds the simplest, most efficient and direct route to his goal and plods forward with his head down until he achieves it.

The advantage to this tactic is that he cuts out all the extraneous steps that might interfere with the completion of his task. The disadvantage is that he will often consider morality, other people's feelings, rules, and decorum as extraneous steps. I am no paragon of moral virtue by any means, but I at least try to hide the fact that I'm exploiting or taking advantage of others. I wield a quiet power. I take great pains to make my strings of control invisible. I pretend to care.

I wish I could abandon that need for etiquette, that pervasive need to keep up appearances, to make everything look placid on the surface. I wish I could tell people what I want from them, exactly what I think of them, without a filter. Without edited, softened, or rehearsed words. Without platitudes or regret. I wish I could be scathing, brutal, the one people love to hate. I wish I could walk away without wondering what they thought of me, if they are mad at me, if I have somehow tarnished my reputation.

Eddie is fearless in this way. As much as I am a narcissist, Eddie exists as a pure, unadulterated creature of self. There is no self-admiration, no self-aggrandizement. He does not need to feed an oversized ego. There is no self-importance for Eddie. He doesn't believe he is God's gift, entitled by hardship, deserving of special treatment. Nor does he feel that he is deserving of a larger share of the pot than anyone else. Eddie simply believes he is alone. Separate, different, and outcast from the rest of the world, Eddie believes he is free.

I am going to miss him most of all.

***

After a shower, I feel moderately better, more relaxed and in control of myself. I throw on a light summer suit, brush my teeth, and join Eddie out in the living room. He's contented himself playing X-Box, the room filled with a haze of bluish pot smoke. He pats the spot next to him on the couch.

"Come on, hook in for some Halo."

I sit down and he tosses me a controller, eyes never leaving the television. I stare at him for a moment.

"How did you get in here anyway?" I ask.

"Evelyn let me in. She was on her way out."

"Did she have any gems to pass along?" I ask.

"Yeah," he says. "She says Happy Birthday."

I am incredulous.

"Really? Evelyn said that?"

He laughs and hits me on the shoulder.

"No, dude. I'm just fucking with you. She *hates* you."

Evelyn Tai is my downstairs neighbor. I swore up and down I wouldn't do it. Don't shit where you eat. Rah. Rah. Rah. But I did it anyway, because I have the self-control of a five year old. I slept with her eight months after I moved in and it turned into an utter disaster.

It started off innocently enough. She met me in the throes of moving my stuff in and introduced herself. We chatted on the stoop and she offered me a cold beer. We did the small talk thing and I was really too worn out to take in just how attractive she was. I'm not into Asian girls as a rule, but Evelyn is a mix of Japanese and French that defies explanation. She was cute enough, but she was my neighbor and I absolutely knew how badly it would end.

Life went on as usual for the first couple months. I'd see her coming in or pass her on the stairs. We'd catch each other waiting for the same train some afternoons or run into each other at the bars. Then I went to New York City for a weekend and I asked her to catsit Cora. I didn't have to ask her. Someone else could have done it. I don't know why I did it. I imagine I wanted her in my space where she could snoop and poke around and become intrigued.

After that, we were buds. The formal neighborly platitudes were dropped. She'd stop in from time-to-time. Sometimes she'd bring me cookies if she was baking or we'd hang out on the roof and smoke weed. Real palsy. But it wouldn't have taken much effort, and both of us knew it. She was lonely, had just been through a breakup, and liked the security of having someone in her building she could pal around with. In short, a recipe for disaster.

One night I came home and she was having a party. She was talking with some girl in the hall and saw me. She squealed and pulled me drunkenly inside. Two hours later we were fucking in the back stairwell while the party raged inside.

The next couple of months were blissful. She'd bang on her radiator three times if she was home and wanted me to come over. She'd come up or I'd go down. Sometimes she'd stay or I'd stay and others we'd say goodnight and sleep in our own beds. She had a key to my place, I had a key to hers. Some days I'd come home from work to find her cooking us dinner or well into a bottle of wine. She was an admin assistant in an office downtown and I was mostly on nights at the restaurant, so we had this perfect limited window when we just met for sex. We fucked and hung out. It was an ideal setup.

Then I met Paige and it all went to shit. I managed to slip around Evelyn's schedule for a while. She had said she was fine with our arrangement, but I could tell she was getting attached and I knew the "are you seeing anyone else" discussion was looming in the back of her mind.

I think to a certain degree, I baited Evelyn. I think I wanted to get caught. The whole thing was becoming a little too domestic and Ozzie and Harriet for me, claustrophobia had gripped me. I'd begun to feel restricted. So, one day Evelyn unlocked my front door to find me fucking Paige on a table in the hall. From then on, it was *War of the Roses*.

Evelyn controlled the heat for our building from a thermostat in her apartment. She'd try to smoke me out during the early mornings and freeze me solid in the middle of the night. We started competing with each other. She'd bring some random guy home from a bar and fuck him as loud as she could so I'd be sure to hear and I'd take Paige right over her bedroom with the same enthusiasm.

Late at night, when I knew she'd be sleeping, I'd make as much noise as possible and stomp around like I had two club feet. She, in turn, would pound on her ceiling with a broomstick or bang the radiator with a wrench in the mornings when she left for work. She tried messing with the fusebox downstairs and blew the power out for the whole building and she'd called the cops on me for no reason at least half a dozen times.

I let Cora take a shit on her welcome mat. She superglued my door locks. I stole her mail. She stole FedEx packages that were left for me. She broke my button on the buzzer. I knocked off the doorknob of her front door with a baseball bat. I gave her phone number and e-mail out on porn websites. She threw a bottle of clothing dye at Paige. I started sending information packets for herpes and syphilis treatments and adult diaper samples to her work.

On and on. *For months.* And neither one of us would move. Once I got so drunk I passed out on the landing in the hallway and she shaved one of my eyebrows and wrote CHILD MOLESTER across my forehead in permanent Sharpie marker. I had to wear a hat for three days.

After that, we settled into an uneasy truce. She started dating some weak guy who bows his head and complies as she shrilly bosses him around. I always see him carrying armfuls of her shopping bags with a resigned look on his face. He passes me dirty looks on the stairs, but he doesn't have the balls to say anything. When she finally breaks the kid, I'm going to have to take him out for a beer and we can commiserate and share battle scars. Hell hath no fury...a good lesson.

Eddie teases me about her relentlessly.

"You remember when she tied your front doorknob to the stair railing so you couldn't get out!" he shouts, elbowing me in the ribs, cracking himself up.

"Christ, she used a bicycle chain so I couldn't cut my way out," I say. "Lunatic. I had to go to *work*."

Eddie is rolling around on the couch now, tears streaming down his face.

"She's focused, I'll give her that," he says, reaching for the bong.

"Focused? She's fucking crazy."

He takes a hit, starts laughing again and coughs, smoke sputtering out of him like an old steam train. I clap him on the back a few times, but he waves me off, laughing and coughing simultaneously.

"I'm okay, I'm okay," he wheezes, face red.

"I had to call the frigging fire department."

That sets him off again and now we're both laughing hard, the video game forgotten, the two of us howling like little kids who just heard a riotous fart joke. Cora pads into the room, stares at us for a moment as if to ask what all the ruckus is about, decides we're not worth her time, and saunters off to the kitchen with her tail swishing.

What are you going to do with Cora?

The thought sobers me instantly. I truly hadn't thought about that until this moment. In fact, I hadn't given thought to what would happen to any of my stuff: my clothes, my furniture, the television, all my books. Eddie can't take her because Harriet's allergic. And none of my girls will want that kind of burden.

I have a vision of Cora in some awful pound somewhere, pacing behind bars, staring out at her doomed cellmates, crying out for her father, wondering why he abandoned her. And in seven days some callous attendant will put her in a room and gas her. Can I leave her with Sarah? Can I impose like that? Even as a last request? Even after-

(Don't ever call me again.)

-all that's happened?

(Not ever, Jared.)

The thought makes me ache with the fresh void that is Sarah's absence and I force myself to push it aside before all the good humor in me goes sliding off to the floor. Eddie has regained his composure and he's staring at me.

"What is it, man?" he asks. "You look like somebody died."

The chill returns.

That's two, Eddie. Get out of my head.

With every ounce of will I can muster, I make myself act nonchalant and meet his eyes. I wave a hand in front of my face.

"It's way too smoky in here," I say and he relaxes his scrutiny. "It's bugging my contacts big time. You want to get some air?"

I squeeze the corners of my eyes and the bridge of my nose to bring the point home and he nods, getting up from the couch and stretching his long frame. After a few pops and crackles he claps his hands together.

"A little roof action?" he asks.

"I'll get some beers," I say, trying to keep that casual tone to my voice.

I vow as we climb the stairs to the roof that if he does it again, if he references death or funerals or anything like that, I'll tell him. I'll spill the whole thing. He's been with me all this time. He's stood by me through all of the shit I've pulled. He's had my back through the thick of it all. God, how can you just leave someone like that? How do you say goodbye when you can't even tell anyone you're leaving? After all we've been through, he deserves to know. Doesn't he?

I think of Sarah.

Where are you?

Doesn't he?

***

"Can I have one of those?"

Eddie raises his eyebrow at me.

"Excuse me?"

"You heard me."

He looks down at his cigarette, then back up at me.

"Yes, but I'd really like to hear you say it again."

"Just give me a damned cigarette, will you?"

He reaches into his jacket pocket and pulls out a pack of Marlboro Lights. He shakes one out and fishes around in his pants for his Zippo. Looking at me with a mix of amusement and concern, he lights it and hands it to me. I take a deep drag and instantly I feel better.

"Thanks," I say.

He nods and points to it.

"How long?" he asks.

"Two years," I say.

He shakes his head.

"Is this your first one? I don't want to hear shit later that I aided and abetted your return to the fold. You asked, I gave you one. Fair?"

I nod.

"Fair," I say. "And it's not my first. I had a few this afternoon. I didn't even cough. How sad is that?"

"Harriet's going to be *pissed* at you."

I take another deep drag.

She's going to be pissed at me for a whole hell of a lot more than this in the end, I suspect.

"She'll live," I say.

He takes a sip of his beer and he looks out over the Boston skyline, now lit up and hazy in the heat of the summer night. When he turns back, the time for games is over.

"Are we done dancing yet?"

I blink at him.

"Are you going to tell me what's really on your mind?" he asks. "Or are we going to keep dancing?"

I sigh and run my hands through my hair like I'm trying to push my broken skull back together again.

"I told her," I say at last.

"Told who? The MIL-"

"No."

"Oh," he says, understanding dawning on his face. "California. When?"

"Earlier this afternoon."

He turns up his lip and scrunches his forehead.

"How did it go?"

(You're sick.)

"Not so good," I say. "We're all done."

"Are you sure? Because girls talk a good game, but-"

(Not ever, Jared.)

"I'm sure."

He is quiet for a moment, looking out over the roof, then up at the hazy sky. When he speaks, it's not what I was expecting.

"Well, good. Fuck her," he says.

"Eddie-" I start, but he cuts me off.

"No, fuck her. You're always jumping to her rescue, always defending her. She's been stringing you along for how many years now?"

"It's not like that-"

"Bullshit it's not. She knows no matter what she does, she's always got lovesick Jared to charge in on a white horse to be her emotional tampon-"

"It's really not like that-"

"Let her go cry to her boyfriend about it. You're better off without her anyway. Do you really want to be some California chickie's backup? Come on, grow a spine."

"Are you all done?" I ask.

He turns and looks out over the city again, deflating a bit, shoulders relaxing. I sidle up next to him and we look out at the skyline, smoking in silence. After a while, he puts his arm around me and squeezes.

"There's over three billion women on the planet, buddy. Don't waste your time getting hung up on one. Especially not some fucked-up scatterbrain like Sarah."

"You don't understand. We're..." I struggle for the word. "Connected."

Eddie launches into it again.

"Here we go," he says, rolling his eyes. "The soulmate shit again."

"We *are* connected."

"Why? Because you can Koon or Kunt or Kyke or-"

"Kine."

He waves his hand.

"Whatever. You think this Vulcan Mind Meld of yours makes you soulmates? She didn't even try to stop you from leaving. She's made no effort to visit you here. She only calls you when she's fucked-up-drunk or coming down off a coke binge-"

"Ed-"

"No," he says, raising his voice. "Parlor tricks alone do not a soulmate make."

"But you weren't *there*, man. The first time we saw each other, it was..."

He laughs and points at me.

"What? Magical? Will you listen to yourself? Love at first sight? From 'lock up your daughters, it's Jared November'? *This* from a guy who got *chained* into his apartment by a jilted ex? Please!"

"You still don't understand-"

He stops me, deadly serious.

"I understand plenty," he says. "You jumped. And she stood squarely on the dock with her feet planted and watched you fall."

He's right about that.

"We jump together. That's the rules, right? She couldn't be bothered to love you back. So fuck her. Good riddance. I never trusted her anyway."

I want to be angry with him, but I can't. He's right about a lot of it. And the stuff he's wrong about, I can't convince him to change his mind on, no matter what I say. As it has always been, the mysterious realm of my relationship with Sarah remains something only truly understood by the two of us. Or it used to be. I feel the ache rise in me again. I finally feel the bite of losing her.

"Jesus!" Eddie says and claps me on the back. "Is this what's eating you? I thought you were going batshit over turning thirty-five. You've been acting like you're on life-support over here."

That's three, Eddie.

Here it is. I can feel it. My heart quickens and I can feel massive workings and infinite stars spinning above me. I can feel the air pregnant with anticipation. This is one of those defining moments that will determine the course of things to come. This is a moment where I could reach across the gulf, clutch to my friend, and ask him to help me, where I could fill the hollow of being alone. But despite my vows I say nothing.

I stand on the roof and I stare off into the distance and I say nothing at all.

Chapter Six

Curtain Call

When I was a kid, my parents took me to the theater. The play itself was unremarkable, but I left the theater forever changed. Towards the end, during a scene in the kitchen, one of the walls collapsed and the rudimentary construction of the play's backdrop was exposed. The actors tried to play it off, but the illusion was ruined. Stagehands dressed in black leotards scrambled out, attempting to re-attach the missing piece as inconspicuously as possible.

The entire debacle took maybe two or three minutes out of the scene and the audience settled back into their absorption of the performance without a hitch. But I never could. I saw underneath it all. I saw the actors were just people in costume and that the sets were flimsy, slipshod constructions that merely mimicked life. I realized they were just parroting someone else's words and pretending to inhabit a world that wasn't real. From then on, I couldn't look at anything without looking for the trick behind it.

Around this time, I remember talking to my mother about heaven and hell. We weren't a religious family, but we celebrated Christian holidays, had a bible in the house, and went to church once in a blue moon. I was at that age where I wanted to know about God, death, and all the other elusive mysteries that existed in a world outside of my parents.

Hell, of course, was supposed to be fire and torture and regret forever. But for some reason, there was always a concept of redemption. Somehow, you could suffer *enough*. You could realize what you did in your life was bad and genuine remorse could set you free. Even purgatory, while seemingly flat and boring, had the possibility of parole. Heaven was the big end, the ultimate goal. People in hell dreamed of it and people in purgatory waited for it. But if you were good, you got the express ticket. If you were true to the basic laws of morality, the gates would open, the trumpets would sing, and you would be welcomed into the eternal kingdom.

"But what's it *like* in heaven?" I had asked.

I don't know why she said it. Maybe it was because the idea of something being unknowable or unfathomable was like defeat to my parents – everything had to have an explanation. Maybe it was because she trusted her own personal belief on the nature of the afterlife. Or maybe it was simply to shut up a curious kid whose esoteric questions seemingly knew no limits. But in the end, she made the first, formative dents into my sanity with an answer that would haunt me all down the years.

"Jared," she had said. "I want you to imagine the best day that you could possibly have. Everyone you love is there. Everything you've ever wanted is available to you. You can play, and explore, and run around and have all kinds of fun. There's no bedtime and no school and no one is ever mean to you or doesn't want to play with you."

I closed my eyes and pictured shopping sprees at Toys R' Us, ticker-tape parades through the streets of the town, the circus, the beach, and Six Flags all wrapped up into a perfect day. I imagined all my friends from school and camp and our dog and my parents and a buffet of sweets and candy and junk food. There were party hats and fireworks and a whole preserve of wild and exotic animals. I allowed myself to sink into the vision and let my imagination run amok.

"Is that really what it's like?" I had asked, eyes closed, wrapped in the sublime image of a perfect day.

"Yes, honey, that's really what it's like," she had said. "Forever."

My heart jumped and the first sinking feelings of doubt crept into my fantasy.

"You mean it just goes on and on?"

She nodded and stroked my hair.

"Heaven never ends, Jared. It's like the most amazing day you could ever have, and it goes on for eternity."

My young brain balked. How could something never end? How could something just stretch out, endlessly in all directions, with no barriers, with no beginning or end? How could a day, no matter how incredible, never end? Wouldn't you get bored? I mean, how many years would it take before you ran out of things to do? And if you were already dead, how did you get out? What if you didn't want eternity?

I said nothing at the time. I just nodded and tried to fit my finite little mind around the idea of forever. I would lie awake at night and stare up at the ceiling and think, perilously, about going on and on without end. At first there was a distinct sense of awe at the prospect. But the more I tried to conceptualize the massiveness of eternity, the more true terror crept into my thoughts. Heaven began to seem less and less blissful and more and more like a prison for the mind. I imagined my soul, at death, like an insect trapped in amber, frozen forever in a single moment without release.

The night we went to see the play, I couldn't sleep. What if all life was just a series of plays? What if we were just actors on a ramshackle stage, acting out our stupid little lives against a backdrop that was just as fake as the sets in a theater production? What if our lives were just pretend? Worse than that, what if we didn't know we were actors at all? What if we somehow got so lost in our roles, we thought the play was real? What then? What happened when we died and we realized that everything we did and everything we knew was merely to have something to do with ourselves until eternity claimed us once more? What if the religions got it backwards: what if heaven wasn't a peaceful rest after life, but instead life itself was a momentary vacation from the awful, yawning chasm of forever?

I remember that first sense of unreality with life, those first fundamental cracks in a world that, up until this point, I had taken completely for granted. I became fearful and resentful of a God who could conjure up such a twisted master plan. I clung to my parents, terrified of losing them to the black reaches of a day without end. And when she died, I hated her for leaving me to navigate this cosmic conundrum unaided, doomed to walk the earth alone, looking for the trick in everything until the play finally drew towards the final act.

***

In the car, Eddie puts the top down and cranks up the tunes, revving the engine of the old Mustang. He screeches out of the parking spot and zooms down the street, banging his hands on the steering wheel in time to the music. He looks at me, expectant, and so I slap my hands against the door and bob my head to the Stones.

Please allow me to introduce myself...

Contented, Eddie runs a stop sign and pulls out onto Commonwealth Avenue with an angry squeal of tires. When we're stopped at a light, he taps the glove compartment and nudges me in the shoulder.

"Your present," he says. "As requested."

I blink at him.

"I figured you'd stuff a girl in the trunk at least. Glove compartment's a bit unsavory, don't you think?"

The light changes and he lays on the horn. When the woman in front of us doesn't respond, he cuts into the other lane and whips around her, snarling at her out of the corner of his mouth. Another couple of cuts and we're barreling down Comm. Ave. at 70 miles an hour, wind blowing our hair back and flapping our ties. I open the glove compartment and there, beside some maps and a flashlight, is something I had almost forgotten about asking for in the first place.

Not like you'll be needing it now.

I take the little glass vial out and shake it, feeling a confusing mix of conflicting emotions. Inside the vial are two thin paper strips about two inches long. God, where was my head when I asked for this? It almost feels like someone else was speaking through me when I asked Eddie to do me the favor. I never even really expected him to come through. But he never fails. Eddie always comes through. I look at him, but he's anticipated the question.

"I know this guy, Wade," he says. "Has an in with some chemists."

I shake the vial again and before I can ask him the next question, he anticipates once more.

"It's good acid," he says. "And very potent, I'm told. You sure about this?"

I'm not sure. Suddenly I'm not sure about anything. This puts a wrinkle in my plans. For the first time in a long time, I feel something that isn't depression or despondency or grim resolve. It is a stirring, an old, childlike feeling – a desire deeper than skin or distraction. I am starkly curious. It may just be another escape, layers upon layers, but the prospect remains intriguing. Suddenly I'm not sure at all.

"No," I tell him; the first bit of truth from me all night. "But thank you, man, really."

"It's cool. Happy Birthday," he says. "But seriously, if you go crazy off that shit, you didn't get it from me."

He sails through a yellow light and cuts in front of an MBTA bus, narrowly avoiding the backside of a minivan.

"I don't think it's going to matter if you kill us both before I get the chance to take it," I say with a grin and pocket the vial.

"I'm serious," he says.

An old Saturn covered in bumper stickers jacks up the brakes in front of us. Eddie swears and cuts over into the next lane, nearly taking out the front grille of an Escalade. The driver lays on the horn, but he's already accelerating again and leaving the driver to his well-deserved rage.

"So am I, dude. Jesus."

He checks his watch and taps it impatiently at me.

"Lookit, if we're super late to this thing, Harriet will make a car wreck look like blowjobs."

He shoots around a hotel shuttle bus like an Indy driver and I turn on him.

"You have had a blowjob before, right?"

"Gobble gobble, gorgeous," he says and his laughter fills the car.

I close my eyes and sink into my seat, trusting Eddie to get us there in one piece. Somehow, despite his curses and the angry blaring of his horn, I know he's in control. At breakneck speeds, in the lurching missile of his car, I have never felt safer.

***

On some nameless side street in the North End, we sit in Eddie's car and pass a joint back and forth. It's 9:30 and both of us are ignoring our phones. I'm lingering because I always feel like I have to be "on" when dealing with other people and this requires preparation. Eddie is letting me linger because he knows I need it and because he knows it's driving Harriet nuts. The glint of antagonism between them keeps the spark bright and alive in their relationship.

"So who's going to be at this thing?" I ask. "I need the briefing."

Eddie takes a toke and hands me the joint.

"Harriet's people. I think she invited some of the crew from your work. And your best friend is going to be there."

"Lena," I sneer under my breath, taking a deep, resentful pull on the joint.

Eddie smiles at me.

"Well, at least you're finally using her name instead of expletives. Perhaps there is some maturity at thirty-five after all."

"I hope that cunt get hits by a city bus and dragged on her ass for blocks," I spit.

"Perhaps not," Eddie says.

I stare out into the alley, trying not to seethe and failing. I feel the quick poison of hatred course through my veins and my fists clench before I can stop myself. There is a sudden pulsing at my temple and a bitter metallic taste coats my mouth. I fumble around in my pockets for cigarettes that aren't there with growing frustration. Eddie pulls one from his own pack, lights it, and passes it to me. I take it from him and suck on it greedily.

"You okay?" he asks.

"Why the fuck is she even at this thing anyway?" I ask, realizing that my voice is louder than it should be in the quiet of the car.

He shrugs.

"Her and Harriet go way back. There's no escaping her. And I think this is Harriet's way of punishing you a bit. You know, making you face unrequited love and all that."

I take a breath to launch into a tirade, but Eddie holds a hand up.

"You should know that she's engaged."

The words hang, cloying and heavy like the night outside, saturating me. I get why no one told me; the less I know about Yelena Soroskova, the better. But the news feels like a lead pipe to the gut and I'm suddenly paranoid.

"Anything else I should know about?"

Eddie reaches over to turn down the radio and refuses to meet my eyes.

"Well?"

"We should go," he says and kills the engine.

I grab his arm, but he ignores me and busies himself with putting the top up and closing the windows.

"We should go," he repeats and pulls away from my grip.

He exits the car and I follow him. He's stooped over and fussing with his tie in the reflection on the window glass. My paranoia demands acknowledgement and now I feel like he's messing with me just to be a bastard.

"Ed, what the fuck?"

He looks up from his fussing and considers me. There's a twinkle in his eye.

"Okay," he relents. "There *is* a surprise, but I can't say anything else. I promised Harriet."

I'm not sure I can handle any more surprises this night and I've always trusted Eddie for full disclosure, so I call him out. I pull the guy card.

"Woah," I say. "So much for bros before hos then, eh?"

His eyes narrow and he draws himself up to his full height. The twinkle becomes a blaze.

(*Don't look at the flash.*)

"Let's get one thing straight, Jared," he says, sharp. "Harriet is not a whore."

I open my mouth to say something, but he jams a finger in my face.

"And if you spout some bullshit about me being pussy-whipped, I will knock you on your ass right here and now."

The tension is thick and for a second, I'm pretty sure he's actually going to deck me no matter what I say.

"I'm sorry," I manage. "I know she's not."

The moment hangs and he bores into me with his eyes, searching my face for whether I'm being truthful or pretending and feeding him what he wants to hear. The line is so blurred for me these days, I can't be sure either way and I brace for a good swift pop to the mouth. But he sees something there that deactivates the alarm and his face breaks into a smile. It is a genuine smile that is so disarming-

(*You'll go blind.*)

-that I find myself smiling too in spite of myself.

"Well good," he says and buttons his jacket. "Let's go get drunk, birthday boy."

I awkwardly fall into step beside him, not entirely sure what just happened, but relieved beyond measure that Eddie's good humor has returned.

"You really love her, don't you?" I ask.

He puts an arm around me.

"It's called an adult relationship, buddy," he says and shakes me. "You'd understand this if you got over yourself and stopped fucking idiots."

I dismiss him.

"So, do I have to act surprised to protect your adult ass from getting chewed out?"

He laughs and shakes me again.

"Jared, I think for the first time in a long time, you won't be acting anything."

Maybe it's the weed, or my guilty conscience on overdrive, but I have a vision of walking into the restaurant and having Boston PD there waiting for me with my shotgun and shells laid out on the table like evidence in a murder trial. I see all my friends fanning them, intervention-style, looking at me with a disgusting mix of pity and fear. A doctor stands up and calmly walks over with a hypodermic of Thorazine hidden behind his back. Outside, there will be an ambulance with the engine running and some burly orderlies preparing a special suit jacket that's just my size.

I choke down panic and try to clear the vision from my head, but it is doggedly persistent. I feel myself reaching out for-

(*Sarah*)

-some kind of tether so I don't fly apart. But Eddie is teasing and cheerful and ignorant and there's no way any of them can know. I have been careful. I have minded the cracks and the little slips and I have made certain that it at least looks like someone is still minding the store. But if I can put on an act this way, why can't they? How good am I, really, at playing pretend? And for how much longer? Can I hold it together, just for a few more hours? Can I fool them all before the curtain comes down?

Eddie skips up the steps to the bistro and holds the door for me.

"After you, sir," he says with an extravagant wave of his hand.

I look up and down the street, at the door, at the lobby inside, the walls, the paintings – searching for the trick. I can feel myself hesitating, and that open feeling of unreality washes over me. I feel unprepared. Unscripted. It's as if some huge unseen force is going to suddenly rip the entire building and the street surrounding it up into the sky, leaving me exposed and alone, with absolutely nothing to hold on to. I make my way slowly up the steps, trying to chase away visions and wondering at the same time if I don't deserve every one.

**

Harriet is standing just past the hostess desk with her hands on her hips. Her lips are drawn into a thin, dissatisfied frown and she is tapping her foot impatiently.

"Hi Harry," I say, but her face is stone.

Eddie comes up behind me and she looks back and forth between us, the frown deepening.

"You assholes are baked out of your tree," she says. "Great."

I look at Eddie and we both shake our heads. Our voices blend together into one pathetic chorus of denial. Harriet shushes us and turns to the hostess, who is watching this display with amusement.

"Do they look high to you?" she asks.

The hostess nods and smirks at us.

"Cheech and Chong," she says. "Big time."

Harriet is one of "those people", meaning she has to have everything just so or everybody suffers. It's like Type A slept with OCD and had a perfectionist baby so tightly wound, she crawled out of the womb on her own. Harriet loves checklists, goes berserk when things are messy, and has an impossibly long memory for disorder. Match this with a Texas temper and you have something that roughly resembles Martha Stewart's Id. Between Eddie always doing what he wants, independent of her plans, and my constant chaos, doctors will most likely blame her future stroke on the two of us.

She can't really lay into us because there isn't time; this night has been orchestrated with the precision of a Swiss watch. And the beauty of Harriet is that she'll let the anger go once we all come together. But she won't forget and right now, both of us are in the hot seat. She whips a hand out to point to the hostess and then it's back on her hip. I am weirdly reminded of my mother and have to suppress laughter.

"See," she says. "You're busted."

"Dave's not here, man," I say to the hostess in my best Tommy Chong and she lowers her head, fixing me a sly smile that tells me I should revisit the hostess desk later this evening.

"You know it's my birthday," I tell her.

Harriet shoots her an annoyed look and lurches forward and grabs my arm.

"Come on, Romeo," she says. "Everyone's waiting for you."

She pulls me past the hostess, who is still eyeing me, and out across the floor. She looks over her shoulder at Eddie.

"And you," she says. "Don't you have your goddamned phone?"

He gives her an easy grin and reaches into his pocket, pulling out his phone and showing it to her like a little kid proudly displaying art to his parents for the fridge.

"Yeah, it's right here."

She mutters something obscene under her breath.

"Did you need to make a call, baby?" he asks.

She mutters something else and her grip on my arm tightens. We round a corner and they're all there, sitting at a long table. They stand up as we approach and it happens. The roof tears off the restaurant. The walls collapse and the tables and chairs fly up into the air. I no longer feel Harriet's vice grip on my arm and the music coming from the speakers falls away. My breath catches in my throat and my legs turn to rubber.

No.

He pushes his chair back and comes to me.

No, it can't be.

Dapper, almost unrecognizable to me in his neat suit and tie, he comes to me. With a broad smile, arms outstretched, beaming at me with those big, liquid eyes of his, he closes the distance.

"Happy Birthday, Jared," he says.

"Dad," I say, still not trusting what I'm seeing.

But then he's hugging me and the old, familiar smell of him overpowers me. I fall into the sheer warm reality of him and emotion floods through me like a dam burst open. I close my eyes and pull him tight to me and Eddie is right. For the first time in a million years, I am not acting.

***

"You ready for this?"

"Whatever you say, Dad."

I was cold, sullen, and blinking tiredly in the gathering light of the dawn. My life jacket was pinching at my ribs and the helmet they gave me was too big for my head. The other people on the raft trip were all much older, mostly out of shape, and it was painfully obvious that I was the youngest person there.

They were polite enough to me and smiled when I looked at them, but I could see the irritation in their eyes. *Who brought their fucking kid along for the ride?* I hated them, but at thirteen, I hated pretty much everybody and everything. The team leader was the worst kind of perky, jazzed up with the forced enthusiasm you only saw in Disneyworld employees and lunatic asylums.

"Okay troopers!" he shouted. "Let's get to it! Everybody grab a paddle."

Four times a year, the power company in Maine opens the dam on the Kennebec River Gorge to test its turbines. It used to be at random intervals, but now they are scheduled and whitewater rafting companies have capitalized on the surges for trips. The brochures promised thrilling adventures in class three and four rapids – fun for the whole family.

Since my mother died, my old man had been desperately trying to recapture his youth and make up for all the lost time he spent caring for a slowly dying woman. We had traipsed around Europe, gone hang gliding in upstate New York, deep sea fishing in Miami, and had taken up skiing –

gear, roof-racks, season lift-tickets – the works. That year, he was positively tickled by the idea of white water rafting and after a dozen brochures and a mess of phone calls and referrals, he packed us into the car and took us up to Maine.

I listlessly picked up a battered paddle, dented and scraped up from seasons of abuse, and sidled up next to my father. The water looked freezing and this crew of weekend warriors was decidedly uninspiring. But our guide was undaunted, hopped up on good cheer and possibly medication. He looked down and gave me a winning Tom Cruise smile with his perfect teeth and manic eyes.

"You're going to be my first mate. Think you can handle it?"

I looked frantically to my dad, hoping he'd finally snap to his senses and get us the hell out of there, but he just saluted me solemnly and everyone laughed. I was trapped.

"Aye aye, Captain," I said sarcastically, but the group thought it was cute and I found myself urgently wishing for an embolism.

We lifted the eight-person raft and carried it to the rocky shore of the river and piled in. The guide broke into the safety lecture.

"Most of the time, you guys are going to be paddling. But when we hit the rapids, and we're gonna hit 'em hard, I'm going to tell you to hold on. When I do that, I want you to hold your paddles against the side-wall with one hand and hold on to the raft with the other and tuck in. You got it?"

I was honestly scared, but I didn't want to admit it. I passed a nervous glance to my dad, but he was engrossed in the lecture and I was forgotten. It dawned on me, acutely, that this trip, like all the others, was really for him. Bitterly, I wondered if he'd rather be here on his own, instead of dragging some dead lady's kid around with him like a gimp leg. I was too young to know all he'd done for me; for us. I was still too raw to be able to see who he really was. By the time we pushed off and floated out into the river, my anger was ripe. By the time we hit the rapids, it had fruited into rage.

"Hold on!" came the command and we were besieged by water.

The boat crested and crashed, lurching through the violent water, and I was terrified. The river was a gaping mouth, frothing with white rapids, rocks for teeth, poking up on all sides, threatening to chew us to pieces. We hit a huge wave and the raft went vertical. Suddenly, I felt a terrible weight pulling at my arm, threatening to tear me over the side. I screamed and turned to look at what was happening and my dad was almost out of the boat, flailing for purchase, eyes wide with fear.

I felt myself going over, my fingers slipping off the guide ropes, the river rising hungrily to devour me. I tore my arm away from him with a brutal shake and I saw his face change from fear to shock as he fell. I turned my back on him and clung to the boat, hunkering down into a tight little ball, holding on for dear life, and he was over.

I don't know why I didn't reach for him. I should have. I know I should have. And I can't escape it. It's easy for me to rationalize it by saying that I was just a kid, and scared shitless, and maybe I was too damned young to be put on such an intense expedition in the first place. I can point to the general self-preservation instinct that short-circuits the most noble of intentions when the chips are down. All of us have it, as much as we try to deny it and puff ourselves up about selfless gestures, but the truth rears its ugly head when the building is on fire and everyone tramples each other for the exits.

But a deeper me, an older me, won't accept this. Even simple cowardice, as painful as it is for anyone to really see in themselves and admit, isn't enough. The more I poke at the wound, the more I wonder if I wanted him to fall. If, in that moment, I made a stark decision not to follow him down into the depths. Not just the raging water, but the depths of his life – a lost man, aimless without his wife, broken by forces beyond his control, trying to recapture some ephemeral hurrah once felt in a youth where things were so much simpler. I wonder if I hated him because some part of me knew that he wanted to follow her and that the only thing that tied him to his life was a kid who was just as lost and broken as he was.

It was just the two of us, trying to make it, to navigate in a world that had moved on. If there was ever a time to reach for him, a time to pull him back to life and show him that solidarity ran blood deep, it was that moment. But I didn't. In the center of this wound, surrounded by hurt, I wonder if I was just numb to it all. After the slow, wasting tragedy of my mother's death, what did it matter? Once you get hammered by the big loss, all the others seem paltry in comparison. After the great one is in the ground, all the others go in with terrifying ease. Turning your back is all too easy.

They all scrambled to recover him. The guide marshaled the two rafters nearest the back and they extended paddles to him. Two others reached over the side and fought the surging whitewater and the bucking raft to haul him, sputtering and battered, back into the boat. Strangers went out of their way to rescue a man they barely knew while his own son cowered in a corner, burning with shame and rage.

He laughed it off, probably to take the heat off of me, God love him. But the look he passed to me when he resumed his perch at my side scared me more than any rapids. The rest of the day passed without incident. The river quieted as we passed out of the rough patches and into calmer waters and there was a barbecue at a campsite waiting for us when we finally docked the raft to join the other boat crews.

The afternoon was lost in burgers and dogs and smell of campfires. My dad's story had circulated among the travelers and the guides and had become the stuff of legend – he was a hero by the time we left. But unless other people were around, he was silent to me.

Back at the car, I finally mustered up the courage to ask him if he was okay.

"Selfish prick," he spat and the sheer disgust in his voice made me cry.

He said nothing on the ride back to the hotel, but those two words were enough. He was cool to me the next morning, but it melted by the afternoon and he was his usual, Stuart-self by the time we rolled back into Rhode Island. He would always tell the story with laughter and it was clear that he'd left that moment of bald contempt on a narrow wooded trail in moose country. But I never forgot; those words never left me. They became a title, a naming, a label by which I came to identify myself. Indeed, I have modeled my life after them. And I think a part of me is still crying.

***

He breaks my embrace and puts his hands on my shoulders, looking at me with a mix of tenderness and pride that lovingly sees deep down to a place I have long forgotten.

"Not too shabby, Jared," he says. "Not too shabby at all."

He spins me around to face the others and his voice booms through the restaurant.

"Ladies and gentlemen, my son is thirty-five."

The table erupts in cheers and my stomach flips. Other tables join in and pretty soon the entire restaurant is caught up in our revelry. The cameras come out and he holds me to him and beams at them. I imagine that I must be smiling, but my insides are in freefall. I love him so much and somehow, despite my dreadful plans, it is utterly fitting that he is here now. It should be him at the end. It should be all of them. I pass Harriet a look of simple gratitude that erases all the little annoyances and hurts of the evening and she blows me a kiss.

Surprise, she mouths and I finally see what Eddie sees every time he looks at her.

He nods at me, as if telling me it's okay to love her a little and they all crowd in for hugs. I lose my dad among the well wishers and I feel the loss acutely. I realize with startling clarity that our roles are now reversed. I have lost my hold. I am falling off the raft, out and over, pitching into icy water. Would he reach for me? Would he try to pull me back? Would he try to drag his-

(*selfish prick*)

-mess of a son back to life? He catches my eye among the tangle of people and I know, with that same startling clarity, that he would. Again and again and again. No one hears my heart break, but it does just the same. Because I just can't reach him. A darker part of me wants to fall and no matter what I do, I can't extend my hand.

"Speech! Speech!" Eddie shouts and now they're tapping their wine glasses with their forks.

The stage lights dim. The crowd falls silent. The curtain opens and I stride out onto the stage. The audience stares up at me with expectant wonder. The spotlight shines down and I am all the world. With the very last of what I have, I take a bracing breath and throw myself into my last performance. When I am finished, there is a riot of admiration and there isn't a dry eye in the house.

Chapter Seven

Exit Strategy

I am outside, leaned heavily against the wall of the restaurant, smoking a cigarette when Lena finds me.

"I thought you quit," she says.

Her accent isn't as thick as it used to be, but it still comes out *qvit*.

"So did I," I tell her.

She stares at me, her eyes steady and dark, a teasing half smile on her lips. Her exquisite hands reach into her clutch and she pulls out a slim silver case. Her long fingers flick it open and pluck a cigarette out. Her lips part, just so, and she slides it between them with a controlled slowness that makes me want to knock it right out of her mouth. Everything she does is about five seconds slower than it should be. The way she talks, the way she moves, it all has a maddening hang-time like she's working the camera for some unseen director.

"Light?" she asks, though I saw a perfectly good lighter in her clutch.

I feel my hand reaching into my jacket before I can stop it and I loathe myself for the subtle, but all-pervasive power she's always had over me. She is so cold. She betrays nothing behind half-lidded eyes. Nothing is ever forced, nothing is ever spontaneous. Lena is never unscripted. Part of it is that icy mystique all Russian women embody, that smug hotness the Europeans love to flaunt. But much of it is just her way. She is perpetually amused or bored-to-tears, perfectly still as other people's emotions swirl around her. Forever fucking unaffected.

She is striking in her own way, but not beautiful. When you really look at her, she looks underfed and scrawny, like the runt of the litter. But the way she embodies her flesh, the way she wears her tawny darkness transcends strict definitions of beauty. She is a true feline, assessing, toying, and lethal. She makes me feel like a fly that's gone off course, trapped between the screen and the window, banging helplessly in ever-increasing desperation to escape. I want to punch her in the face and fuck her rudely at the same time and I bang between these states, knowing I am powerless to escape, but unable to stop.

I pull out the lighter and hold it up to her. She won't reach for it. She'll never come to me, for anything. She just stares at me with hellish patience and waits. In a fit of frustration that has been building all night long, I clench the lighter in my fist and pitch it out across the street, where it bangs off the windshield of a car and skitters down onto the sidewalk.

"Light your own fucking cigarette," I snap.

She says nothing, but the smile arches up and I want to scream. She takes her own lighter out and snicks it on. I feel my hand twitch and I wonder if it might ruffle her feathers if I chucked another one across the street. But she'd just melt up to me, close enough to kiss me, surrounding me in her wicked stench of *Amerige de Givenchy* and almost. She'd wrap her hand around mine, peeling back my fingers, liberating my smoke so she could light her own. And I'd do nothing to stop her.

She tosses her head back and exhales smoke like a movie star. She's cut her hair since the last time I've seen her, short, up to her jaw and it's dead sexy. That perfect swan neck of hers lies open and exposed and I can actually feel saliva pooling into the bottom of my mouth. When she knows for certain that I am captivated, she brings her left hand up and runs it through her hair so I can fully see the brilliant sparkle of a diamond that could probably be seen from space.

"Do you like it?" she asks, the double question.

"I liked it better the other way," I tell her, the double answer.

She frowns. There is a ripple of uncertainty somewhere deep in the vacant blackness of her eyes.

"You're different," she says.

"Think so?" I ask.

I'm exhausted from the party and done with these games, on a soul level. My cigarette has burned down to the filter and it finally occurs to me that, in every single way, I am free to leave this situation at any point. I look at her, really look, boring the naked intensity of my gaze past her cool exterior and into that deeper place where the ripple is growing. And just like that, I see her trick.

"What are you hiding, Jared?"

Vut are you hiding?

I laugh, the first real laugh I've had all night and she is unsteady.

"Pity," I say and flick the dying cigarette butt at her.

It passes inches from her face and she flinches as if I struck her. The laughter spills out from deep in my belly, feeding itself and growing. She begins to wither before me. Liberated, I turn and make my way back up the steps to the restaurant, leaving a joyless woman to sit and stew in an unscripted moment that I hope will last long after I'm gone.

***

My dad and I are up at the bar, sipping Glenlivet 25, watching the servers slowly take the bistro apart for the evening. Lena left in a huff shortly after our exchange and the others have been slowly filtering out since then. Eddie and Harriet are lingering over cake and after-dinner drinks with some of her friends at the table. It's after midnight and the staff has been kind enough to let us hang out while they close up shop.

"I missed you at Christmas."

I make up some excuse about work, but it's weak and both of us know it. Also, I think he senses that it isn't what I need to talk about anyway.

"I'm sorry I let you fall," I say at last.

He looks at me, not understanding.

"Out of the boat when I was a kid," I say.

He still hasn't made the connection.

"What are you talking about?" he asks.

"When we went white water rafting in Maine. Remember?"

Realization dawns on him and his face is a mix of surprise and concern.

"Jared, that was almost twenty-five years ago now," he says. "Don't tell me you're still holding onto that."

I say nothing and spin my glass absently in my hands.

"You were just a kid," he says. "No one could have expected you to rescue me. I would have gone over, no matter what you did."

"But you were…" I trail off. "You were *so angry*."

"But not at you," he says. "I was just angry back then. With all of it."

"Do you remember what you said to me?"

He laughs.

"No, Jared," he says. "I can barely remember the damned trip."

"Really?" I ask.

He shakes his head. I am incredulous and accusatory, searching his face for deception, but he is open and truly unaware.

"You said-"

(*selfish prick*)

"-some hurtful things."

He takes a sip of his drink and sighs heavily.

"Do you remember what you said to me when I forgot to pick you up from soccer practice?"

I search my memory, but I come back with nothing.

"Sixth grade," he goads. "Right before your mom got sick the last time. She'd had a seizure and we'd been at the hospital all afternoon. I forgot you."

There is a dim picture of the day, but it's cloudy in my head. The details are a gray fog that slips away from me from when I try to zero in on it. I stare at him blankly.

"You said that God was killing the wrong parent."

Blood rushes to my face and my ears burn. I shrink to about three inches high and shame tightens into a thick lump in my throat. I'm close to tears and I'm disgusted with it because I feel like I've been close to tears my whole life. He can tell I'm getting flustered and he puts a reassuring hand on my arm.

"Jared, I'm not telling you this to make you feel bad about yourself. I'm saying it because people say things they don't mean all the time. People get upset and lash out. It's part of being human. If you take everything that comes out of someone's mouth as a personal assault, you'll never be able to get out of bed."

He squeezes my arm.

"Memory is subjective. We cloud it with our own beliefs and judgments. Even if what we remember is accurate, it still gets filtered through our own views about life. We choose what and how we remember. Maybe it's time to let this one go."

It's my turn to sigh and he pats my hand.

"Maybe it's time to let a lot of stuff go."

I slap my hands on the bar and turn on him.

"How?" I demand.

My dad nods to the bartender and holds up a peace sign. She comes over with the bottle and refreshes our drinks.

"Drink up," he says. "Because you're probably not going to want to hear what I've got to tell you."

I take a healthy pull of Scotch.

"You think too much, Jared," he says. "You're all about the next angle, the next chess move, and how you can get what you want out of people. You assume no one is worthy of trust and you take everything so *damned personally*."

"Wow, Happy Birthday to me, Dad," I say sullenly.

He holds up a finger and I see a stern flash of Professor November in his eyes.

"Don't pull that crap, son. Don't hide behind it. You shouldn't ask the question unless you really want the answer."

"Fine," I tell him. "Enlighten me."

"You need a woman."

I balk at him.

"*That's* your sage advice? I have girls, Dad. And believe me, they're more a part of the problem than they are the solution."

He shakes his head in frustration.

"You never listen," he says. "I didn't say girls, I said: a woman. A real woman. Someone you actually care about."

He's right, I don't want to hear this. Not even a little bit.

"All this. The girls, the games, the walls you've built up to keep people out. It's the mark of someone who's very isolated. You're lonely, Jared. I can see it. I think your friends can see it too. And I think they're a little worried about you."

They fucking should be.

I'm getting that trapped, exposed feeling again and I find myself questioning just how well I've been hiding the cracks after all. I want to dismiss him altogether, but he is undaunted, shining with veracity, and sure of himself in a way I've never seen before.

"I need you to trust me on this one. I've been alone a long time since your mom and I know what I'm talking about. Keeping your own counsel is a double-edged sword after a while. You start shutting away all the parts of you that you're supposed to share with someone else. When's the last time you had a girlfriend?"

That blonde hair. Those storm-gray eyes. *How can you do this to me, Jared? How?*

"College," I say.

He nods.

"Gayle was a nice girl. It's a shame it all went down the way it did. It's okay, you weren't ready. But all this hurt and resentment? You carry it around like someone told you that you have to keep it. It's not healthy and it's not who you really are. Whatever happened to that girl from California?"

(*You're sick.*)

"Trust me, that's never going to happen," I say with a little more angst than I'd like.

He picks up on it and sips his drink.

"Well, maybe that's for the best. A woman who won't fight to keep you isn't worth it."

He is larger somehow. It's not just the suit and tie either – he is a greater man. There is more of him.

"All I'm saying, son, is that maybe it's time to start letting some of these things go. Don't forget them, don't deny the impact they've had on you, but just let them be so you can start living your own life out of their shadow."

He pauses.

"Like your mom."

Now I know something is up. He is softer, more peaceful than I've ever seen him. He is accepting in a way that can only come with putting darkness behind you and turning the corner. This advice is so out of character that I intuitively realize that it isn't solely his own.

"Where is this coming from?" I ask.

He looks off, out beyond the bar, and his face lights up.

"Well," he says. "It's actually a large part of the reason I'm here. I wanted to tell you in person."

He's suddenly shy, like a little kid who's embarrassed to share some swelling secret.

"I've met someone," he says. "It's pretty serious."

"How serious?"

He locks eyes with me; they are shining.

"We're getting married."

He is hesitant, expectant, searching my face for a reaction. Both of us are anticipating shock, anger, maybe even outrage. But what comes over me is a sweeping relief without measure. I reach over and pull him into my arms, hugging him to me tightly. Locked in his embrace, I reach down through all the years and pass to him all the things I can't say out loud. He will never know. He will never know how important this moment is to me and how thankful I am for all the years he has been my lighthouse. No one is more deserving of love than my father.

For all the presents and well-wishes and warmth that have gone into this night, I have received perhaps the most treasured gift of all. I know he won't be alone. There will be someone there to watch after him and keep him steady through the coming months. I have agonized over him, horrified over what will happen to him when I go. The fact that he was all alone down there in Florida made it that much harder. That I got to see him now is a blessing, that he has someone who loves him enough to finally carry him away from the ghost of the past is a miracle. He is my last thread to tie. He loved my mother in a way I never knew existed. She has haunted him loudly. But now I know. I know that, in time, he'll let me go too.

The last key snaps into place and a great cosmic door swings open.

Goodbye, Papa.

***

When we get outside, Paige is sitting on the hood of a car, reading a book under a streetlamp. Harriet elbows me in the ribs, but says nothing. Paige snaps the book shut and hops off the car. She plants her combat boots and squares off in front of us, book at the ready like a six-shooter. I break from the others and approach her.

"I know," she says. "I'm not supposed to be here."

We both pass a conspiratorial look at Harriet.

"It's okay," I tell her. "It's late. What are you doing here?"

"I was in the neighborhood," she lies. "I thought you might need a rescue."

I wonder how long she's actually been lurking out here and I'm curious what kind of finagling she's pulled to get a car, but I'm so emotionally drained and worn out that she is truly a sight for sore eyes. *Deus ex machina.*

"I kind of love you a little bit right now."

"I know," she says and steals a kiss.

Harriet coughs loudly and I turn around.

"So I take it you don't need a ride?" she says.

My dad gives me a knowing smile and I look to Eddie.

"Don't worry, we'll get him back to the hotel. Brunch tomorrow at noon."

Not for me, old friend.

We did all the hugs and thank you-s before we left the restaurant, but there's always the last minute round up before everyone drives off. I don't want my last interaction with them to be an empty wave on an empty street, but I can't bear to touch them again. Paige seems to sense this and takes my hand and leads me over to the car.

My arm goes up and we all wave. I watch them pile into Eddie's mustang, laughing at some inside joke that is certainly at our expense. Eddie peels out of the parking spot and zooms down the alley, laying on the horn as they fade into the night. I want there to be more. Tears, longing, closure, I want there to be something. But there isn't.

"You ready to get out of here?"

(*Ready Freddy?*)

"Ready Betty."

I open the door and sink silently into the passenger seat. Paige settles in beside me and starts up the car. I close my eyes and listen to her grind gears mercilessly as she pulls out into traffic in angry fits and jolts. I listen to the jangle of her bracelets as she works the stick shift and let her plot the course back home. I think of Sarah and Gayle and my father's advice. I try to make sense of it all, to find some sort of peace. I want there to be more. I want there to be a reason to stay.

But there isn't.

***

She lingers outside of my building. The car smells like burned-out clutch and her perfume. The silence stretches between us and I don't want to leave her this way.

"Where are you?" she asks.

"I'm here," I try, but there is no conviction to it.

She shakes her head and puts a hand on my leg.

"Where are you really?"

I can't tell her that I'm going, so I make excuses.

"I'm sorry, honey," I say. "Too much booze, too many drugs, too much-"

(*pretending*)

-social interaction. I'm just fried."

She perks up.

"Let's get you inside and I'll take care of you. We'll get you out of that suit and I'll make us some tea and you can just be naked with me."

"Honey, I-"

"You don't even have to do anything."

She is suddenly a little girl.

"I just want to be with you tonight."

Under the black of her mascara and eyeliner, her eyes are wide and perfectly naïve. The urgency of her desire is plain and I am touched by the longing of her youthful infatuation. She has done so much for me in the past few months that has gone unrecognized, unappreciated and I know I can make this right in an instant by taking her upstairs. But where I'm going, she cannot follow and to take her in now will only drag out a night that has gone on for thirty-five years.

"I'm sorry. I can't. I just need to be in my own space right now."

Her face falls and behind hectic red lipstick, her lips tremble.

"Fine," she says darkly.

She reaches down and opens her bag angrily, rummaging through its contents with wounded indignation. She pulls out two small parcels and sets them into her lap, tossing the bag carelessly into the backseat. She laughs, nervous and bitter at the same time.

"I had a whole plan for this," she says. "But you're having a bitch moment here, so…"

She throws a plastic package at me with a stuffed catnip toy inside.

"I know it's not Cora's birthday, but we sort of bonded last night while you were up on the roof yelling at the moon. I was going to wrap it, but it's not like she'd appreciate that sort of thing. Then I figured she might want to play with the paper, but I thought that would take away from the actual gift and…"

She trails off, shaking her head in frustration.

"I'm retarded."

"Paige-"

"Shut up," she snaps and throws another gift at me, wrapped carefully in soft blue tissue paper with a white ribbon on it.

I pick it up and heft it.

"A book," she says. "Real original coming from me, I know. But you should read it. It's about love. You need it."

"Paige-"

"I mean you really fucking need it."

"Paige."

"*What?*" she shouts.

"Thank you."

She waves me away.

"Yeah yeah, I'm the best. Get out."

I lean over for the kiss, but she turns her face away. I grab the gifts and let myself out. I look down at the little catnip toy. It's a calico mouse with curly-cue whiskers that are going to drive Cora bonkers. Paige's simple thoughtfulness strikes me and I see how to fix this and kill two last birds with one good stone. I poke my head through the open window and grin at her.

"Hey, can I ask you a favor?"

Her eyes flash anger.

"You never quit, do you?"

"Come on," I tease.

"What, Jared?"

"Listen, if I ever had to get rid of Cora, would you take her?"

"What?" She is incredulous. "What the hell are you talking about?"

I roll my eyes and lie.

"The landlord has been giving me shit. New pet policy. It's a long story. Look, would you take her or not?"

Her face fills with suspicion.

"Why are you asking me? I'm sure there's plenty of other people you could ask."

I wave the catnip toy at her.

"Because this stupid mouse is the nicest thing anyone's ever done for her and it means a lot."

She softens.

"I know you'd take good care of her."

She nods, relenting, inflated and mad at herself with equal intensity.

"Read that book," she demands.

"How about a kiss?"

"Goodnight, Jared," she says and starts to close the passenger window on me.

I duck out of the way with a start and she laughs triumphantly. She grinds the car into gear and I watch it convulse down the street in fitful jerks. Alone at last, I stand out on the sidewalk and go down the checklist in my mind. It didn't all come out like I'd planned. Some things came out better, and some a whole lot worse, but all my threads are tied off. I have done all I can to set things right. When the sun comes up tomorrow, I can at least know that.

I take a last look up at the stars and drink in a huge swallow of air. Strangely settled, I head inside to die.

***

I take off my shoes and socks first and relish the warm grainy feeling of the hardwood floors on my toes. I ball my tie up and toss it carelessly onto the unmade bed. Cora cries and comes up to weave between my legs, whiskers tickling my feet. I go into the kitchen and put a fresh can of tuna on her plate, a special treat, and set it down in front of her. She purrs with delight and buries her face in the fish. I sit down on the linoleum with her and stroke her back while she eats.

I love you. Stupid cat.

When I can't stand it anymore, I go to the bathroom.

***

Sheikh Ahmad was continually in debt.
He borrowed great sums from the wealthy
and gave it out to the poor dervishes of the world.
He built a sufi monastery by borrowing,
and God was always paying his debts, turning sand
into flour for this generous friend.

The Prophet said that there were always two angels
praying in the market. One said, "Lord,
give the poor wanderer help." The other, "Lord,
give the miser a poison." Especially loud
is the former prayer when the wanderer is a prodigal
like Sheikh Ahmad, the debtor sheikh.

For years, until his death, he scattered seed profusely.
Even very near his death, with the signs of death clear,
he sat surrounded by creditors. The creditors in a circle,
and the great sheikh in the center gently melting
into himself like a candle.

The creditors were so sour-faced with worry
that they could hardly breathe.

***

I stare at myself in the mirror and I don't recognize the
face that stares back. For the first time, I begin to think
about some sort of ritual. Should I shower? Shave my head
and face? Adorn myself in flowers and the perfume of

exotic spices? Should I shed my clothes and don the robes of the aspiring acolyte? Don't I owe them something? The ones who find me? The ones I leave behind? I realize I have no will or legal documents. I wonder, amused, what will become of the $130 in my checking account and the hundred dollar bill my dad slipped into my pocket after dinner. I crack myself up at the thought of the hyenas at Capital One and Sallie Mae fighting over the arid bones of my debt. I wonder, with some consternation, about the poor sucker who's going to have to sift through all the porn on my computer and what's going to happen to all my weed.

In the end, I just run cold water over my face and through my hair and retreat to the bedroom.

***

"Look at these despairing men," thought the sheikh.
"Do they think God does not have four hundred gold dinars?"
Just at that moment a boy outside called,
"Halvah, a sixth
of a dirhem for a piece! Fresh halvah!"
Sheikh Ahmad, with a nod of his head, directed the famulus
to go and buy a whole tray of halvah.

"Maybe if these creditors eat a little sweetness,
they won't look so bitterly on me."

The servant went to the boy, "How much for the whole lump
of halvah?"
"Half a dinar, and some change."

*"Don't ask too much from sufis, my son.
Half a dinar is enough."*

*The boy handed over the tray, and the servant brought it
to the sheikh, who passed it among his creditor guests.
"Please, eat, and be happy."*

*The tray was quickly emptied, and the boy asked the sheikh
for his half a gold dinar.*

***

I lay my suit jacket over my desk chair and survey the room. It looks like a bomb went off in here and I debate whether I should clean. God knows what story they'll concoct about me when I'm gone. *Crazed, messy shut-in kills himself in squalor.* I wish I could give it all away. I wish I could sit down and carefully go through each CD and piece of furniture and childish memento and make sure they get to the right people. Maybe if I left them each with something special, they'd forgive me for my exit. It seems grossly unfair to me. When it comes right down to it, all they really want me to be is happy. And it's the one thing I can't give them.

***

*"Where would I find such money? These men can tell you
how in debt I am, and besides, I am fast on my way
into non-existence."*

The boy threw the tray on the floor

and started weeping loud and yelling,
"I wish
I had broken my legs before I came in here!
I wish
I'd stayed in the bathhouse today. You gluttonous,
plate-licking sufis, washing your faces like cats!"

A crowd gathered. The boy continued, "O sheikh,
my master will beat me if I come back without anything."

The creditors joined in, "How could you do this?
You've devoured our properties, and now you add this
one last debt before you die.
Why?"

***

They're going to want to know why. I mean, I think it's pretty obvious and doesn't bear explaining, but people need a reason, for closure. I debate whether I should sit down and draft a note, but recognize almost immediately, that it would be an exercise in futility. When you decide to eat or shit or have a baby, no one asks you why – the answer is implied by the act. I eat because I'm hungry. It's a logical progression. Cause and effect. Besides, what kind of a person will I look like if I leave a note that simply says: *I have collapsed because I am hollow inside.* I'm pretty sure they'll be able to figure out my message in the Rorschach of my brains against the wall. For some things, there are no words that will ever be good enough.

***

The sheikh closes his eyes and does not answer.
The boy weeps until afternoon prayers. The sheikh
withdraws underneath his coverlet,
pleased with everything,
pleased with eternity, pleased with death,
and totally
unconcerned with all the reviling talk around him.

On a bright-moon night, do you think the moon,
cruising through the tenth house, can hear the dogs barking
down here?

But the dogs are doing what they're supposed to do.
Water does not lose its purity because of a bit of weed
floating in it.

That king drinks wine on the riverbank
until dawn, listening to the water music, not hearing
the frog talk.

The money due the boy would have been
just a few pennies from each of his creditors, but the sheikh's
spiritual power prevents that from happening.
No one gives the boy anything.

***

I have a mini freak-out over where to actually do this.
Should I sit on the bed? The chair? I think about the poor

forensic guy who is going to have to scoop bits of my skull and sloppy trails of my brain into a plastic baggie, and the cleaning people who are going to be scrubbing blood off the walls. How ripe will I be when they find me? How long will it be before the cops bang down the door? Only one other person has a key to this place and she's not coming. Should I go up on the roof and give Boston PD a courtesy call and bang bang? It would probably be the most polite suicide of all time. It dawns on me how truly ill-prepared I am for this project.

I keep waiting for some kind of divine intervention, a signal or sign – no matter how crazy – to tell me I'm doing the wrong thing. Just a fucking trickle, a single bead of sweat from the universe to tell me that I matter. That my stupid life is worth something. That behind the mask and costume and the lifetime of faking, there is something buried in me that's worth saving.

Please. Please help me.

But there is nothing. Just a silence of abandonment so loud it could shatter the windows.

I take the shotgun out of the closet and pace the house, deciding on the floor in my bedroom at last. I sit down, Indian-style and lay it across my lap with my hands on my knees. I can see Paige's gift, sitting on the edge of the desk with the cat toy and, despite everything, I am curious. Cora pads into the room and meows at me, sated from tuna snacks and ready for some tummy rubs. I can't have her watching me; it's somehow sacrilegious – too much for impressionable young eyes. I put the gun down in frustration and get up. I pry the catnip toy from its packaging and hold it up. Her nostrils flare and she tries to climb up my leg to get it, paws waving in the air. I throw the mouse way down the hall and she sprints after it in delight.

Be good, baby.

Jesus, why don't I shoot myself in the heart? That's what hurts so damned much anyway.

***

At afternoon prayers a servant comes with a tray
from Hatim, a friend of Ahmad's, and a man
of great property. A covered tray.

The sheikh uncovers the face of the tray, and on it
there are four hundred gold dinars, and in one corner,
another half a dinar wrapped in a piece of paper.

Immediately the cries of abasement, "O king of sheikhs,
lord of the lords of mystery! Forgives us.
We were bumbling and crazed. We were knocking lamps over.
We were..."

***

Afraid. For the first real time since I started taking this endgame seriously, I am afraid. Still, after all these years, I fear the gaping chasm of infinity more than fire and brimstone and divine retribution. I don't want to be forever. I don't want to be endless. But I justify this, right down to the bitter end, by the tacit understanding that we are mayflies in the eyes of the universe. We live for a day and then we return to the ocean of the beyond. Our lives are limited, tiring, and brutally short and if I am one mayfly among many, who cares what I do? What impact am I going to have? What can I possibly do that's going to affect the larger timeless universe? What does my life matter anyway?

My only wish is that the lead shot from the shell spreads through my skull with enough force to completely eradicate me and drive out the very last shreds of who I am. I am trapped in my head and I can't make it stop. I want out with a yearning that frightens me more than infinity itself. Even now, I feel my mind spinning, ceaselessly looking for things to identify, analyze, and hold on to. It seizes on Paige's present and I find myself unwrapping it in my lap.

It is the Coleman Barks translation of *The Essential Rumi*. (*It's about love. You need it.*)

One last thing to read, one last game to play, one last cigarette before we go. I open to a random page and my mind dives in hungrily. *The Debtor Sheikh*. Words and voices and impressions and thought-forms spin through my mind, blending with the poetry to form a single cacophonous scream that makes my temples pound.

FOR GOD'S SAKE DON'T LET ME DIE!

Infinity has to be better than this. I pump the shotgun and a fresh shell slides smoothly into the chamber.

FOR GOD'S SAKE!

I turn it on myself and stare down into a bore so big it looks like a missile silo. It smells like oil and metal and release.

PLEASE!

I put the weapon under my chin and the voices overpower me.

***

"It's all right. You will not be held
responsible for what you've said or done. The secret here
is that I asked God and the way was shown,
that until the boy's weeping, God's merciful generosity
was not loosened.

Let the boy be like the pupil of your eye.
If you want to wear a robe of spiritual sovereignty,
let your eyes weep with the wanting."

***

"-you think too much-"
"-you're sick, Jared-"
"-you're different-"
"-selfish prick-"
"-you make me feel like a slut-"
"-got them all fooled-"
"-who are you?-"
"-you're the Great Pretender-"
"-I am yours and you are-"
"-don't ever call me again-"
"-how can you do this me, Jared?"
"-acting like you're on life-support over here-"
"-don't look at the flash-"
"-heaven never ends, Jared-"
"-you'll go blind-"
"-ready Freddy?-"

BELIEVE

***

You that come to birth and bring the mysteries,
your voice-thunder makes us very happy.

Roar, lion of the heart,
and tear me open!

***

"Ready Betty," I whisper.
Hands shaking, I close my eyes and pull the trigger.

Interlude
DURING

"I don't want no future.
I don't need no past.
One bright moment
Is all I ask."

-Florence and the Machine

Gayle

There is a flash of white and I am-

"Hey."

He blinks.

"You're back."

He is impossibly hot and his mouth is parched.

"You had us worried."

There is a cool hand on his forehead.

"Gayle," he says, voice hoarse and surprisingly weak.

She looks down at him sweetly and strokes his hair.

"Who were you expecting, silly?"

I know this conversation. I know what comes next. He's going to ask-

"Am I dead?"

She laughs and it fills the room.

"No," she says. "You just went out for a while. But…"

She trails off and I feel dread collect and tighten in his chest.

"…we called the hospital and I sent the boys for ice."

He tries to get up off the bed, but he can't and I know it. So does she and gently pushes him back down. There's a blizzard outside that has all but paralyzed the city and the hospital has told her that even if they took an ambulance out their way, they'd just do the same thing at the hospital that they could do at the apartment. It would take at least an hour to get out to them and time is a factor. They told her to go get some ice or collect snow and draw some cold water for a bath. And here come the excuses.

"I feel better, Gayle. Honestly. I don't need this. I just need to rest. It'll pass, I swear to you…"

I want him to shut up. They're going to dunk him anyway and there's nothing he can do about it. He's been running a fever up around 105 for the last two days and he'll cross over into the danger zone pretty soon if he hasn't already. I want to reach out and run his hands through Gayle's perfect blonde hair and touch her cheek. I want to pull her face to his and kiss her so badly I am practically shouting inside, but he just keeps talking.

"…gotta trust me, honey. I used to get sick like this as a kid. It looks worse than it is…"

I realize that I am not just watching him, and that this isn't just a memory. I am *in him* somehow. I have snapped into him, as cleanly as a puzzle piece snaps into a bigger picture. There is a doubling, like déjà vu, where I am vividly living his experience presently and yet completely aware of what's going to happen next. This isn't a reliving, either, and it's not a dream. Gayle is really next to him and I could reach out and touch her if I could just make him move. The swirled stucco of the ceiling, the rough weave of the coverlet on the bed, the hot damask cotton of the pillows, the smell of the shampoo in her hair, it's all so saturated with details that can only exist in reality. I am *here*.

She's going to give him one more chance, and he will summon all his internal powers to meet the challenge, but the end is still the same.

"When they come back, we're going to check your temp again. If it's dropped, we'll wait and see. But if you've spiked anymore-"

He reaches for her.

"Gayle-"

But she is resolute.

"-we've got to bring your fever down."

She loves him. Perhaps more now than she ever has and I marvel at how close she is. How real. Her love has always been innocent, somewhat careless, but she is fierce now. She is protective of him, grim-faced, ready to do whatever needs to be done. She's going to make a good mother someday and I feel an overflowing admiration for her single-minded toughness. She is an amazing girl. But he can't see it, he's obsessed now only with-

(*selfish prick*)

-avoiding the discomfort of his predicament.

He is twenty, a junior in college, down in New York City for New Year's Eve. One of Gayle's friends offered up her parents' apartment on the Upper West Side for a gang of them to spend the weekend. The parents are overseas for two months and the kids have free reign over the place. He started getting a tickle in his throat on the drive down and by the time they'd hit the city limits, he was running a fever. By the time they'd gotten settled in the apartment and the sun went down, he was weak, achy all over, and his temperature was climbing. That night, the first of the snow started to come down heavy, blanketing the city in a whirlwind of thick white. By dawn, there is almost a foot and a half on the ground and no end in sight. By mid-morning, the city is at a standstill and he is burning up.

There is commotion at the front door and Eddie and his two friends come bustling in, arms overflowing with bags of ice. He directs them down towards the bathroom at the end of the hall and pokes his head into the bedroom.

"We cleaned out the liquor store and hit the bodega down on 57th," he says. "How's he doing?"

Eddie is so young. He's about twenty pounds lighter and lean from another season of swimming. He is handsome and vigorous, face tightened into the same grim-faced expression as Gayle's. He, out of all of them, has been the most concerned and has been pushing for measures to bring the fever down for the last twelve hours. In the throes of delirium, Jared hasn't noticed how worried they are and still believes the fever will break without intervention. But they are right to be worried. I can feel him, fading in and out, his consciousness blinking on and off like a light switch. His thinking is muddled and the heat is literally cooking him from the inside out. He is hours away from brain damage and I can feel his tether to his body slipping away.

Gayle shakes her head. Jared doesn't see it, but I do and try to push forward and inhabit him so I can talk to them. Eddie nods.

"I'll be back with the thermometer."

I don't know how I got here. I don't remember anything before I woke up in this bed, but I know it's wrong somehow. I don't belong here. Where I came from, this time has passed. This isn't my timeline. This isn't *when* I should be, but I can't recall how I know this. Somehow, I am overlapping him, laid over his existing life like an artist's transparency. I know what he knows and his memories are mine, but I am separate from him. I am older, later. Displaced. It is growing hard to think inside his head and my own memories of his/my future are beginning to fade. The thought comes and the first trembles of uncertainty and fear ripple through me.

How long can I stay here before I forget who I am altogether?

With real urgency, I try again to come forward and use him to communicate. He is unresponsive, but Gayle seems to sense a change and leans down close enough so I can see the pores of her skin and the wide, swimming gray of her eyes.

"What is it, baby?"

This isn't in the script. This is outside of the memories I have of this day. She will remain with him, silent and steadfast, until Eddie and the others come back to take his temperature and the circus begins. She will kiss his forehead and feel his cheeks and mumble to herself-

(*Please don't die on me, Jared.*)

-but this moment is outside of the pattern and I sense a warning gathering in the air, like I am about to break a set of rules so set in stone that to violate them violates all other rules in the process. But I am beyond that and heedless of the consequences. With all my focus, I push into him and try to speak. His throat tightens and his lips open. I feel him fighting me, trying to assert himself and tug away from my emergence. He is confused and feels like he's falling, but he is too weak to combat it. I wrestle with his consciousness and push him *behind* me. With titanic effort, I make his vocal chords vibrate.

"Ga…" he sputters. "Ga."

The color drains out of her face and she grabs the sides of his head.

"Jared. What's wrong?"

I cry her name inside his head.

"Gay…"

"Eddie!" she shouts. "Get in here now!"

I hear heavy footsteps crash down the hallway and he sprints into the bedroom.

"What is it?"

"Something's wrong."

I try again.

"Gaaay…"

Her face is drawn. Eddie shakes out the thermometer and hovers over him, patting him on the shoulder.

"Hang in there, buddy. I gotta check your temp."

Eddie shoves the thermometer into his mouth and I feel him trying to push me out.

"Under your tongue and hold it. Can you do that for me?"

Jared nods, frightened now that hallucinations are setting in. I rise up and will him to spit it out so I can try and talk through him again, but his tongue settles over the metal, bitter with the taste of isopropyl alcohol. I change tactics and try to move his hands, but it's like trying to swim through molasses. Even with all my focus, I can barely wag one of his fingers. Once Eddie checks his temperature, everything is going to move quickly. I'm running out of time.

Gayle and Eddie stare at each other as the moments tick by. I don't know if it's his delirium or a part of this strange overlapping double-mind, but it feels like there are other people in the room with us. I hear whispering, and sense others crowding in around the bed. I don't know what's being said, but it seems like an argument is taking place. He reaches out and grabs Gayle's arm tightly. Eddie plucks the thermometer out of his mouth and holds it up to the light.

"People are here, Gayle," Jared says and opens his eyes wide as shadows coalesce around them.

"Eddie, he's hallucinating."

He grimaces at her.

"He should be. He's at 107. Get his clothes off. I'll be right back."

Eddie looks down at him.

"I'm sorry, man. But it's time."

NO!

He takes off down the hall and Gayle turns to peel off his soaked tee-shirt and shorts. It feels like there are more of the invisible others here now. They have filled the bedroom, spilling out into the hall and the other rooms. The apartment is filled with whispering, sibilant chatter and now there are distinct shimmers in the places where the light is low. I hear the taps go on in the bathroom and I lurch forward, summoning all my force to push him back.

"Gayle."

She stops.

"Lissin…tooo…."

He resists, struggling against me, wrestling for control.

"…mmmeee."

I feel his mind, now fully aware of the violation, and he surrounds me like a white blood cell targeting an alien invader, blasting me out and behind him. The strain shakes through his body and he starts to seize.

"Eddie!" Gayle screams.

NO!

I am losing hold and tumbling inside him as the convulsions wrack through him one right after the other. His eyes roll back in his head and all I can hear is the rising chorus of whispers in the apartment and Gayle's terrified screams. Eddie barrels into the room with the other two boys and takes charge.

I need more time.

"Get his arms," he commands them. "I'll get his legs. Gayle, protect his head."

I have to tell her.

They surround him and hoist him up, flailing and kicking. With one great final shake, the strength collapses out of him and he folds, limp and exhausted into their arms. His mind is drained and he lacks the presence to keep me out, but his body is too weak to sustain me. I feel us both sliding toward the darkness and I am powerless to do anything but stare out of his eyes and wait.

They walk him down the hallway and now the nameless others have solidified from shadows and shimmers into rough humanoid shapes that line the hall from end-to-end. There must be forty or fifty of them, tall, thin, ethereal with rough smudges on their heads that resemble faces by the loosest of definitions. All at once, the whispering stops and they bow their heads, parting to let us pass, reaching out after us as if paying their respects.

The friends cross the threshold into the bathroom and carry Jared to the tub. The strangers crowd in behind them, but they don't come inside. The room is shockingly white, walls and tile gleaming. The bare bulb hanging from the ceiling is painfully bright, banishing all shadows from the room. The bathmat has been kicked away and the tub looms, peppered with ice chunks, vapor rising up from the water. He notices the monograms on the bath towels hanging on the shower rack. He sees the bright pink shell soaps on the dish by the sink. He feels them shift around his body and hears the raw edge in Eddie's voice.

"You're going to have to hold him."

Then he is plunged into frigid agony. The cold sears his flesh. Shock rushes through him and he gasps for breath. His heart thunders and he fights to escape. Black spots dance in front of his eyes. He screams.

And I am cast out.

***

I am floating.

I have no sense of my body. I am dimly aware of cold, screaming, and flailing somewhere way out beyond me, but it is so far distant that I can't hold onto it. I can't orient myself, there is no up or down and I am in a place where all my outer senses are useless. But I sense endless space, stretching out beyond my comprehension. I drift, un-tethered, in cavernous emptiness. But I am not alone. I feel a presence that, while unseen, seems to fill and surround the void like water in a lakebed.

I am protected. More than that, I am couched in a loving kindness that permeates every part of this place. Thousands, millions of arms caress me in the darkness and wrap themselves around me, pulling away hurts and stresses and sorrows like an army of ants carrying away a treasure trove of crumbs from an immense picnic. There is no judgment here, no derision or condemnation, only a patience and infinite understanding that would make me weep if I had eyes. Nestled in the thousand arms of this distinctly-

(feminine)

-benevolent presence, I feel everything I've been holding onto all this time begin to melt away. Tenderly, the clothes of mortality that I have clung to so tightly are removed and discarded. Gentle arms wash me and clear off the years of grime and shame and hatred that have roughly worn themselves into my flesh. I feel myself begin to cry, and-

(she)

-the presence holds me and silently encourages me to release it all. Raw, jagged emotion swells and, with a great cry that pierces through all of the darkness, it surges out of me in immense waves. Free of a body, unlimited, tears the size of planets shake out into the enormous void in all directions. Brick by brick, walls as big as galaxies crumble away. Walls I have so stridently protected fall to ruin and uncover a me that has been hidden since before I was born. Decades of pain and loathing shake loose and something light and new, naked and fragile, pushes out.

I almost remember. Intuitively, I almost understand. But my intellect, the part of me that is distinctly and irrevocably *me*, calls out into the emptiness.

Where am I?

The voice that returns is gigantic, booming, seeming to come from everywhere at once.

YOU ARE IN BETWEEN.

I see a flicker of a young man writhing in a tub.

In between what?

There is another flicker – an older man, sitting on the floor of a room with a shotgun under his chin.

STATES.

Am I dead?

There is a ripple in the darkness, an enormous, teasing laughter of pure joy.

THAT IS BEING DECIDED.

How did I get here?

YOU HAVE BEEN HERE BEFORE.

When?

THE FIRST TIME. WHEN YOU HAD A FEVER. IT WAS THE FIRST TIME YOU DISCORPORATED.

Where is this place?

WE ARE OUTSIDE OF TIME.

My intellect rejects this and struggles with concepts, trying to frame the experience.

I don't understand. Why here? Why now?

The joyous laughter shakes through the darkness again.

YOU HAVE DISCORPORATED AGAIN.

But I was in New York. I was back in-

YOU HAVE CHOSEN TO RETURN TO THAT MOMENT TO SAY WHAT REMAINS UNFINISHED.

I see a flash of blonde hair and the lilt of her laughter sings across the expanse.

Gayle.

YES.

Something that is not my intellect spills out and guilt consumes me.

I have to tell her. I have to tell her that I'm sorry. Oh God, I'm so sorry.

There is a heaving in the void and I sense something that is not anger, but an immense sternness that shrinks me to atoms.

NO! YOU MUST TELL HER SOMETHING FAR MORE IMPORTANT.

Emboldened by the shame of my actions, I rise in defiance.

She has to know that it was all my fault. She has to hear it from me. I can't let her think I meant to hurt her.

YOU ARE WRONG! YOU SPEAK FROM THE MIND WHILE THE HEART IS SILENT.

She meant everything to me. I have to apologize for what I did.

There is a distortion in the darkness and the arms pull away from me.

YOU WILL MAKE A CHOICE.

I've made my choice.

THE CHOICE WILL BE MADE IN THE MOMENT AND YOU WILL NOT REMEMBER THIS ENCOUNTER. BUT YOU WILL KNOW. IN A SENSE BEYOND MEMORY, YOU WILL KNOW.

Please, I don't understand.

WHAT YOU TELL HER THEN WILL DECIDE WHAT HAPPENS NOW.

Why?

There is another heaving and the voice booms with grim finality.

THAT IS YOUR LESSON.

Something shifts and I feel myself pulling away.

Wait! I don't understand-

Suddenly I am moving, rushing at impossible speed through the space. A point of light appears on the horizon and grows. I see the outline of what looks like an enormous grid, flat up against the void like a massive painting hanging on the wall. As I hurtle closer to the point of light, I see pictures of other lives, other times, other days, other me-s displayed on the grid like shows on a television. There are endless squares, each displaying a different place and time, each alight with activity. My speed increases and now I see that the point of light I am racing toward is one of the squares on the grid. I can hear countless voices, rising behind the wall. I am not slowing as I approach the square of light and real terror rises in me as I contemplate the totality of impact.

I'm going to crash!

The pane of light rises up to meet me, the one square easily the size of a city block on a grid that must contain millions of them. The sheer size is awesome and I am brought, dizzy and low, to the feet of humility. The whole grid trembles and the light spills out, pulling me towards it like a black hole, sucking all of me into its gaping brilliance with a force beyond anything I have ever imagined. There is a great bellowing hum and my consciousness breaks apart. The last thought I have before I slam across the window pane is a tiny cry in white infinity.

I'm going to break-

***

-through.

His eyes fly open and I am fully behind them. I gasp and draw a huge sucking blast of air into his lungs. I inhabit his body and make him sit up in the tub, gripping the sides with freshly realized strength. I have come forward and taken control. I turn his head and look around. The others are gone and it's just her, sitting on the edge of the tub, watching him furtively. I reach out to her and she grasps his hands and I feel the warm wonder of her skin. Not behind him, not through him, but as *me*, I feel a touch I never thought I'd experience again.

"Gayle," I say, voice trembling with relief and gratitude.

"I'm here," she says and squeezes. "Eddie's getting blankets and changing the sheets on the bed. You're ready to come out."

The water is tepid, the ice completely melted. The fever has broken and the relative chaos of the day has subsided. The two of us hang suspended in a spanning moment of quiet and tranquility. Again, I can't remember how I got here. I don't know where I was before I woke up. There are threads, wisps like a dream, but they are fading. Yet, I sense great power pooling around us and I know what happens next is crucial.

(*YOU WILL MAKE A CHOICE.*)

I can't stay here much longer.

"I don't have much time, Gayle."

She squeezes again.

"What are you talking about?"

A tremor passes through him and I feel him rising behind me.

"I'm not the Jared you know. This isn't my time. I'm speaking to you from a future when."

He rails against me, trying to eject me with all his fury.

"Jared, you're scaring me."

That doubling comes again, a splitting of two consciousnesses, vying for ownership of this moment. My memories overlap with his and I know what comes next. In four months, he will lie to her. He will confide in her, pulling her aside after class on a bright afternoon in April, and tell her he has cancer. He will do it because, subconsciously, he has never properly dealt with his mother's death and he wants to experience the drama from her side. He wants to understand it, not as an observer, but as a participant. And, in a misguided way, he wants to test her. He wants to see if she'll stay, even if things go wrong, even if he breaks down. He needs to know if what is between them is real. He never suspects that it is and she never once believes that it isn't.

He has lied about many things in the past, but this crosses a line he never expected to cross. While his underlying intention is not a malicious one, the lie will grow. It will expand and bloom outward and soon encompass his entire group of friends. She will suffer. She will suffer most of all. And while their time before graduation will actually be among the happiest of their lives, it is only such because of the looming shadow that hangs like the sword of Damocles over their heads.

He will flee to California after graduation and the lie will unravel. The betrayal, the deception, the wasted worry. The ease of his lies. It will cleave Gayle's heart in two as cleanly as a guillotine blade. She will never be the same. In the end, he will lose all of his college friends, except for Eddie. But the wound of losing Gayle will never heal. For Jared, it is the worst thing he has ever done in his life. It is his most savage regret. And in all that time, for all that he put her through, he never told her.

"You need to listen to me, Gayle, please. You need to hear me now."

She pulls away, badly frightened.

"I'm going to get Eddie."

I grip her arm.

"No," I command. "This is only for you."

It's getting hard to think in him and I feel his memories flooding me on all sides. I feel him in the background, roaring, tearing away at me, trying to regain control. His fists clench and his throat tightens as he tries to speak. I am slipping.

"Gayle. Please. *Hear me.*"

I can't stop what comes next. I can't change the timeline no matter how hard I try. I am already losing ground to him and I have minutes left at best. What can I do? How do I set this right? How do I make amends to the one person who I have wronged the most? How can I tell her how sorry I am? Do I apologize? Do I throw myself at her and beg forgiveness? Do words even compare to what I've done? Can anything be said that will alleviate her agony in the coming months? Can I even apologize for something that hasn't happened yet? My God, how can I give her what she needs the most? What would you say if what you said had to reach across time? What would you say if you only had minutes left? What would you say to the person who matters most?

The ethereal unseen visitors crowd in the doorway of the bathroom, silent and expectant. The entire apartment hangs on this moment. Outside, the city swells and power gathers over the skyscrapers. The air grows thicker. The gravity gets heavier. Time slows. Storm clouds swirl away and through a break in the clouds, the moon shines down over our building. A great wind rises and shakes the windows and in it there is a legion of voices. Pressure builds and his ears pop. What comes next will reverberate across worlds.

She stares at me, and behind the apprehension is a wonder and a tenderness that eclipses all that I could possibly say. She sees me. She sees *me*. And she is unafraid. In that trembling moment, I decide.

"You need to know…"

***

In another when, a shaking finger squeezes the tempered metal of a shotgun trigger. A catch releases and a bolt shoots forward. The hammer slams down, striking the firing pin and driving it forward with a definitive snap. In milliseconds, the firing pin travels a quarter of an inch and launches out of its sheath, punching into the primer at the center of the shotgun shell with perfect killing efficiency.

***

"…that I love you."

Her eyes fill.

"Jared…"

"I've always loved you."

He is battering at me, screaming himself to the front again and I can't feel his legs anymore. He thunders into me, and I feel myself starting to fracture. With the last of my strength I grab her and pull her to me. She slides off the side of the tub and lands on top of me, water splashing everywhere over the sides. Her hands are in my hair and she is laughing and tears spill freely from her eyes. Then her lips are at mine and for a splendid eternity we are kissing. I lose control of his arms and feel myself going, but she holds me and the sweet familiar taste of her mouth is the last thing to go. For the first time in my life, my heart is open.

I love you, Gayle.

"I love you too."

His eyes roll up in his head and his eyelids flutter. I hear the mighty din of applause and cheers from the unseen visitors outside of the bathroom and the room fills with light. She touches his forehead with her own and I stare out at those gray eyes, impossibly huge and pregnant with delight.

I will always love you.

The light explodes around us. And I am gone.

***

Floating in the darkness between space, I sink into a thousand tender arms and cry. Filled impossibly with stark, simple love, my heart swells, blooms, and bursts open and golden pollen as big as suns spreads out across the universe. The tears melt away the very last of my shell and a being of light emerges and blinks in the new brightness of a trillion suns. I hear bells and singing and the laughter spreads out through the expanse, tickling me with ecstatic affection.

YOU HAVE OPENED!

The arms draw me in further and caress me with enormous pride.

Please, I don't want to forget this. I don't want to lose this again.

YOUR HEART HAS SPOKEN. YOU HAVE CHANGED EVENTS ACROSS WORLDS. THAT, YOU CAN NEVER LOSE. BUT YOU WILL FORGET.

Why? Why will I forget?

IT IS THE NATURE AND THE BEAUTY OF YOUR EXPERIENCE. YOU MUST FORGET IN ORDER TO REMEMBER.

What?

WHAT YOU REALLY ARE.

I want to stay here.

That boisterous laughter.

YOU WILL RETURN SOON ENOUGH.

Why can't I stay?

THERE IS MORE FOR YOU TO SEE.

But I want to learn here. I want to know this.

YOU ARE NOT FINISHED YET.

The universe shifts and I feel myself starting to move once more.

No, please. You can't leave me like this. You can't leave me all alone.

YOU ARE NEVER ALONE.

My voice is tiny and afraid.

I'm so small.

YOU ARE GREATER THAN YOU CAN POSSIBLY KNOW.

I am accelerating and the connection to-

(*her*)

-the presence is fading.

Please.

YOU ARE NOT FINISHED YET.

A pinpoint of light appears on the horizon and the grid rises like a monstrous cosmic mural, washed across with all the stories of my lives. The window pane sucks me forward with devastating speed and my consciousness dissolves into white. The last thing I hear before I am propelled through is the voice, rich with mirth, overflowing with exuberance-

YOU ARE NOT FINISHED...

Book Two
AFTER

"Your task is not to seek for love,
but merely to seek
and find all the barriers within yourself
that you have built against it."

-Rumi

Chapter Eight

Satori

. . . $Y_{ET.}$

Click.

The sound echoes through a great, all-encompassing silence. As he gradually comes back into himself, other sounds break in – the hum of the air conditioner, the rustle of papers fluttering by the vents, the thump of a radio from the upstairs neighbors, the sounds of drunk people laughing outside. But though he recognizes the sounds and understands their origin, they are alien to him, new somehow, as if he is hearing them for the first time. He becomes aware of intense pain in his face and with a mixture of horror and awe, he realizes his eyes are squeezed tightly closed and his jaw is clenched hard enough to make his teeth ache. He hears his heart thudding in his ears and realizes he has been holding his breath.

He gasps, still convinced that he has died despite the act of breathing, when the smell hits. He has soiled himself and the smell of it is richly pungent and alive. Wildly afraid, uncertain of what awaits him, he opens his eyes. The bookcase, the office chair, the bed, the room materialize and he blinks in amazement. Everything is exactly as it was mere seconds ago, but he feels like he is seeing it with new eyes. It is like he is waking up from an impossibly long dream. An air of unreality hangs over everything. He was somewhere else. He knows it. He was-

(floating)

With a start, he pulls his head away from the gun barrel and a shudder runs through him. His hands are gripping the weapon so tightly that his knuckles are white and the sinews stand out in stark relief against the flesh of his hands. Did it jam? Instinctively, he pumps the shotgun and the shell ejects into his lap, another loading seamlessly into the chamber. Oiled and precise, designed to operate under the harshest of conditions, the gun should work flawlessly. But there is only one way to be sure. He forces his hands to unclench and lays the weapon gingerly on the floor. He picks up the shell and holds it tightly in his fist. It is a long time before he can open his hand, but eventually the need to know overpowers any superstitious fears.

In the middle of his palm, the shotgun shell sits. Heavy, deadly, awaiting inspection. He picks it up with his other hand and slowly turns it over to examine the bottom. In the very center of the primer, there is an unmistakable divot in the brass where the firing pin struck, exactly as it was supposed to. Misfire. In a panic, he throws the shell into the corner of the room and kicks the shotgun away, skittering back on his haunches, dizzy with terror. He should be dead. His head should be blown out. He should be-

(YOU ARE NOT FINISHED-)

His stomach rolls and vertigo converges around his head. Before he realizes what he is doing, he is staggering into the bathroom, throwing open the lid of the toilet, and vomiting the remnants of dinner violently into the bowl. He grips the sides of the toilet, heedless of the thudding in his head and the shit running down his legs, blissfully free of thoughts of any kind, and purges the last of his old life out into the musty water.

(-YET.)

Exhausted, empty, he falls away from the bowl and collapses onto the tile. Black spots pop and sputter in front of his eyes. The room bends and wavers. The floor pitches forward. And he passes out.

***

She rushes. She is always rushing. Clothes are strewn about her bedroom in errant piles and her dresser drawers are open, spilling out tee-shirts and panties onto the floor. The clothes do not matter, but she needs to have some semblance of prudent packing or she fears she will descend fully into panic. She has been sorting through her wardrobe for the better part of an hour and she still has to catch a cab and get to the airport, but she cannot escape her apartment.

She stops in the middle of the room and presses the heel of her hand to her forehead. Tears are close and behind them, a gnawing absence in the pit of her stomach that terrifies her. She takes a deep breath and forces herself to compartmentalize the feeling, shutting it off from the tasks at hand. She surveys the room, not really seeing anything and feels the futility of her efforts threatening to dismantle her. Her mother's voice, tough and serious, rises in her head and clears out some of the clamor.

Well this isn't getting you anywhere, is it?

"I know, mom," she whispers under her breath.

This isn't a vacation, honey. What do you need?

She stares down at the empty roller luggage in the center of the pile and feels some control return back to her. No, it definitely is not a vacation, is it? With renewed vigor, she frees a pair of jeans from the wreckage and folds them carefully, freeing a clear spot for them beside the cart on the floor with her foot. She plucks two blouses from the tangle and adds them to her jeans. Momentum gathers and soon she is collecting order out of the chaos. Clothes assembled, she rummages through the bathroom – hair dryer, makeup, moisturizer, shampoo, conditioner. Before long, she is zipping all of it into her suitcase and going down the last of the checklist in her mind.

She wraps her hair up into a ponytail and checks the room one last time. Satisfied, she takes her keys and sunglasses off the bureau and rolls the luggage out into the hall. She locks the apartment and takes the elevator down to the street. For over an hour, she stalks down the avenue, trying to flag down a taxi with growing irritation. She has called three cab companies already and they have told her drivers are scarce in the pre-dawn hours of a Sunday morning, but if she would be willing to wait…

Squeezed by the pressure of collapsing time, she lets loose a cry of rage and frustration and wills a taxi to materialize with all of her might. When nothing happens, she resigns herself to walking to the corner and waiting for a bus. At least that will bring her closer to the city, where hopefully, she will have a better chance of catching a lift. As she approaches the bus-stop, a car sidles up behind her and toots the horn. She turns on it, hostile, ready for a fight, when she sees the taxi light and the commercial markings. The passenger window comes down and a gruff voice, thick with the accent of another coast, calls out to her.

"Hey, yous need a ride?"

Her heart leaps in her chest.

"Yes! Thank you!" she cries and throws open the back door.

The driver tries to get out and help put her bag in the trunk, but she stops him.

"No time," she commands, heaving the bag unceremoniously into the backseat. "SFO. And fast."

He looks at her through the rearview with a bemused look on his face.

"You want I should put on the sirens and the lights too?"

She fishes into her bag and pulls out a fifty. She stuffs it through the slot in the plastic divider.

"I don't care what you do. Just go."

The cabbie shrugs and clicks off the meter. He slips the cash into his breast pocket and drops the car into gear. He floors it, forcing her back into her seat, sending them flying with a scream of tires. He tears around the corner and they barrel down the boulevard towards the highway. He launches up the on-ramp and winds his way through tangles of early morning traffic. When they are well underway, he chances a look back at her. She is pensive and silent.

"Hey, you okay lady?"

"No," she says flatly and stares at him until he looks away.

She leans back in her seat and rolls her head to the side, staring out the window at the passing traffic. As they approach the airport, the first, faint shine of the dawn appears at the horizon, and her thoughts are thousands of miles away. She wonders if she can get a ticket, and what will be waiting for her on the other side. If there is still time.

***

He awakes to sun streaming through the bathroom window and a ringing phone. He is curled into a ball with puke dried into a crust on his face. The smell in the bathroom is awful and he realizes he has passed out in shit-stained clothing. He feels absolutely disgusting and revolted to find himself in such a sorry state. Embarrassed, unsteady, he makes it to his feet as the machine kicks on. He waits for a message, but there is only a click and a dial tone. He finds himself curiously musing if the phone would have rung in an empty apartment if he had actually been successful in killing himself. Would there have been a message if there was no one there to hear it?

The idea of a ringing phone in a vacant apartment freaks him out and as a chill runs through him, he wonders for the second time in a few short hours if he is actually dead. He bites his tongue as he sometimes does in dreams to be sure of what's real, half-expecting the Novocaine numbness that will tell him he is wrapped in a dream. Or worse. But the pain is acute and with it there is a rancid puke taste and a furry feeling over his teeth.

He suddenly wants nothing more than to be clean. He feels like nothing else can possibly move forward until he washes the fetid stink of last night's experience off his body. He peels his clothes off with a mixture of relief and disgust. Without hesitation, he throws it all – socks, underwear, pants, even his shirt –into the wastebasket. He turns on the taps and runs his hand under the water, making it as hot as he can stand. Something about the noise of water running into the tub triggers a strange feeling of trepidation and, for a moment, he sees a mental picture overlapping into his current space. In his imagination, he sees a tub filled with ice. He feels a weird doubling sensation and he has to shake his head violently to clear it.

As solidity returns, he pulls the lever on the faucet and the shower roars to life. He pulls back the shower curtain and steps into the tub. He closes his eyes and walks under the torrent of water. A fall of almost scalding heat pours over him and he loses himself. He scrubs away shit and fear and lets the heat work out the kinks and knots in his muscles. He stays in the shower until his skin is tender and pink and the bathroom is completely filled with steam. Outside, the phone is ringing again, but he cannot hear it.

***

"What do you mean, there's nothing?" she demands.

The Delta ticket agent looks at her as one would look at an obstinate child.

"I'm sorry, ma'am," he says. "But I already told you – the earliest flight I can put you on into Logan is at 2pm."

She is adamant.

"How is that even possible? There must be a thousand planes going that way this morning alone. You're telling me you can't put me on *any* of those flights?"

He leans over and looks behind her to the other people waiting in line. She taps her finger on the desk impatiently.

"I'm not going anywhere, so focus on me please," she snaps.

"This is holiday travel time, ma'am," he says. "There are a lot of people flying and they made reservations weeks or months in advance. The earliest flight I can put you on is-"

"What holiday?" she says, aware of her rising voice and the growing annoyance of the agent, but unable to stop. "Fourth of July was a month and a half ago and Labor Day isn't for another two weeks. This is insane!"

The man behind the desk glares at her.

"I'm going to ask you to lower your voice when speaking to me, ma'am, or I'll have to summon security. All right?"

She nods, holding back tears.

"Now, as I was saying. This is summer vacation for a lot of folks and there aren't too many flights, especially for same-day travel. If you want, I can put you on standby and you can try your luck."

"Listen to me," she says. "You have to get me on a plane. You have to find me something."

The ticket agent looks out past her into the line again and sighs.

"I've already explained what's available to you. Perhaps you'd have better luck with another airline."

"No!" she shouts, slamming her fist on the counter. "I've been to three other airlines already. You have to *help* me."

The tears come now and she is powerless to stop them.

"Please."

The agent's face softens.

"Take it easy. Let me check something."

He taps some keys on his computer, nodding his head slowly. Finally, he looks up at the crying woman with a tight smile.

"I can put you on a 6:30am direct flight to JFK in New York. That puts you on the ground around 2:30 Eastern Standard Time. You could rent a car and drive the four hours to Boston and still come in a few hours ahead of any of the other flights landing at Logan. It's the fastest solution I can give you."

The ticket agent looks at his watch.

"And you're going to have to run to catch it."

She pulls out her license and an Amex card from her purse and tosses them onto the counter.

"Book it."

The agent processes the ticket and prints her boarding pass.

"I'll call ahead to the gate, but you better fly, girl."

She thanks him profusely, wiping tears from her cheeks, and hurriedly gathers her things.

"I hope he's worth it, honey," he says.

But she is already out of earshot and sprinting for the gate with everything she has got.

***

He sits on the edge of the tub, staring out the window at the gathering morning. The birds are singing and the green of the leaves on the trees is luminous. The detail is so crisp and sparkling with life that he cannot look away. He has seen this view a thousand times, but today he is finally seeing it without filters, without opinions, or the discordant swirling of his inner monologue. He is clear inside, open in a way that allows him to truly absorb the beauty of the morning and let it pass through to his heart.

He forces himself to stand and go over to the sink. He is a foggy outline in the mirror and he is strangely afraid to see himself clearly. He fears he will see a gaping hole at the bottom of his jaw and that the back of his head will hang open in flaps where his skull used to be. He raises his hand and swipes away a stripe of condensation from the mirror. The eyes that stare back at him are larger, open wider, and have a shine to them, a luminous quality that he has never seen before. The crow's feet and the laugh lines over his lips have somehow faded away and the permanent scowl between his eyebrows is gone.

Before he really knows what he is doing, he is reaching for the shaving cream and his razor and freeing his face from a goatee he has worn for fifteen years. With each careful scrape, more of his true face emerges and the old mask falls away and collects in a heap of whiskers at the bottom of the sink. As he chisels the hair away, his lips, full and proud, come forward and dominate his face. He works to clear his chin and he uncovers a hectic red circle about the width of a quarter where the gun barrel was pressed tightly into his jaw. He knows that it will fade with time, but he almost does not want it to. Something has changed today, and he wants a reminder of that with a vehemence he does not fully understand. He is terrified of losing this knowledge, of forgetting the feeling of this transformation.

He washes the last of the shaving cream off and pats his cheeks dry with a towel. He runs his hands over his face, marveling at the smoothness and the clean slope of his chin and mouth. He looks much younger and wondrously alert. The gray pallor, the shadow that used to hang over his face has been lifted and even his skin glows, iridescent in the light of the morning. The face looking back at him is benevolent and new.

What the fuck is happening to me?

But the face in the mirror only looks back at him with a playful smirk that betrays nothing.

***

Out and over middle America, cruising at thirty-eight thousand feet, she listlessly stirs her coffee and tries to lose herself in the blue sky outside the window. The Xanax should have kicked in by now, but she feels nothing. There is only a buzzing static in her mind where there used to be a distinct and solid connection. The 757 is moving at over five hundred miles an hour, but she feels like she is standing still. Time has slowed to a crawl and there is only emptiness, like a radio station that has gone off the air.

What the fuck is happening to me?

The answer, like the dead air that hangs between her and Boston, remains shrouded in silence.

***

He cleans off the rim of the toilet bowl and ties up the plastic trash liner with his ruined clothes in it. He brings the bag out to the bin in the back hall and tosses it with a welcome sense of finality. Cora is prowling the kitchen, meowing at him, demanding food. He picks her up and holds her close to him, amazed at how soft she is and how green her eyes are. With amusement, he plucks one of the whiskers from the mouse toy out from between her jaws. She paws at it and squirms, not in the mood for being held one bit. He sets her down and scoops another fresh can of tuna onto her plate.

She hesitates and looks up at him for a second, as if trying to decide what the trick is here.

"Well go on, eat it," he says.

He realizes this is the first time he has spoken aloud in many long hours and his voice seems alien in his mouth. He becomes aware of a splitting, a schism between what he perceives as himself and another *I* who is more than the personality that is Jared. *He* has spoken these words, seemingly from nowhere, apart from this other I. The cat looks at him. It is *his* cat. Her name is Cora. She belongs to him. She loves him and he loves her. She thinks he is her father. But there is another I, separate and yet inhabiting him, who can flip through his mind and memories like a rolodex to understand these associations, yet remains distinctly apart from him.

He looks down at his hands and the schism widens. These are not *his* hands, he does not possess them or own them or even make them work. They are just hands, they do not belong to him and they will operate independently of that other I. With a lurching sort of separation, he realizes he is not only looking at his hands, but looking at them *through* his eyes. He is an observer. He is *behind* himself. Suddenly, it feels like he/I is/are falling and there is that yawning feeling of doubling again. He feels himself become unsteady and sinks heavily into one of the chairs at the kitchen table.

"What the fuck is happening to me?" he says aloud.

With a real sense of urgency and panic, he wonders if he's even really there. Can *I* hear him? Or is he truly outside? Is he trapped in his head, with only himself for company? Is he locked in, like a train on rails, predestined to carry out his life in a certain, inalienable order while I ride along inside him, watching? Is he my passenger? Am I his? Does he contain me, or do I contain him? What am I? Who is he? He sees the larger I is far bigger than just his body for the first time and we both come to the realization at once.

There's really no one here!

"Who's there?" he almost shouts into the empty kitchen.

And I force myself to come *forward*.

"I am," I say at him, through his mouth, through his voice.

He falls silent and I peer through his eyes. The doubling shakes through us both and he falls away, dumbfounded. The voice that is him, the chatter of his mind and the scrutinizing, analyzing part of him recedes and I come to the front and fully into him. The personality that is Jared November collapses and there is only the one. There is only *I*. Here, present, and thoroughly immersed in *being*. I squeeze his hands into fists and release them repeatedly, now wholly in possession of him.

"I *am*," I say.

The words echo and there are no thoughts behind them. No inner commentary rises to challenge me and no personality intrudes to dilute the force of the statement. The cat chews through her tuna. Some cars pass by on the street outside. The laughter of children echo past the windows and a warm breeze rolls through the kitchen. I sit in the center of a perfect expansive quiet. Completely absorbed in the spacious present, I sit, awakened, and there is nothing at all.

***

"You're kidding me, right?"

The kid, who cannot be more than twenty and is so damnably perky she wants to smash a fist through his face, grins at her.

"I'm sorry, miss, but it's been a busy week here and it's all I've got left on the lot."

She does not know how anyone can be sorry with a grin like that on their face, but this is the last car rental kiosk and she is exhausted. Budget, Dollar, Thrifty. Nothing. Avis had only gas-guzzling monster SUVS left. Hertz had a Cadillac and a tricked-out Mercedes Benz for about a thousand dollars a day. And now this chipper kid at the Enterprise desk was making her consider throwing in the towel and taking the Acela train.

"Not even a little Mazda or a Civic or something?"

With infinite patience, he explains it to her again.

"Everything's been rented out, I'm afraid. I can give you the pickup or the caravan. Which one do you think will best suit your needs?"

Somehow, his smile gets even wider and she feels her hand twitch at her side. She was not going to IKEA or to soccer practice and both of these cars were about as impractical to her as a snowmobile on a Baja sand-dune. Defeated, she throws her hands up into the air.

"Which one gets better gas mileage?" she asks.

"Oh, definitely the caravan," he beams. "And it's got nav and a rear-seat DVD entertainment system. It's pretty hot-"

She arches an eyebrow at him.

"-you know, for a family car."

She slaps her credit card and license on the counter.

"Fine. Just give me the damned van and let's get out of here."

Delighted, he punches away at his keyboard, humming to himself as he prints out the rental agreement. She signs it, declining his earnest entreaties about the insurance package, and snatches up the keys. He leads her out back to the lot. Planes roar overhead as they walk down the rows of cars to a gleaming cherry-red eyesore at the very end. She squeezes the bridge of her nose.

"Really?" she asks.

"Yeah," he says. "Isn't it great?"

She wants to shake this kid and scream in his face, but she is pretty sure that nothing short of a nuclear holocaust could wipe that obsequious smile off his face. She forces a smile of her own and wrestles with the side door. He shakes his head, comes to her, and pulls the keys out of her hand.

He hits a button and the door slides open on its own. She blinks at him.

"Right? I *know*," he says excitedly and lifts her suitcase into the back.

He hits the button again and turns the keys over. She climbs aboard and leans out the window.

"How do I get to 95 North from here?"

He points past the lot.

"Just follow the signs when you get out and you'll be all set," he says. "And thank you for choosing Enterprise!"

She puts the van in gear and backs out of the spot. The kid waves after her as she pulls away and she suddenly feels very alone.

Where are you? Where?

She navigates onto the expressway and merges into the afternoon traffic. With the gleaming spires of Manhattan towering in the distance, she follows her inner compass north to an uncertain future.

***

He loses the rest of the day in Boston Common, wandering among the fragrances of flowers in high bloom and the salt air coming in off the ocean. He has appointments, a brunch with his family and friends, but he does not want to go and I do not know how long I can stay present like this. And there is another. I feel her, somewhere still far in the distance, but approaching steadily, carried by love and fear. He will need to be himself to deal with what she is bringing him.

His ego is strong and will not remain in the background for any extended period. But it is a questing ego, impassioned and curious, and he will not forget this experience. Once one is awakened, they seldom return to sleep. They may slide back into old habitual reactions and inner rationalizations for a while, but the truth, when seen fully, cannot be ignored. He will be rattled by this displacement of himself, but his investigative nature will continue down a road of discovery and expansion. His path has been forever altered. He is a seeker and, in so many ways, has been waiting for this communion his entire life.

He is worried that he has had some kind of psychotic break, but he does not know that I have always been here. This is not possession, demonic or otherwise, but more of an exuberant entrance of consciousness. I am pure awareness. I am the will, the urge to *become*, the animus behind him which gives him vitality, the root *I* that has birthed him into being. I am what he will return to and expand back into when he dies. I provide him intuition, knowledge beyond intellect, creative insight, and compassion for others.

Secretly, he fears – more than psychosis or split-personality –that he will lose this silence, this presence, this totality of the moment. But he will not. The way to me is found through his heart, through his most cherished feelings. Ever since the snapping Zen of the gun misfiring shook him awake in the early hours of the morning, he is experiencing events from a place he can no longer rationalize. He is operating on feelings and the dim instincts of years of operant conditioning. More and more of his ego will fall away as life intrudes into every crevice and feeling overwhelms him, until he is stripped away and only the pure, original I remains.

I walked him down here, opting away from the mechanical things like trains and taxis. I wanted him to experience the feeling of his feet connecting with the ground, the thrilling mechanics of his body, the texture of brick and stone of the buildings, the verdant wonder of gardens run over with color and life. I wanted him to stop and stare, mesmerized, seeing objects in nature as if for the first time. I want to return him to the sense of wonder and awe he knew as a child, so he appreciates not only the value of his own life, but *all* life.

The temperament of mankind is too fast. Cars race down streets, people speed-talk into cellular phones, all is light and motion and immediacy. Too few are present, inhabiting the moment, seeing the world as it is, without filter or interpretation. So many are weighed down by misery. They are caught in the false traps of self-doubt, derision, memory, and expectation. They are not any of those things; they simply *are*. He is not Jared November; he simply *is*. This understanding is not intellectual, it is experiential.

So I walk him through the Common, turning his head to take in swan boats, young couples in love, and children running and screaming with joy in the swelling afternoon. I make him stop and play with dogs and smile at old people. I sit him down on a bench so he can watch it all go by from a place of stillness and know that no matter what happens "out there", he remains a calm and unperturbed center "in here". No matter what happens to him or around him, the original I is unassailable and always accessible.

Finally, as sunset approaches, I find a rolling hill and lay him down in the lush green grass. I run his fingers through the blades, letting him soak in the soft texture of the living carpet. I have him look up into the blazing sky and the sunlight reflecting reds and oranges and violets off the billowing folds of gigantic summer clouds. I have him watch the sun burn down into a glowing red orb that sets the horizon to flames.

Inhabiting this moment, in a very quiet voice, he asks if he is loved. I tell him the only answer, loud and through his own voice, so he will hear it spoken out into the universe and remember.

"You are love."

On a rolling hill, he finally lets it wash over and through him, penetrating across years of anguish, understanding gratitude, understanding joy. And I love him. I have always loved him.

***

She is hesitant outside his door. She frowns at the key in her hand.

What if it doesn't work?

But of course it will work. The one to the front door worked perfectly and she knows this one will trick all the tumblers and open onto-

What?

She flat-out sped all the way up here, making it in less than three and a half hours, even with a gas-up and a stop for the speeding ticket from the impassive Connecticut State Trooper, who clocked her at well past ninety outside New

Haven. She is haggard and strung out and every time she closes her eyes, she sees the vision that sprung her from bed screaming at three in the morning.

There's a shotgun on the floor and he's sprawled out on his back-
The key shakes in her hand.
-and his head is missing. His head is missing! And there's blood-
"Everywhere."

She jammed the minivan up onto the curb and ran out and up the stairs. But now, at the threshold, she is hesitant. She cannot bear the thought of not knowing, but she is horrified to walk inside. A scrabbling part of her brain has already formed the image of seeing first the gun on the floor and then the shadowy lump of a foot and then-

"*Stop it!*" she shouts and it is so loud in the empty hallway it makes her jump.

She hears a cat crying on the other side of the door, pawing at the wood, and this finally drives her into action.

"Please," she whispers, and opens the door.

It is all shadows in the dying glow of the afternoon and she fumbles for a lightswitch. The cat swirls between her legs, purring for attention, but she ignores her. The light comes on and she tries to orient herself. Straight ahead is a bathroom and a long hall to her left that leads to the other part of the house. To the right is an open door and she can see the outline of a big bed. She steels herself and crosses the threshold into the bedroom.

The first thing she sees is a shotgun on the floor and her breath catches in her throat.

No.

Now there will be a foot and a leg and a body without a head. She slaps at the wall, frantically feeling for a switch.

She finds one and flicks it on and there is nothing. She is standing in an empty room. The breath escapes her in a rush and she bursts into tears. The cat comes to her, mewling, worried, and butts against her leg with her head. She kneels down and tenderly strokes her fur.

"So you must be Cora, huh?" she asks, voice high and shaky.

The cat meows with pride, purring into her hand.

"Where's your daddy, baby?" she asks.

The cat looks up at her, expectant.

"Let's find him, whaddya say?"

She gets up and the cat pads out of the room, stopping in the hall and looking back to make sure she is following. They walk, room to room, and she turns on all the lights as they go, already feeling a little bit steadier now that she has banished the last of the shadows from the apartment. But their search turns up nothing and panic has turned to worry. She sits on a couch in the living room and tries the phone again, but it goes right to voicemail like it has been doing all day.

"Okay," she says to the cat. "There's no blood and no dead people here, so at least he's alive somewhere, right?"

Cora licks her paw absently as if this was old news. She debates staying right here and waiting until he comes home, but she feels afraid of staying in an empty apartment with a loaded shotgun less than twenty feet away. Not to mention what would happen if someone came home and found her sitting here. She figures outright surprise is not going to win her any points.

She stands and scans the room, looking for a pen and paper and unwilling to set foot back in the bedroom. After some fruitless searching, she gives up on the idea of a note and settles on a DVD collection next to the television. She walks over to it and pulls out two at random. She pats the cat on the head and exits the apartment, locking the door back behind her.

Outside, she hits the button on the remote and the van door slides open. She chuckles to herself and climbs inside. After some cursing, she figures out how to use the entertainment center and collapses into one of the command chairs to watch a movie.

"I'm paying for the damned thing," she mutters. "Might as well use it."

Before the FBI warning finishes playing, she is asleep.

***

He wakes up, chilly and disoriented. He sits up and hugs his arms to his chest. Fall is already in the air and he feels a pang of loss come over him. Something else is lost too, but still close somehow. Gone, but not gone. He knows he is in the Common, it is all coming back to him now, but it is like a dream. He was someone else there for a bit. He was-

(*You are love.*)

-not alone. A feeling of unreality remains, but there is no fear. If anything, he feels a sort of warm benevolence, an afterglow like the nostalgic memories of Christmas or the Fourth of July when he was a boy. Wrapping paper and scattered boxes. Sparklers and waffle cones. He reaches out in his mind, searching for me, but there is nothing there. Yet, he feels larger, expanded, and like that other I is still there, somewhere, receded but now always available. He feels the need to think about this, to understand what has happened to him, what *is* happening to him. But not tonight. He is bone tired and wants nothing more than to curl up in his bed to sleep for a thousand years.

He catches a cab out on Tremont Street and zones out on the ride home. He is different. He can sense a change, though he is at a loss to explain it in any rational terms. It is more a feeling than anything. A shift. Like after losing your virginity or graduating from high school or getting into your first fist-fight. Nothing has changed, but everything has changed. He feels older. Bigger inside. More open. More grateful. Alive.

The cabbie lets him off in front of his building and he thanks him, passing him a fat tip and wishing him safe travels. The driver toots his horn and speeds off. He looks up at his place, ecstatic about the idea of falling into bed, when he sees all the lights are on.

What the hell?

He is fishing for his keys when he hears a car door open behind him. There is a tickle like a feather across the back of his neck and an unmistakable sensation, like warm tendrils sliding over his skull and then-

(*Turn around*)

-she is there. And she is running across the street. And she is leaping into his arms. And he can feel her heart pounding fast in her chest. And he remembers the scent of her. And she is saying something, but he does not hear it. He does not have to. He knows.

He has always known.

Chapter Nine

Surrender to Me

"What are you doing here?"

I am stunned by the warm reality of her in my arms.

"I came to find you, stop you. I didn't know if…"

She trails off and then her face sours. She whips her hand out and slaps me across the face, hard enough to send me reeling.

"You scared the shit out of me, Jared!" she shouts.

"Jesus Sarah," I say, bringing a hand to my burning cheek.

"Oh my gosh, are you okay?"

When I nod, she grimaces and slaps me again, harder than before, enough to make me see stars. I back away from her, hands out in front of me, laughing off her fury.

"Easy killer," I tell her.

"*It's not funny!*" she screams.

I come to her, but she pushes me away.

"It's not funny," she repeats and her voice breaks.

She tries to wipe the tears away, but they keep coming. I pull her to me. She fights, half-heartedly, and then she's clinging to me, sobbing. I say nothing, I hold her and let her cry until her heart finally slows and the heaves subside.

"I thought I'd lost you," she whispers at last.

I kiss the top of her head.

"I'm right here. I swear it."

She nuzzles into my neck. I feel that channel between us open. I catch a snatch of her thoughts and am transported, almost instantly, back to an alley behind a restaurant in San Francisco that first Halloween.

(-but for how long?)

I wonder how many times we've done this. Across how many lifetimes? How many times have we found and lost each other? What has passed between us in all the eons our souls have been connected? What kind of odds are we fighting to stand here right now? What kind of a miracle has occurred to put her in front of me – again? How long do we really have in the end?

How long?

I pull her tighter to me and I know this is a question that has no answer.

***

A woman out walking her dog gives us a disparaging look and I realize we've been standing locked together out here for a while.

"Do you want to come in?"

She nods and thumbs behind her.

"I gotta get my suitcase."

I look past her to the bright red minivan jacked up onto the curb.

"No way."

"Shut up," she says. "It's all they had."

"It's very…" I pause. "Conspicuous."

She snorts.

"Tell me about it. I have a three hundred dollar speeding ticket from Connecticut's finest sitting in the center console."

I gape at her.

"Connecticut? Where did you come from?"

She rolls her eyes.

"I don't know, Mars."

I push her in the shoulder.

"Tell me."

She doesn't want to recap the saga, but I can tell she wants me to know it wasn't easy.

"I flew into JFK this morning. I had to rent this red piece of shit and do the drive. There were no direct flights into Logan until late and I didn't know…"

She drops the rest of the thought and abruptly pulls out the keys.

"Check this out."

She pushes a button and the side door of the van slides open. She grins at me.

"Pretty cool, right? It's got nav and a DVD system too. And I'm not gonna lie, she's pretty fast for a mommy-mobile-"

I grip her arm.

"Sarah, how did you *know?*"

She yanks her arm free.

"I saw it, okay. I tried to kine you and there was just…nothing. And then I saw you. Dead. Worse – *broken open*."

Her lip trembles and she turns away from me, stomping across the street to the car.

"I'm sorry," I call after her, the words feeling vastly inadequate.

She hauls her bag out of the back and locks up the van. She looks at me and her eyes are shining.

"You fucking should be," she spits. "I hate this thing."

She's laughing, but there's no humor in it, just a supreme bitterness that shames me all the way down to my core. She walks past me and tugs the luggage angrily up the stairs.

"How do I fix this?"

She stops and throws her hand out at me.

"What's to fix? You're fine. Of *course*. And I feel like an idiot. Sounds like business as usual as far as I'm concerned."

I open my mouth, but her hand cuts through the air.

"Don't," she says. "Just don't."

She climbs the stairs and retreats into the lobby, leaving me with the resounding sting of words that burn more than any slap ever could.

***

She stands in the hallway, unsure what to do next, looking fearfully into the bedroom. I come up behind her and try to put my arms around her shoulders, but she shrugs me off.

"You need to get rid of that gun," she says with real contempt. "I don't even want to be in this house knowing it's here."

"Well, it's not like I can just go throw it in the neighbor's yard. What do you want me to do with it?"

You could shove it up your ass. How's that for a start?

"Sarah-"

She brings her arms across her chest and fights a shiver.

"Just put it away," she says. "Please. I can't even think straight with it just lying out like that."

"Okay," I tell her. "Make yourself at home. There's tea and coffee in the kitchen and probably some leftovers in the fridge. Help yourself."

I leave her and go into the bedroom, pulling the door closed behind me. The shotgun lies on the floor, leering up at me like the killer that it is.

"You don't scare me," I say under my breath.

But it does and I am afraid to even touch it. I can picture it jumping in my hands, somehow come to life, turning itself on me, the black bore ejecting death in a shriek, blowing my face away like dandelion spores. With crowning dread, I wonder if anyone can really cheat death. Is the gun somehow sentient? Does it know it misfired? Is it waiting, biding its time until it can get me? Will it keep trying to rectify its mistake? Will it mindlessly continue its mission like those impertinent brooms animated by a sleeping Sorcerer's Apprentice?

The idea that Sarah might be able to hear these thoughts aloud finally makes me move. I sweep the gun up off the floor and carry it, like a heap of hot coals, over to the closet. I tuck it into a far corner and pile dirty clothes and towels on top of it until it's completely buried. I emerge, already feeling better just having the thing out of sight. I hunt around for the dead shell, checking under the bed and behind the radiator, but it's nowhere to be found. I worry that Sarah might stumble across it later on, but I figure if I can't find it, then it must be fairly well hidden in some dark corner of the room.

I have another of those feelings of doubling, like this existing moment is being overlapped with another. I see myself floating, weightless in darkness, outside myself. Is there even a shell in the room? Did I actually pull the trigger? Am I even really here? I feel a splitting of lines, parallel lives, like maybe somewhere the gun did go off. Did I jump a track somehow? Did I slide into another life where there was never any suicide at all? Did someone stop this from happening? A course correction? Maybe someone intervened and-

"What are you doing in there?" she calls and from the tone in her voice, it dawns on me that, in her eyes, I'm still a suicide risk.

"I'm coming, babe," I shout and reality solidifies once more.

But the red circle under my chin burns as I leave the room and I can't shake the feeling that I'm being watched.

***

She's sitting at the kitchen table, nursing a whiskey.
"You don't want coffee or anything?"
She shakes her head.

"After the day I've had, you're lucky I'm bothering with a glass."

I laugh, but there's no heart behind it.

"You okay?" she asks.

"Yeah," I say. "I just feel pretty weird."

"You're pale. You want a drink?"

"No, I'm okay."

"Now I really am worried about you," she teases.

I smile wanly at her.

"Can I ask you something?"

She nods.

"When you saw me, in your head? Did you actually see the gun going off? I mean, was I really dead?"

She sighs heavily, her whole body slouching. Then she gathers her resolve and nods her head, as if in agreement with herself to do something very difficult. I watch her collect herself and she spreads her hands out over the kitchen table. She pulls my hands into hers and squeezes them.

"Close your eyes."

I do and the channel between us opens, stronger and more vivid than it's ever been in the past. I see my hall like I'm looking through the lens of a camera. The camera pans and sweeps over into the bedroom. There, on the floor, clear as day, is the shotgun. The view pans up and there is my foot and then my legs and my torso, and the bottom of my neck and jaw, abbreviated by a tangled mess of blood and bone where my head once was. It's like a hectic red bush of gore has sprouted from the stalk of my neck. The spray of my insides covers the furniture and the back wall like a Jackson Pollack painting.

My stomach lurches and I open my eyes. I come back into myself, panting. I grip the sides of the kitchen table and choke down bile. Sarah looks hollowed out and infinitely tired.

"Now you see why I got on a plane today," she says.

"Jesus."

"How about that drink now?"

I nod weakly. She gets up and fetches a rocks glass and the bottle of Jameson from the cabinet.

"Ice?"

"No, just hit me."

Tempting...

I cover both my cheeks with my hands.

"Heard that one, did'ya?" she asks, some of the warmth returning to her voice.

"Loud and clear."

She pours three fingers out into the glass and sets it down in front of me.

"Drink up."

I take a generous pull from the glass and the burning amber settles my stomach and chases some of the shakiness away. I stare out the window, trying to make sense of it all. She feels my concern and puts a hand on mine.

"Jared," she says. "I don't want to dwell on this. I'm just glad that for whatever reason, you decided not to go through with it."

I look at her, trying to see if she's in denial, but she really doesn't know.

"Sarah, I *did* it."

She stiffens.

"What?"

"I pulled the trigger. I made the shot. The shell just didn't fire."

In a rare moment, she is rendered speechless, but her mind is active and loud.

That's impossible. That's impossible. That's-

"Impossible or not, it's what happened."

She searches my face and deeper for the lie or the trick, but there is only the incredible truth.

"Something happened to me, Sarah. Something's *changed.*"

"No-"

"Hear me out," I insist. "What if there is a timeline where I did successfully kill myself? What if what you saw actually did happen somehow? Or was going to happen? And it got changed."

My mind is a flurry of ideas and concepts and I feel the surging hugeness of occult curiosity behind it, pushing me to engage her in impossibilities. But she squeezes her eyes closed and puts two fingers up to the spot between her eyebrows.

"Stop."

"Why?"

She gets up and walks to the window, leaning on the sill.

"Because it's too weird. It's too much. All this quantum mechanics shit, I can't handle it. It makes me feel crazy."

"You got on a plane today because you had a vision about someone you're telepathically linked to and you don't want to even *entertain* the idea that there might be something bigger going on here?"

She turns on me, fierce.

"No, I don't! I don't even want to think about it. I hate it. I've had this curse my whole life and I *hate* it. I never asked for this. I never wanted to be anything special. I just wanted to be normal. Can't you understand that?"

All too well, my friend. I'm the Great Pretender, remember?

"Well, you're not normal, Sarah. Any more than I am. And that's okay-"

"Okay?" she shouts. "Says the guy who tried to shoot himself because he was fitting in so goddamned well."

Something happened. Whether you want to believe it or not.

"It was a fluke, Jared. Get that through your head."

Do you really believe that?

She resists it in her mind, but the truth comes through anyway.

I don't know-

"-but I can't handle the idea of angels or supreme beings or whatever dangling us on strings for their amusement. I don't believe in fate or destiny or any of that crap."

"Why not?"

"Because it scares me that I'm not in control."

And on the heels of that comes the thought that shines down to the root of all her fears.

Because I don't want to be a part of something bigger than I am.

"But you are," I tell her. "You must be. Or you wouldn't have come here."

She passes me a look I can't decipher.

"You really believe that, don't you?"

I take another big pull of my Jameson, draining it, and set the glass down.

"I didn't. Until today. But yes, I do believe it. I don't think we're here right now by accident. I think we've been brought together for a reason. I told you, something's changed."

Her eyes are accusatory.

You still don't see it, do you? Why I'm really here? Why I'm so scared right now?

"Then tell me."

"What if it changes back?"

***

The silence between us is killing me and I hate that we're fighting like this. After all the time and all the distance, we're finally together and the gulf that separates us is wider than ever.

"Are you hungry?" I try. "I could cook us up something to eat."

She smiles at me with genuine amusement.

"You have condiments and orange Gatorade in the fridge. And something in a take-out box that looks like it was Chinese food before it mutated."

"That's General Gao's chicken. It's delicious. You want me to nuke some up?"

She wrinkles her nose.

"You really know how to make a girl swoon."

The moment spans and I hear her thought-

I need to touch you so I know you're really here.

I get up from the chair and cross the distance in two steps. I grab her face and try to kiss her, but she turns her head.

"Oh no," she says. "I didn't fly out here to fuck you."

"Sarah, I-"

"When you don't understand something, you either try to fuck it or stomp it flat. And I don't want to be that for you. I don't want to be one of your girls."

I take a step back, genuinely appalled at the idea.

"You never could be."

She sees I am genuine, but she is unfazed.

"You say that. You may even believe it. But you still want to possess me, don't you? To *have* me. But you can't have me. Who I am has to be given. Do you understand that?"

I shake my head. She touches my cheek tenderly.

"Good, you're not supposed to."

I feel frustration rising inside me.

"Why are you here then? Really Sarah, why?"

I don't know.

"I don't believe you."

I feel you, Jared. I feel you all the time. It pulls me to you.

I try to kiss her again, but she jerks away.

"You're the one thing in my life that doesn't fit into anything. I can't make sense of it. And it's not going to fuck itself away. I want to be here, in your space. Just be with you. Can we do that without you trying to get in my pants all night?"

I nod, but I am crestfallen.

"What happens now?"

She brightens, as if a switch has been flipped.

"Now I'm going to freshen up and you're going to take me out for a night on the town."

"I thought you were tired."

Still trying to get me into the bedroom, aren't you?

She squeezes my chin.

"I was, but you pissed me off and now I'm getting my second wind."

"I-"

"None of your tricks are going to work with me, Jared. You should know that by now."

She has thoroughly upset my equilibrium and it's making me uncomfortable.

What do you want from me, Sarah?

"This," she says. "This confused, uncertain, surprised thing you're doing here. I want you to remember that. It's genuine."

She hugs me and kisses me on the cheek.

"Don't analyze it. Just be insanely grateful that I'm here."

She releases me and walks out of the kitchen, singing to herself. I am left with the lingering imprint of her lips on my skin and a sneaking suspicion that my tricks have never really worked in the first place.

***

She comes out of the bathroom in a sleeveless black dress and heels. Her hair is up, falling in little ringlets down her neck and for a second I can actually see the faint shimmering outline of wings stretching out, impossibly wide, across her shoulders. I close my eyes and shake my head. The image is gone as fast as it appeared, but an otherworldly quality about her remains.

Tell me I'm beautiful.

"You're beautiful."

She smiles bashfully and it lights up her face.

Thank you, Jared.

I am caught up in her transformation.

"You just had this in your bag?"

She frowns at me.

"Well, truthfully, I didn't know if I was going to a funeral or not when I packed."

"Kind of scandalous for a funeral, don't you think?"

She laughs and her-

(*wings*)

-whole body shakes.

"I wanted you to regret it."

I imagine it, the funeral. Who would be there, peering down at the closed lid of my casket? Would there be tears? Anger? Regrets? What would they say about me? Who would speak over my grave? I start to lose myself in the thoughts, but she pulls me out.

"Don't," she says. "Let's just say I'm very appreciative you can see this in the flesh."

Me too, babe.

She tosses me the keys.

"You're driving."

I grip them and make a victory fist pump.

"The red rocket?"

"She's all yours."

And you?

She says nothing, but color rushes to her cheeks and her wings flutter.

***

We sit at a table at the Top of the Hub in the Prudential Building, overlooking the Boston skyline, sipping overpriced Beaujolais, sated from a rich meal. The kitchen was closed when we got here, but I know the Maître d' and he whipped us up a late night grab bag of apps and specialty plates. The afterglow of dinner is warm in our bellies.

"How come you never left the restaurants?"

I shrug.

"It's easy. Decent money. Mindless. Performing for people. Playing pretend, you know? I walk away when it's over and I don't take it home."

"And your dad hasn't been pushing you to do something more with your life?"

I laugh.

"Stuart-"

(*A woman who won't fight to keep you isn't worth it.*)

"-always pushes. He's here actually. Harriet flew him up for my birthday. He's here until Tuesday. I'm going to catch hell for blowing them off today."

She scowls at me, surprised.

Why didn't you say anything?

I shrug again.

"Jared, you should be with him. Your family is important."

I narrow my eyes at her.

"You think I don't know that?"

She sees through the bravado and catches the trail of my underlying thoughts.

It's just that-

"What?" she presses.

I look around the restaurant, searching for an escape, but she pins me.

Tell me.

I am resentful that I can't hide it, but realize we are well past hiding things.

"All of them. My old man, my friends, all of them. They make me feel-"

(*None of your tricks are going to work on me, Jared.*)

"-exposed. Like I should be…*better* somehow. Being around them reminds me that I'm not."

She puts a hand over mine.

"That's good."

I glare at her.

"How can that possibly be *good?*"

She smiles.

"They see who you really are. They see what you're capable of being."

I pull my hand away, fidgeting, fingering the silverware and my napkin, acutely wishing for a cigarette.

What is this really about?

I sigh heavily.

"I'm a fucking liar, Sarah. Okay?" I snap. "I lied to you, I lie to everyone. It's the only thing I'm good at. I'm just pretend. Everything I do, everything I say is fake. I just pretend to be someone. That's who I really am, I'm nobody."

She sits back in her chair and contemplates me.

"Wow," she says. "That's big of you to admit."

I turn on her, irritated, teeth clenched.

"Don't patronize me, Sarah."

She reaches for my hand, clenched tightly into a fist.

"I'm not, I mean it. I've been waiting for you to say this for a long time."

I slap my hand on the table, my frustration turning to rage.

"Why do you do that? Like you already know what's going to happen?"

There is a thought there, but she won't let me see it. I press her.

"Why have you stayed through all my bullshit when you've known the truth about me all along?"

"I'm like your family, Jared, and your friends. I see more of you – a larger you – that you wouldn't allow yourself to even consider until now-"

(YOU ARE NOT FINISHED-)

"-but you're starting to. I needed to see that change in you before…"

She trails off and again she clouds her thoughts from me.

"Before what?"

She leaves the question unanswered and reaches for the wine.

"You're not like me. I don't want to be more than I am, but you-"

(You shine.)

"-you can't help it. You are more, even when you can't see it. It doesn't matter whether you put on the mask or not, the real you always breaks through. You don't realize the impact you have on people."

I don't have anything. I am empty. I don't have anything to offer.

"Stop trying so hard. Stop trying to *make* anything happen. Don't you get it yet? You already have everything you need. You *are* what you have to offer. And it's enough. Trust me."

God dammit! How can you know that? How can you-

"Because I see you, Jared. I see the truth in you."

***

The clouds between us lift and she is clearer to me. The real, stretching, indomitable source of her starts to peek through in rays. The air around her shimmers and her eyes are huge and clear. The channel widens to a tunnel and then to a portal. I connect with her, and now there are not just words, but images, memories, and an instantaneous, intuitive understanding of who she is. Her thoughts come in a steady stream of consciousness and all at once at the same time. The restaurant dims, thins, and the need for speech evaporates. I lift up and out of myself and the last of the clouds are blown away in a rush. Blazing in the light, I am fully inside her mind.

We can't be together. Not this time. I'm not the girl for you. You know it too. It's in your eyes and your eyes can never lie to me. You'll find out I'm just as complicated and broken as every other girl in your life. This illusion you have about me will shatter and you'll be disappointed. You need someone free and you will find her. I'm too constrained and tight and I manage everything down to the smallest detail. I don't want to expand. It scares me to be big. I know you don't see it now, but you'd outgrow me. We are connected, we will always be connected. Your soul knows me. But this isn't the time for us. Your story is different now.

I don't know what to do with that.

I want to give you something, Jared. Something I don't think you've ever had before.

What?

The reason why we live. Not some high-minded concept. The real reason. But you have to promise me. You have to promise me that it will be enough.

How can I do that? How can I make a promise like that?

Because you see me too.

When I come back into myself, everyone is staring at us. Conversations have stopped mid-sentence and there is an electric hum in the restaurant, a buzzing, like the air in a field before a thunderstorm. With a puff and a whisper, the candles on all the tables have winked out.

***

"We should get out of here," I suggest, looking around.

"I want to get a hotel room. Can we?"

"Well sure, but-"

"I want to be somewhere that's new for both of us. Without attachments. I can't sleep in your room, Jared. Not after-"

She shivers.

"-what I saw."

"The Mandarin is just down the street. We can go check in there. Okay?"

She smiles.

"Okay."

I pay the check and we get up to leave. People stare after us as we pass, whispering in low tones, moving aside to let us through. She stands beside me in the elevator and we ride down to the lobby in comfortable silence. She slips a hand into mine, the air solidifies, and the buzzing stops.

***

I busy myself at the mini-bar with making us drinks. She stands by the window, arms crossed, looking out over the city, alone and impenetrable in her thoughts. I feel awkward and a little sheepish being alone with her in the big hotel room. I get it now – neutral ground. Here we can come to each other on equal footing. It's a spot new to us both, with no memory and no history, where we have no familiar trappings or tricks to fall back on. Yet as I bring her a drink and sidle up alongside her, I am aware that a place like this has no future either.

"Listen," I tell her, trying to be reassuring. "I want you to know that it's okay if-"

Then she's kissing me, forcing me back, breathless. The glass falls forgotten from my hand. Within that kiss is a longing and sweetness I remember from that first night in California. I am stunned by how much I've missed it, the taste of her, and how truly lonely I have been without it. But with it comes something new, a larger sadness, loss, a sorrow that I can't fully grasp and that she won't let me see. She slides her hands across my chest and peels off my jacket, setting it on the chair by the window. I reach for the knot of my tie, but she stops me.

"I'm in control."

She tugs it loose and drapes it over my blazer. Expertly, her fingers pluck at the buttons of my dress shirt, opening me and lifting the shirt loose from my trousers. She fans her hands over across my shoulders and pulls the shirt from my body. She kisses the hollow of my shoulder, lips lingering, hair tickling my skin, and a shiver runs through me. She folds the shirt with a care that borders on reverence and adds it to the pile on the chair.

She gets on her knees and opens my belt buckle, sliding the leather loose from my pant loops with a whisper. She puts her forehead against my belly and breathes into the blade of my hip, her lips just grazing my flesh, and the hair on the back of my neck stands up on end.

"Lie on the bed."

I do it and she removes my shoes and socks, setting them on the floor beside the chair. She hovers over me, pausing at the button of my pants and looks at me.

I'm in control.

She pops the button and curls her fingers underneath my boxers and removes the last of my clothes in one swift motion. When everything is neatly folded and piled, she climbs on top of me and brings her face close to mine.

"I only have one rule," she breathes.

"You're in control."

She nods.

"It's the only way that-"

Her face darkens.

"It's the only way that I can do this."

In my mind, I see a cruel shadow lurking over a small, cowering child.

"I will never hurt you, Sarah."

"I know."

"Never."

I know.

She reaches up and pulls off her dress.

"You're so beautiful."

Thank you.

"So-"

She grips me firmly in her hands and squeezes. I am straining and impossibly hard and the feeling of her is charged and unreal.

"-beautiful."

"Have you ever made love before?" she asks.

"I don't know," I tell her truthfully.

She laughs sweetly and squeezes again and a rush runs all the way up my spine.

"That means you haven't."

I am suddenly shy.

"I don't know what I'm doing."

She leans down and kisses me.

"I've got you."

I promise.

She slides her panties to the side and rubs herself on me in crawling, aching circles. She is so wet and the heat that is coming off her is almost too much to bear. She moans, kissing me with greater passion, her mouth covering me, devouring me. I slip inside her and I gasp, my whole body lighting up like a circuit has been tripped. She cries out in a thick, heady bellow and clings to me, shaking.

She brings her hips up with maddening slowness and then thrusts them back down and my vision blurs. I am seeing colors and trails of lights and the hot tightness of her seems to grow and spread and saturate my entire body. The smell of her enfolds me and her hair is in my face, her body melding into mine.

"What's happening?"

"Open the channel," she urges, writhing over me.

"Sarah, I-"

Let go!

My body starts to transform, skin, muscle, and bone beginning to liquefy and merge into hers.

"What's-"

She puts her lips to my ear and compels me.

"Let go."

We are vibrating and the bed, the whole room, is shaking.

Surrender.

She kisses me and the flesh of her lips fuses to mine. There is no pain.

Surrender to me.

The room rips open in a blast of blue light. The barrier between us tears away and we are run together in a forge that burns the last of us to cinders. We burst apart, atoms exploding out in a buoyant expression of universal joy. There is only light and motion. We are one.

***

She is bucking at me with her hips, urgent, burning. Her breath escapes her in harsh pants and she is dripping with sweat. She puts her hands on my chest and drives into me, head thrown back, mouth open into a wide and vital O. Her cries fill the room and I feel myself swelling and building.

"I'm gonna come."

"Yes," she says. "Come with me."

She slaps into me, faster, eyes tightly closed. Red blooms across her chest and I feel her clamping onto me in great rolling waves. She sucks in breath and her legs shake. She shoots open her eyes and pierces me with her gaze.

Come home. It's time. Let me take you.

I am in awe of her.

"What are you?" I whisper.

She arches her back and now there is no mistaking it. She spreads her wings out to their full span and draws in a great, shuddering breath.

"I am love."

And I come for what feels like the first time in the whole of my short, stunted life.

***

She snuggles into me and I bring my arms around her tightly. She kisses my neck and rests her head in my shoulder. We doze like this, drifting in and out for hours, sweat drying off our bodies, carried on a tide of affection that seems to stretch out across time. There is no need to speak, our thoughts spill into each other seamlessly and without borders.

Thank you, Sarah.

You will always have this moment now. Always.

I want to be with you.

This is all I am able to give you. Promise me you won't forget it.

I-

Promise me.

I promise.

I love you. So much more than you can know.

I love you too.
Promise me.
I promise.
Jared?
Yes.
Do great things when you wake.

***

I think I hear crying coming from the bathroom in the middle of the night. I reach out for her spot on the bed, but she isn't there and the sheets are cold. I try to summon the strength to get up and seek her out, but I am unable to move. I attempt to call for her, but the words, forceless, fall away just past my lips. I speak to her with my mind.

Come back to bed, Sarah.

But the channel is closed and in another minute, I fall back asleep.

***

In the morning, she is gone.

I search the room, but there's no sign of her. I dress quickly and go out to the hall, checking by the ice maker and the candy machines. I go down to the lobby and look into the restaurant and the lounge, but she's not there. The concierge knows nothing and the staff at the front desk have no memory of seeing anyone pass by. The valets tell me they didn't see her or a mini-van when they came on for their morning shift. Finally, in a last ditch effort, I take the elevator to the top floor and run up the fire-stairs to the roof.

I throw open the door, blinking in the bright sunlight, expecting her to be standing there, watching the day break over the city, waiting for me to join her. But I am alone on the roof, the breeze whipping my tie, the sound of horns and Monday morning traffic reverberating off the buildings. I reach into my jacket pockets, searching for my phone, and I feel a folded piece of paper. Heart sinking, I pull it out and unfold the hotel stationary. There, in the looping scrawl of her handwriting, I know that she is truly gone.

Jared,

This is all I am able to give you. But you will always have it now.
I hope someday you will understand that I came to give you everything.

All my love,

Sarah

The morning is hot and bright and I turn my face up to the sun, reaching out to try and find her again. But there is nothing. I am left with a gaping hollow in the pit of my chest, the fading smell of her in my clothes, and the giant echo of beating wings.

Chapter Ten

Escape Velocity

I stand outside the Mandarin, sucking down a cigarette I bummed from one of the valets. I want to rage, to scream. I want to throw things, tear them down, smash them into irreparable pieces, to revel in wanton destruction. I seek amnesia, chemical or otherwise, to cleave me from this bottomed-out feeling in my chest. I want to go back. I want to go back to the old November. But I can't. Too much has changed, too much has grown out of the last few days that I don't even recognize myself anymore. So I stand outside the Mandarin and suck down a cigarette and try to figure out what to do next.

I feel like I am poised on the center pivot of a giant seesaw. Behind me is all my past, stretching out, put into perfect balance by the uncertain fog of a new future I can't even begin to discern. I feel like what I do next is going to tip those scales forever. In so many ways, I *have* died. All of who I was is no longer valid and what I'm supposed to do remains a mystery as unfounded to me as why the gun didn't go off in the first place. The past is no longer an accurate representation of who I am and the future is a perfectly clean slate, like freshly fallen snow, unmarred by clumsy footprints. I feel both fragile and thoroughly free, released out into a new state of becoming by an experience-

(*You have to promise me-*)

-that has unchained me.

(*-that it will be enough.*)

I stamp out the cigarette and start walking, not choosing a direction through any conscious effort, but surrendering to the tone of my inner compass. I bob along among the morning commuters, winding their way down the sidewalks to work, buzzing around in their cars, scurrying from the T-station like wind-up beetles. They lug bags, backpacks, and briefcases like the stone of Sisyphus, mired in all the gear to run a race no one ever really wins. Their faces are pinched, strained, and they wear dark circles under bleary-eyes.

They talk too loud and too fast into i-Phones and Blackberries and Droids, so desperate to prove to everyone around them that they are connected, that they are worthy of connection, but ignoring the very people who walk beside them. They move purposely, but without purpose. I want to tell them that there's more, that they are missing out on a true connection to the continuum that gives them life. I want to tell them that the door to their prison has always been open. But I know they won't hear me. I know they can't. For whatever has shifted in me, I am still apart from that world. I am only myself.

I know what I have to do.

***

I walk upstairs to the restaurant. If I'm lucky, they'll be setting up for brunch with only a skeleton crew and I can avoid drama. I am hoping that Marcus will still be waiting for his morning coffee to kick in and be too sluggish to fight me on this one. But as I come up onto the landing, I hear a mighty crash, cursing, and Marcus' distinct furor ringing throughout the restaurant.

"You fucking idiots!"

I make eyes with a waifish blonde girl I don't recognize at the hostess station and she smiles at me nervously. She puts down the schedule she's been working on and comes around the podium with her hand out.

"Hi," she smiles. "Welcome to-"

Marcus launches out of the kitchen, slamming the revolving door loudly. His chef jacket is covered in a lurid pink goop that he is swatting angrily off him with a towel like a swarm of bees. He nods at me and passes her an annoyed look.

"Put your clit away, Stephanie, he works here."

She flushes, embarrassed, and he pushes her out of the way. He grabs a cardboard box filled with carnations off the top of the dessert cooler and shoves them at her.

"Here. Make yourself useful and go down and tell that prick florist if he keeps sending me dead flowers, I'm going to make his competition rich."

She lingers, looking at him, uncertain.

"Do you really want me to say that?" she asks.

"Go!" he shouts at her and she starts, as if struck, and skitters past me and down the stairs.

He goes over to the schedule and looks down at it, wrinkling his face in disgust. He picks up a pencil and starts crossing things out like a ruthlessly correcting headmaster.

"She seems nice," I try.

He looks at me over the rim of his glasses.

"She's a bubble-head. I give her a week," he says, tossing the pencil aside and coming out from behind the podium, wiping at his jacket. "You want some raspberry beurre blanc? Help yourself, it's all over the fucking floor."

"Um, no thanks."

He looks me up and down.

"Why are you here, Jared? You're not on the schedule until Wednesday night."

"I need to talk to you," I say. "If you have a minute."

He pushes his glasses up on his nose and glares at me.

"If this is about your shift, forget it. We already gave you a break for your birthday and Nicole is still giving me shit about working a double on Saturday."

"It's not about that. Do you have a minute?"

He considers me.

"Fine," he says. "I'm due for a cigarette anyway. Step into my office."

He tosses the soiled towel over the schedule with a malicious grunt and pats himself down for cigarettes. He charges through the revolving door and I follow him into the kitchen.

***

In the kitchen, the sous chef and two of the cooks are sullenly mopping up a soupy pink mess into a yellow industrial bucket. I wave and say hello to them, but Marcus cuts me off.

"Don't talk to them, they should be stirring up goat ass at a Taco Bell."

I pull my lips back and mouth a *yikes* to the sous chef and he shakes his head. Marcus ignores them and heads out to the dishwashing station. Past the washers, tray jacks, and stacks of thick plastic glass racks, there is a door that leads out to a little deck. Dotted with overturned buckets, littered with overflowing ashtrays, it looks out over a small parking lot and an alley. Marcus uses it to wheel-and-deal on his phone and the staff comes out here to smoke, gossip, and vent about unruly customers.

Outside, Ricardo leans against the railing of the stairs, smoking and talking excitedly to Nicole about the weekend. She is perched on a bucket, immersed in his story, hanging on his every word. The two of them are peas in a pod. Ricardo is very tall, very dark, and very gay and Nicole is a willowy, pale, chain smoker who was born bitter and rambunctiously vocal about her lot in life.

The two of them feed off each other and, when they're not screaming like an old married couple, they spend most of their time ragging on everyone who crosses their path. I thought she was in love with him for a long time and that Ricardo just kept her around because he enjoyed the attention. But he is sweet with her and takes care of her in his weirdly dysfunctional way. They are part of the old guard who have been with Marcus since he opened the restaurant ten years ago.

Ricardo whistles when he sees me.

"Damn chulo, you clean up nice."

Nicole is much more snarky.

"What's with the suit?" she asks. "You look like a Ponzi scheme."

Marcus lights a cigarette and turns on them.

"You two," he says. "Setups, done. Polishing, done. Menus, out. Bar, unpacked. Cooler, cleaned out. Am I correct, or do I have to start yelling?"

They nod in unison.

"We're set, boss," Ricardo says.

Satisfied, Marcus settles onto one of the buckets and crosses his legs primly.

"All right then, you've earned your gossip," he says and turns to me. "Jared has something to tell us."

Ricardo leers at me.

"You look different."

He can smell sex from miles away and I don't need him sniffing around today.

"I shaved," I tell him and pull at my chin.

He shakes his head, smiling, eyes twinkling.

"Nah, that's not it," he says "I think some puta is walking sideways this morning."

I look to Marcus to save me, but he only eggs them on.

"You know, he *does* look kind of rumpled in this light."

They're about to start in on me and I need to keep this conversation serious or I won't go through with it.

"Marcus, I don't really want to do this in front of an audience…"

He points at them, wagging his finger.

"We're all family here. Dish."

I realize this is going to be a lot harder than I expected and that I can't do it alone.

"Does anyone have a cigarette for me?"

Nicole's face breaks into a savage grin.

"Ha!" she shouts and punches Ricardo in the leg. "I told you. Pay up."

His face falls.

"I believed in you, man. How could you do this to me?"

"I'm sorry," I tell him. "It just happened."

He reaches into the pocket of his pants and glumly counts out five twenties. Nicole cackles and makes gimme gestures until he slips the wad of cash into her hand. Marcus, who is keener on a bad day than the two of them combined, passes me a cigarette and looks at me with shrewd eyes.

"Nothing ever just happens, Jared. Out with it."

I light the cigarette and Ricardo jumps in.

"Oh my God, you're getting married." He turns on Nicole. "You better give me that money right back, girl."

She rolls her eyes.

"Aw, is that it, Jared? Are you in *love*?" she asks.

(*I am love.*)

"No," I tell them. "I'm quitting."

***

Marcus flies off the bucket, kicking it over in a rage.

"Who poached you?" he demands. "Was it those assholes over at The Palm?"

"No, it's not like that-"

His eyes narrow.

"Don't tell me it was those cunts over at Legal! I will slit those bitches from ear-to-"

"Marcus, *calm down*," I say sternly and Ricardo and Nicole visibly shrink behind him, holding their collective breath.

He falls silent, gaping at me. Telling Marcus to calm down is the equivalent of telling a hysterical woman that she's acting crazy. It also crosses a line of respect that people don't cross unless they're really ready to move on. I brace for the onslaught, but his shoulders sag and the anger drains out of him like a deflating balloon.

"After all these years," he says, so quietly I can barely hear him. "You're really leaving me."

He is a small, wiry Jewish man from New York, bald with a sharp birdlike nose and piercing eyes. He has a penchant for horn-rim glasses and turtlenecks and his love of all things epicurean is rapacious. He is made infinitely larger through his temper, his passion, and the indomitable fire he exudes, demanding life to conform around him. But now he looks small and lonely, suddenly and starkly old. My heart goes out to him.

"I'm sorry, Marcus," I say. "But I need to do something better."

He draws back at once, hugely offended, a combative glint snapping into his eyes like a switchblade.

"Better? You come here to quit and now you're insulting me?"

I put my hands up, as if trying to calm a maniac with a weapon.

"No, of course not. I would never do that," I say. "I mean better for *me*."

I reach for him and he relents.

"Better for me."

He looks up at me and his eyes are wet.

"Bubbe," he says and bursts into tears.

I pull him into my arms and he embraces me with surprising strength, sobbing freely. Nicole comes over and finally Ricardo moves away from the landing and joins her. Standing in a rough circle, they hug me and Marcus' sobs are huge on the little deck.

(*You don't realize the impact you have on people.*)

No, but I'm beginning to. Isn't that what you wanted, Sarah?

A breeze breaks through the trees and travels down the alley, ruffling through my hair.

Isn't that all you really wanted in the end?

***

Out on the street, I realize that I have nothing to do and nowhere to go. I cut most of the strings to my old life in preparation for my exit. But with this last thread untied, I finally feel myself floating free and giddy out the open window of possibility. There is a part of me, still rigid and rational, still obsessed with material concerns, that is worried about how I'm going to feed myself in the coming weeks. But my rent is paid up through the end of the month and I've been living off credit cards for the last few weeks anyway and I still have some wiggle room.

"I am thirty-five and I am unemployed with no prospects and no discernible skills," I say.

I feel like saying this out loud should incite some kind of protective instinct and some healthy panic, but the giddiness rises up and I start to laugh, hard enough that I have to cover up my mouth so I don't look like a lunatic. The fact that I'm even capable of laughing after waking to find Sarah gone fuels more laughter and soon there are tears streaming down my face. A cop car rolls down the street. The uniform in the passenger seat looks at me with a little too much scrutiny for my tastes and I realize I have to get it together. For about the hundredth time in the last few days, I question if I'm really here.

There is one person who'll know for sure. But it's going to cost me. And I'm going to have a lot of explaining to do. I pull my cellphone out from my jacket pocket and turn it on for the first time in two days. There are twenty-two missed calls and sixteen messages. Most of the ruckus is from Harriet and while I'm deleting messages and screwing up the courage to call her, she buzzes in. A cartoon picture of Dot from Animaniacs fills my screen: Harriet Calling.

"Speak of the devil," I say and put the phone up to my ear. "Hi Harry."

"Thank God," she breathes. "Are you okay? I've been calling you forever."

"I'm okay."

Her tone changes in an instant.

"Good, because you're in a whole heap of trouble. Where have you *been*?"

"Look, I'm sorry, something came up."

She chuffs in my ear.

"I'll bet it did," she says. "You missed brunch. Your dad's been worried sick."

"Where is Stuart anyway?" I ask.

"He's golfing with Eddie. He took the day off of work so they could go play because *you've* been MIA."

I try to picture my dad in pleated golf pants and I can't do it.

"Well he can't be all that worried then," I say. "Since when does my dad play golf?"

"Since I have no idea," she says. "Eddie doesn't even know which end of the club to hold. They're probably drinking Scotch in the clubhouse or racing the golf carts. You can probably catch them if you head out there now. I think they're in Newton."

"I actually called to talk to you."

"Oh, okay. What's up?"

"Where are you right now?"

She laughs.

"I'm at work, like a normal person."

"Do you know anything about guns?"

There is silence on the other end of the phone.

"Harriet?"

"You assume because I'm from Texas I know a lot about guns. That's racist."

"How is that racist? You're white."

"It's culturally racist. Shame on you."

"Look, do you know anything about guns or not?"

"Of course I do, I'm from Texas. Now what's this all about? Are you in some kind of trouble?"

I want to call her on her bizarre circuitous logic, but it's just easier to move past it, so I opt for simple answers.

"No, I'm okay."

"Are you calling me from jail?"

"No."

"Do you have a gun on you?"

"No. It's at home."

"Wait, you're not at home?"

"No."

"Where are you?"

"I'm downtown. I just quit my job."

There is a long pause.

"Harriet?"

"Are you going to hold up a bank?"

"No.

"Then what do you need a gun for?"

"I just have it, okay?"

"Is it stolen?"

"No, I bought it. I think it's broken anyhow. But I want to go shoot it off and see."

"Don't you think you should have seen to that before you bought it?"

I put a hand up over my forehead and squeeze my temples.

"You're exhausting to talk to, you know that?"

She is exasperated.

"Why are you calling me, Jared? This is Eddie's department, not mine."

I don't know if she'll do it, but I have to ask.

"I know you guys do foreclosures where you work. I thought you might know a place we could go and not attract any attention. And…"

"And?" she presses.

"I really need your advice right now."

"My advice is that you shouldn't have paid for a busted gun."

There's only one way to stop this *Who's on First* runaround and as much as I don't want to get into this with her over the phone, I can't take much more of this.

"I bought it to kill myself, Harriet."

She draws in breath and says nothing.

"Harriet?"

Silence.

"Are you there?"

She sighs.

"My boss is in arbitration all day. I can probably sneak out for a few hours. I think I know a place. Can you catch the 11:30 train into Winchester Center?"

I check my watch, it's just after ten.

"I'll make it. Thank you, Harry. I mean it."

"Don't thank me yet, Jared. I'm ornery. And you have a lot of ground to cover."

"I know."

"A *lot*," she snaps and hangs up the phone.

***

I stand in North Station, with a shotgun and a box of shells in my gym bag, waiting for the Commuter Rail to take me out to Winchester. The dead shell-

(*It's just a fluke, Jared. Get that through your head*)

-retrieved from under the bookcase, sits heavy in my jacket pocket like a stone. I have passed four cops, one with a big, panting German shepherd, and at least a dozen MBTA workers and no one has given me a second glance. A guy in a suit with a gym bag during the lunch hour – I look like every other corporate raider downtown trying to get in a quick run on the treadmill and a steam before afternoon meetings. It strikes me just how easy it is to walk around a major city with a weapon and come and go in and out of transportation hubs with perfect anonymity.

I board the train and a blue uniformed conductor punches my ticket and tucks a receipt on top of my seat with a friendly smile. He makes small talk with me, something about the run of nice weather we've been having, and moves on to take care of the other passengers. He has no idea that I could unzip the bag, pull the gun out, and hold the entire train hostage. Or worse, go on a killing rampage until the transit cops put me down. Everyone can see my face plastered up on Fox25 news at ten with a Maria Stephanos voiceover: *Tonight, tragedy on the Commuter Rail outside of Boston...*

I played guns as a kid and I've never really grown out of that boyish awe and admiration for the bad-ass special ops dudes and CIA intelligence agents who rappel out of Blackhawks and neutralize threats in the middle of the night. What boy doesn't want to grow up to sip martinis and play baccarat in the South of France with a Walther under his tuxedo jacket and a cavalier attitude in the face of imminent danger? But under the cool gear and the mystique of that kind of training is a familiarity with violence that I know I will never possess.

I have been in exactly three fist fights in my life, two of them before I even got to high school. I've never had to fight for my survival, much less been in a situation where I've had to take a life. Like all men, who always live under the threat of random violence, I like to think that if the chips were down, if it were him or me, I would act and be the one to walk away.

But, like all men, there is the gnawing fear in my heart that I am a coward, and when it really came down to it, I would just freeze up or curl up into a ball. The worst part of this uncertainty is that you can't really know the answer until you're faced with it. So much of a man's identity is based on how tough he is, not muscles and strength, but the ability to stand and deliver, to protect when the world falls apart. It is a part of the male experience that women will never understand.

Having a gun at my side *is* empowering, I won't lie, and I can see how the gun nuts and the Columbine rejects get a jones over possessing control over life and death. But there is a frantic dread to it that eclipses any kind of superhero mojo. It is instant judgment, an immediate sentence with no possibility of reprieve. The gun is designed for one purpose and one purpose only: to kill in the most efficient and expedient manner available. It's not like flowers or some trick flag that says *BANG!* are going to pop out of the business end when I pull the trigger. This thing at my side, it's a one-way street.

It's making me paranoid, how easy it is to walk around with a gun on my person. It makes me wonder how many other people, less conscientious and far more comfortable driving down that one-way street, are packing heat in the train stations, the malls, the movie theaters. I guess there is some truth that an armed society is a polite society, but just having the gun near me is starting to make me feel crazy. No matter what I do, as long as it's in my presence, I can only think of death. What was I thinking? Where was my head when I bought this contraption? Who did I think I was? And why did I think it was a good idea to drag Harriet into this?

I feel my mood turning, souring, and I debate, for long enough to scare me, whether I should just go and turn myself in. I could just find the nearest PD or transit cop, surrender the bag, and admit that I am unhinged and suicidal and a marked danger to myself and others. I could let them fit me for a white coat and spend the rest of my days up in Worcester State doing macramé and drooling out the side of my mouth. I see, really for the first time, how easy it is to let things spin out of control. More than that, I see how easy it is to get locked onto a track and feel like there is no escape.

By the time the train stops in Winchester, I am jumpy, sweating profusely, afraid of myself. My heart is racing and in my head is a screaming litany of voices, telling me I'm crazy, unstable. Dangerous. I step off onto the rail platform and I feel like everyone is looking at me. I look straight down at the ground, not making eye contact with anyone, and work my way stiffly through the straggle of commuters with my shoulders hunched. In my suit and tie, with my dark sunglasses, my Italian loafers, and a bag of assassination at my side, I want to feel like a secret agent. But I just feel like a sweaty, cornered coward with the walls closing in.

***

We're standing out in a cow pasture on a farm in Western Massachusetts. The sun is shining. The overflowing cumulus clouds of summer roll past us. There is a battered farm house and a pair of grain silos up the hill, looking down at us like the lost sentinels of a forgotten war who, out of some stubborn sense of duty, refuse to leave their post. Green meadowlands, cut up into plots marked by ancient piled rock walls, stretch out around us. The farm is untended and overgrown, wild vines and weeds rising from the earth to reclaim the land. Patches of wildflowers blow in the breeze.

Harriet marched her little blue Corolla right past the main gate with all the NO TRESPASSING signs and off the battered dirt trail out into the middle of the abandoned pasture. All her doors are open and music is blaring across the field and out into the afternoon.

Admit that the waters around you have grown.

We're sitting on the hood of the car, me smoking a cigarette, her sipping sweet tea out of a thermos with Hello Kitty on it.

"I can't believe you're smoking again."

"I can't believe you never told anyone about this place until now."

Harriet works as the head paralegal for a law firm in Winchester. They handle a lot of property cases, mostly foreclosures and estate sales, and she's the boss' go-to gal – running basically the entire operation. She has keys to some high-end locales, and she's toured us through some pretty swanky digs. But nothing like this. Tucked away, out past the interstate, miles away from anything but forest, this place is a gem. I feel so far removed from the city and all its trappings that I don't want to go back.

Keep your eyes wide, the chance won't come again.

"You want it?" she asks. "It goes up for auction next year. I can probably get it for you for a steal too."

She points up the hill.

"The buildings will probably have to come down, they're pretty shot. But the soil is good and the land will be worth a lot to a developer someday."

I balk at her.

"What do you know about soil?"

She draws herself up proudly.

"I grew up on a farm, thank you very much," she says. "My Daddy taught me how to hunt and fish and farm the land."

"Really?"

"Yes really. I'm the girl you want to hang with after the Zombie Apocalypse goes down."

She passes me the thermos of tea, but I decline. She calmed me down a lot on the car ride out here, and just being out in this open space is making me feel much better, but my stomach is still queasy. She keeps telling me the tea is special and that it will settle the nausea, but I've never been a big fan of teas.

It'll soon shake your windows and rattle your walls.

"Do you think you could shoot someone?" she asks. "I mean really shoot them, put them down?"

"I don't know," I tell her. "I guess if they were trying to kill me and I had to defend myself."

"But not in cold blood?"

I turn on her.

"You mean just off somebody for no reason?"

"Yep."

"No, I couldn't."

"Never? Not even for money?"

"No, never."

"How come?"

I struggle for an answer beyond simple morality, looking out into the meadow, not sure where this line of questioning is going.

Your sons and your daughters are beyond your command.

"I couldn't just cut a person off, "I say at last.

She nods.

"Like you'd have no way of knowing if you might stop Gandhi from becoming Gandhi. Or Martin Luther King Jr. from becoming Martin Luther King Jr., right?"

I lie back on the hood and stare up at the clouds.

"I guess so. Every person gets a shot, right? Where are you going with this?"

"What about your shot? You're a person. How can you know what's in store down the line."

The order is rapidly fadin'.

"Are you telling me I'm Gandhi, Harriet?" I tease.

"I don't know," she says and grins. "Knowing you, I would say probably not. But the point is you don't know either and it's not up to you to decide."

"Who then, God?" I scoff.

She gets up off the hood and passes the Thermos to me again. This time I take it.

"Before you start mocking God, you better remember that someone spared your life so you could sit out here and give me a headache."

I take a long sip from the Thermos and say nothing.

"You're not apart from this experience, Jared. You are *here*, in life, covered in shit just like the rest of us. Stop scrambling for higher ground and just get used to it. Look around you. Is this really so bad?"

I stare out at the pasture, absorbing the day, breathing it into my lungs, admiring the teaming life that surrounds us and the rolling sky above. I take another sip of the sweet tea. It's cool and delicious. Harriet smiles at me, and for a wonder, my stomach feels better.

The times they are a'changin'.

***

"Gimme this thing, you big baby."

She snatches the shotgun from my hands and puts the stock to her shoulder. She pulls the slide back and looks through the opening and down the barrel. She cocks it all the way back and dry fires it, repeating the action several more times.

"It seems fine," she says. "These guns are built tough and it's well oiled."

She flips it over and starts to load a handful of shells into the breach.

"What happened with the shells?"

I shrug my shoulders.

"I don't know, they just didn't fire."

She turns the gun over and trains it up. She leans her head down so she can look over the barrel and rakes the slide back and forward again.

"Unless you get them really wet, these should be able to fire for years. Did they get wet?"

"Not that I know of," I tell her.

She squares her shoulders and settles into a shooting stance. The image of this girl in a pressed business suit with a floral blouse and earrings with a twelve gauge in her hands is a surreal one, and I'd laugh if all my fears weren't suspended on the end of her finger. I want to stop her. I want to slap the gun out of her hand and retreat in the car and never look back, leaving the weapon to rust and warp until the field swallows it and buries it like a fossil under centuries of dirt and clay. I want to stop her, but I have to know.

"Well, here goes nothing," she says, and pulls the trigger.

BOOM!

Her shoulder wrenches back and the sound echoes over the field, scattering birds from the trees in angry squawks. She jacks the slide back and a smoking shell ejects out onto the ground. She looks at me, supremely satisfied.

"That was fun."

She rakes the action again. Cha-Chunk. *BOOM!* Cha-Chunk. *BOOM!* Cha-Chunk. *BOOM!* Cha-Chunk. *BOOM!* She pulls back the slide and the last shell pops out and lands on the grass with the others.

"SEEMS FINE TO ME," she shouts.

The air is filled with blue smoke and smells like cordite. My ears are ringing and my throat is dry. With the gun empty, I reach into my jacket pocket, pull out the dead shell, and toss it to her.

"Try this one," I tell her.

"What?" she calls.

"TRY THIS ONE!" I yell and motion using the gun.

She nods and loads it. I close my eyes and hold my breath.

Cha-Chunk-

(*Jared-*)

BOOM!

(*-Do great things when you wake.*)

Chapter Eleven

Touchdown

"Damn," she says, nodding her head to the music on the radio. "I think *I* need a cigarette after that."

I have been silent, sullen, lost in my thoughts and staring out the window for most of the drive back. Harriet has been trying to lighten the mood, but I'm too immersed in trying to salvage some meaning out of what's happened to me to let my spirits lift. It still feels like a dream – unreal – like none of this is really happening. Like I'm not really here. And how can I be? By all rights-

(Cha-Chunk-)

-the weapon is infallible. I suspect something then, something mighty, but I can't let myself imagine it to be true. It's far easier to remain distracted by thoughts than to face it.

"Eddie's going to get raped tonight," she says. "Big time."

I make a face, but I don't say anything.

"Where is your head right now?" she asks.

I'm actually thinking about-

(*BOOM!*)

"You never met Gayle," I say. "She was good to me and I did her wrong. She's been on my mind a lot these last couple days. I don't know why. I haven't thought about her in years."

I tap the window glass absently.

"I never told her how much she meant to me and I should have. You know?"

She pats my leg gently.

"She knows, Jared. Girls always know."

She winks at me.

"Always."

I bang my head into the headrest a couple of times and close my eyes.

"I should be dead."

She turns down the radio and puts a hand on my shoulder.

"But you're not."

I bang my head again.

"How come I got spared? What's so special about me?"

She squeezes.

"I can't answer that, Jared," she says. "But I do know that most people never get a second chance in this life. My Daddy didn't. And I know your Momma didn't either."

"What happened to your dad?"

She returns her hands to the wheel and her lips draw down into a frown.

"That's a story for another day. Let's just say I know a thing or two about suicide myself."

Harriet never talks about her father and now I know why. I suddenly feel selfish and very small.

"Why didn't you say something? You didn't have to do all this."

"I know I didn't," she snaps. "I did it because I care about you. I'm not willing to let someone else who's close to me slip away."

"I'm sorry, Harriet. I feel stupid."

She laughs and her voice softens.

"Well good, you should. But there's something I do want you to know. In case you ever go back to that place again."

"Okay."

"I won't come. To your funeral. I will not attend."

"That's a little harsh, don't you think?"

Her lips are drawn into a thin angry line.

"No," she says. "Funerals are for people who've earned it."

***

She pulls up in front of the Lennox hotel on Exeter Street.

"What are we stopping here for?"

"This is where you get out."

She unclips my seatbelt and leans over me to open my door.

"I don't get it."

"This is your dad's hotel. You're going to march up there and find him and tell him you're flying out with him tomorrow."

"But-"

"You wanted my advice, here it is: go home, Jared. Get out of the memories and the drama you have here and go be with your family."

"In Florida? I can't just *leave* Boston."

"Why not?" She asks frankly. "You have no job now. What's stopping you? I'll send Eddie to get your mail and feed your cat."

"I…I don't know."

"Good, then it's settled. Now get out."

I vacillate over the open door, uncertain what to do next. I reach out to hug her, but she turns away and puts both hands on the wheel.

"Nope, not doing it. Now get out before I start crying."

"I don't know what to say."

"Go be Gandhi," she says. "Get."

I exit the car and reach back to close the door. I wave, but she's already pulling away and out into traffic, the radio jacked back up to full volume. I watch her go and pull out a pack of smokes. I open the pack and look inside, rolling the remaining few around like marbles. I feel Harriet in my head and that feeling in my chest lifts a bit. I wonder if everything might be okay after all. I close the pack, return it to my pocket, and head inside to find my father.

***

I find him in the restaurant pub, sitting at the bar over a plate of steak and potatoes, reading a newspaper. His white hair is disheveled, poking up in errant tufts, and he absolutely looks like a tourist in his plaid shorts and Tiki-bar shirt. I stand in the doorway and watch him pluck through his paper for a bit, consumed by a mixture of shame and love.

He senses someone concentrating on him and he looks up. His eyes find me and he beams. He waves me over and motions to the bartender. I pull out a stool and settle in beside him. The bartender brings me a menu and I nod to my dad's Scotch.

"I'll take one of those."

He folds his paper and puts a hand over the back of my neck.

"Where have *you* been hiding?"

I can't even begin to tell him about what happened between Sarah and me, much less her flying all the way out here because she thought I was blown apart.

(*Cha-Chunk-*)

"It's a long story, Dad. Can I just leave it there?"

The bartender sets a glass in front of me. I haven't even opened the menu, I just hand it back and point to Stuart's plate.

"Well, I hope she was worth it," he grins.

(*This is all I'm able to give you.*)

"I need to talk to you."

He waits for me.

"I just quit my job and…"

Can I tell him? Should I? He looks so expectant and I can see how much he wants to be helpful and supportive, but he can't be expecting what's gone on in the last three days. How could anyone really? Wouldn't it break his heart? And doesn't some part of him already know, even if he can't fully see it for himself? I feel something larger move inside me that tells me that for all the protecting he's done for me over the years, it's time for me to return the favor. I make the choice to go with sanitized honesty.

"...I'm pretty shaky right now."

The fixer in him rises to the surface and he's all about the game plan.

"Tell me what you need, Jared. Name it. We'll figure it out."

I am almost afraid to ask him. I don't know why, but I fear he'll say no and I'll have nowhere to go. For the second time since I've seen him, I feel like the roles are reversed and this time it's me spilling out of the boat and into hungry waters. I take a chance and reach my hand out.

"Can I come home with you? Just for a little while."

Professor November looks back at me.

"Are you all right, son? Don't lie to me."

I wonder, in the light of his scrutiny, how much he actually does know.

"I will be," I tell him, no lies there. "I've just got to get out of here for a while. Is it okay if I come stay with you?"

I pitch and spill and, helpless, he catches me fearlessly and hauls me back into the boat.

"Of course you can, Jared," he says. "The wedding isn't for another three weeks. I was going to fly you down for that. But we've already got your room set up for you and everything."

He pulls his phone out of his shirt pocket and holds a finger up to me.

"Hang on. I'm going to call my travel agent down there and we'll see if we can't put you on the same flight with me tomorrow."

"Dad, you don't have to do this now-"

But he's already dialed and barking into the phone.

"Connie. Stuart. I need a favor. No, it's for my son…"

I watch him take charge with that same marshaling gusto that has always made him seem superhuman. Even in his tropical getup, he still ripples with authority. The bartender sets a steaming plate of food down in front of me and cocks a thumb over at my dad with a smile. I nod and hold up his famous peace sign for another round. My stomach rumbles loudly and it dawns on me that I haven't eaten anything since last night. Pretty soon I am diving into my steak with abandon while Stuart moves the world to get me down to Florida.

He clicks his phone shut and turns on me, triumphant.

"It's done. You fly out with me tomorrow at 9am. We should get into Palm Beach International around twelve, twelve-thirty. What's left?"

I look up from my food.

"Nothing. We're cool. Two questions though."

He unflips his phone, ready for anything.

"What have you got for me?"

"Since when do you golf?"

He laughs and folds the phone back up.

"What? I have a life. Next question."

I reach out and finger a sleeve that is covered in parrots.

"Seriously, what's up with this *shirt*?"

***

We spend the rest of the night sipping Scotch at the bar and regaling with the people around us. Stuart plies them with war stories of his old days at Brown or embarrassing tales from my childhood. He keeps telling everyone he meets that it's still my birthday and random drinks keep showing up in my face. We've collected quite a crowd by the end of the night and I'm pretty drunk. I know if I'm going to catch a plane in the morning, I have to call it quits.

On the way up to his room, a tipsy woman with a bad spray tan and an obnoxious sundress purposely collides with him and gives him a complement on his shirt. He throws his hands up at me.

See?

Outside his room, he puts his arm around me.

"You can stay here tonight if you want. I'm just going to watch Letterman and go to sleep."

As much as I'd like to remain with him, I don't know if I can deal with another hotel room right now. Anonymous, suspended in time-

(*Lie on the bed.*)

-I can't do it. Maybe not for a long time.

"I gotta go home. I have to pack and sleep in my own bed for the night."

He nods and hugs me.

"Okay. Get home safe. Ed says he's picking us up here at seven. Don't be late."

I turn to leave and he calls after me.

"Jared."

"Yeah, Dad."

"It means a lot to me that you feel like you can come to me when you're upset. I never could with my father. And…it means a lot."

I find myself wondering again how much he really knows. I feel like the moment should be punctuated with hugs or some other kind of acknowledgment, but I don't know what to do. I can only nod and be grateful. I leave him standing in the hallway, swaying and fumbling with his room key, flush with drink and a kaleidoscope of tawdry parrots.

***

The cab drops me off in front of my building. I pay him and get out, looking over to the curb, hopeful that there will be a red minivan there. But there's just a white, beat-up Subaru Forester with New Hampshire plates, loaded up with camping gear. I hover on the stoop, stubbornly wishing for a psychic whisper along the back of my neck, but it's just the stoop. Whatever magic took place here is over.

I head upstairs without much enthusiasm and let myself in. Cora is screaming at me, protesting neglect and demanding food. Automatically, I follow her into the kitchen and heap out a plate of food for her. Continuing on auto-pilot, I walk around the apartment, turning on all the lights to chase away the last of the shadows or maybe to uncover her, hiding playfully behind a curtain. It feels vast in here, empty without-

(*Tell me I'm beautiful.*)

-any company, and for the first time since she left, I allow myself to feel lonely.

In the bedroom, it still looks like a bomb went off and I know I'm not going to pack tonight. I strip off my clothes and toss them on the chaise. I feel like I should shower and brush my teeth, but the energy saps out of me with every movement. I set an alarm with the last of my strength and collapse onto the bed. I sink into the pillowtop with a contented sigh. After two nights on the bathroom floor and a night of God-knows-what at the Mandarin, my bed is akin to heaven. I know I should pull the covers over me at least, but while I'm thinking about doing it, I fall asleep.

***

In my dream, Gayle is picking flowers in a meadow surrounded by trees. She is so young, maybe seventeen, long and coltish, with her hair – almost white in the sunshine – tied up into a French braid. She is skipping around in the grass, the hem of her dress rising up and out with her steps, her bare feet scarcely touching the ground. She is singing and her voice is clear and high.

She sees me and her face breaks into a joyous smile.

"You're here!" she cries.

She runs over to me, throws her arms around me, and kisses my cheek.

"I knew you'd come."

I try to speak to her, to tell her how happy I am to see her, and how much I've missed her, but the words won't come out. I try, over and over, but there is only terrible, voiceless silence. My mouth strains, my diaphragm heaves, but no sound escapes me, not even breath. I feel panic descend on me as I try to force the words out with increasing futility. She frowns and touches my lips.

"It's okay," she says and kisses me again. "You don't need to speak here."

But I want to. I must. I haven't seen her in so long and my heart aches just looking at her. I want to pull down poems, sonnets, give voice to all the days she's given me happiness. But I am impotent and mute, stripped of my most basic form of communication. I clutch at her, frantic now, trying to rip the words out from deep inside.

I love you. I love you. I love you.

She touches my face, tender, adoring.

"It's *okay*," she repeats. "I know."

She laughs, a sweet soulful sound that has always driven demons from me.

"Girls always know."

Her laughter deepens and it rises, wrapping itself around me, lifting me up until my own feet leave the ground. It tickles through me, swoops out and around the field, and all of the leaves on the trees shake, falling from their branches in a wondrous shower of green.

***

I shoot awake. Cora, curled into a furry ball at the foot of the bed, makes an annoyed meow and tucks her head back under her paws. I leap out of bed and stare at the alarm clock. *Dammit.* Of course I somehow forgot to set the alarm right last night and I've got about twenty minutes to pack and make it to the hotel before Eddie picks us up. I call a cab, throw on jeans and tee-shirt, and go to the hall closet to dig out my suitcase. Behind a battered vacuum cleaner, winter storm boots, and a scuffed-up pair of roller blades, is a suitcase I haven't even looked at in ten years. I wrestle it free from the back of the closet and haul it into the bedroom.

I throw it on top of last night's clothes on the chaise, and unzip it. Cora, no longer dozing, hops down off the bed and cries at me angrily. This is a "going away" bag and I'm going to catch hell for pulling it out without consultation. There are varying degrees of "going away" bags that promote increasing levels of separation anxiety, from the messenger bag all the way up to the long-weekend backpack. But the last time she saw this luggage, she got tossed into a kitty carrier and flown three thousand miles against her will. She cries again and her look is plaintive and clear: *you didn't tell me we were moving.*

I pick her up, she is trembling.

"Easy girl. You're not going anywhere this time. Calm down."

I stroke her fur until she gets it that we're not moving, but she is still slighted that I'm leaving and she squirms to get down. I let her go and she immediately hops into the open suitcase and looks at me defiantly: *go ahead, try and leave me now.*

"Why are all the women in my life so difficult, huh?"

In seeming answer to my question, she circles the bottom of the bag and settles down in the middle of it, contentedly licking one of her front paws. I close the lid of the suitcase on her and rifle through my closet, pulling out clothes and stacking them on the bed. I collect toiletries from the bathroom and prowl the apartment, turning everything off and unplugging all the big appliances. Back in the bedroom, I pause over Paige's Rumi book, finally tossing it onto the pile with everything else. I open the suitcase back up and Cora stares up at me, making herself as cute as she possibly can.

"Sorry kiddo, time to go."

She fights me, whining miserably, but I scoop her out and set her onto the floor. She gives me a wounded look and leaves the room, tail swishing up at me like a middle finger. I transfer the piles into my bag and have just enough time to zip it closed before I hear the cab honking outside. I am positive I've forgotten something, but it's too late now. I grab the suit coat hanging off the back of my office chair, throw it on, and race down the stairs to catch my ride.

***

Eddie drops us on the curb at the American Airlines departure terminal and helps us with our bags. Stuart will only fly American Airlines, no matter what the price difference is or if it means layovers and inconvenient stop-offs. With very T.S. Garp logic, he believes that the airline has already been "pre-disastered" by the 9/11 attacks and that the odds of terrorists choosing the same airline to do the same thing again border on astronomical.

Think that airline will get caught with its pants down like that again? Those planes are safer than a kangaroo pouch, I'll bet my life on it.

American lost a lot of business after the attacks and rewarded him with all kinds of bonus miles and vouchers for staying with them. He has access to the Admiral's Club at all the airports, a credit card that stocks him up with free vacations he never takes, and he gets upgraded every time he sneezes. He's already glad-handing the curbside check-in guy and chatting him up about the Red Sox chances for the series this year.

Eddie pulls me aside, out of earshot.

"So I have shotgun sitting in my hall closet," he says.

"How do you feel about that?" I ask him.

"Well, it's incentive to do the dishes, that's for sure."

I laugh, but his face is drawn and serious.

"You should have told me."

"I know."

He looks at me sharply, the answer isn't good enough.

"I shouldn't have had to find out secondhand from Harriet."

"I know."

"You keep saying that, but I don't think you do."

"I didn't want you to find out at all. *Either of you*. But there it is."

His anger is bright, but underneath it, I can tell he's hurt.

"Dammit, man. We've been friends a long time and I've seen you through some *shit* in our day. How come you thought you couldn't come to me?"

"I didn't go to anyone, Ed," I tell him. "Nobody."

Eddie, like my dad, is a fixer and I can see his wheels turning, trying to figure out what he can say or do to just move us past this.

"I know you want to fix this. But it's mine. It's my burden."

Stuart is calling to me and waving me over and my window with Eddie is closing.

"You have to let me have it."

I turn my house keys over to him and he finally smiles.

"Now there aren't any surprises in your house I should know about? No hand grenades or land mines or anything?"

I smile back and shake my head.

"Cora gets wet food once a day and kibble in a big bowl – you can just leave it out."

"I got it."

"I change the litter box every other day and don't forget to change out her water."

"I got it."

"She's got some toys in a box in the pantry. Make sure you play with her a little and-"

"Jared, I got it."

"Hey," Stuart calls. "Let's get this show on the road."

I thumb over to the curbside check-in.

"I gotta…"

I put my hand out, but he charges into me and embraces me in a heavy bear hug.

"Go get right in your head," he says. "Everything will be waiting here for you when you get back."

"Thanks, Eddie."

He waves to my dad and gets back into his car. He tips me a quick, knowing salute and pulls away.

(*Go get right in your head.*)

"Roger that, buddy."

I go over to the curbside counter and show my license and the agent gives me tags for my suitcase and my boarding pass. *BOS to PBI, Flight 1536, non-stop.*

"Gate B-34, just past security on the right. Enjoy your trip."

My dad grins at me.

"Ready, Freddy?"

(Ready, Betty.)

"Ready, Dad."

Together, we walk through the automatic doors into the airport.

***

"Shoes, belts, jackets in the plastic bins."

Stuart reaches down to pull off his boat shoes.

"Boxcutters brought us to this. Can you believe it?"

I can actually. Considering how easy it was for me to hop a busy commuter train with a shotgun, I figure that trick shoe bombs and plastic explosives in a tube of toothpaste are the least of our worries. It seems like all these extraneous steps are just a way of appearing bigger than we are. It's like putting an alarm on a car. It may make someone think twice, but if they really want it, no alarm is going to stop them. These inconveniences may stop the guy writing manifestos in his mountain cabin from trying anything, but the big sharks will never stop. With enough will, someone, somewhere, is going to figure out a way to pull it off.

"Laptops need to be out."

I slip out of my shoes and drop them into the plastic bin. I work my belt off and start digging through my-

"Nothing in your pockets, please."

My wallet and phone go into the bin. I'm checking my jacket when my fingers slip around a glass vial and my heart stops.

No.

My mouth goes dry and the pulse thuds in my temples.

No.

A TSA agent makes eyes with me.

"Jacket in the bin, sir."

I nod automatically, palming the vial, and shrugging out of my jacket. I lay it on top of my other things and look around the line. Can I escape to the bathroom and dump it? Wouldn't it look even more suspect if I jumped out of line? With my shoes already in a plastic tub? No one has to pee that badly. Could I feign a weak bladder? Food poisoning? The line inches closer to the conveyor belt and I feel an invisible noose around my neck tighten. In my mounting hysteria, I wonder if I could just take them, toss the vial back and swallow before anyone can say shit to me. But even the terrifying thought of sitting in my skivvies in a little white room while some overzealous TSA agent slips on a latex glove pales in comparison to the thought of my first acid trip at 35,000 feet.

What the fuck am I going to do?

Stuart is saying something about the humiliation of being fondled by the TSA, but I have tuned him out. I think the humiliation of having his son arrested for trying to sneak a Class A controlled substance on board a 757 is going to be way worse. I can't imagine what the penalty is for pulling a stunt like this, but I know it's not going to be a slap on the wrist.

Jesus Christ, I'm going to jail.

The line moves closer and the woman in front of me slides her bin onto the conveyor rollers. She smiles at me and says something about how they'll be asking us to take our pants off pretty soon, but I am already standing in front of a judge and getting sentenced in my mind. With hands that don't even feel attached to me, I place my bin on the rollers and slide the vial into the waistband of my underwear. A voice rises in me, mean and thick with derision, mocking me in my greatest moment of peril.

Did you really want to die, Jared? Or did you just want to be free? Too late now. Serves you right for not appreciating what you've got.

"You okay?" Stuart asks.

"Yeah," I say. "My damned pants are just falling down."

I laugh, but it comes out more like sharp bark and far too loud. What happened to Jared? Oh, you didn't hear? He tried to kill himself and then got arrested trying to get on a plane with six hits of LSD. Shotguns on trains, acid on airplanes? What the fuck is the matter with me? Who is this person living my life? The woman ahead of me goes up to the body scanner and I feel sweat break over my brow. Jesus Christ, I'm losing it. Another voice comes into my head, older and far more serious.

Keep it together, kid. You hear me? Or you've got no chance at all.

The machine is going to detect the glass and the agent is going to nod to someone and I'm going to get pulled out of line. *You got a prescription for these balls-out hallucinations?* And the look on Stuart's face is going to kill me-

"Step up, sir."

I force myself to choke it all down and walk up to the agent with an almost perfect easy smile on my face.

"How you doing?" I manage, and my voice is strong.

"Anything in your pockets, sir?" he asks.

I shake my head and pat myself down, like maybe I might have forgotten something. I know this game. I've-

(You're the Great Pretender.)

-dealt with scrutiny before. He waves me into the machine.

"Stand with your arms above your head. Okay?"

I lift my arms, the vial shifts in my waistband, and my heart kicks in my chest. It's going to fall out and through my pant leg and roll out onto the carpet and *look-here, boys-*

Is this really how my story is going to end?

I close my eyes and try to pray.

"Sir."

Here it comes. I had a chance. I actually got another chance and I fucking blew it. I realize, with crowning irony, that it isn't when life actually ends that you realize how precious it is, but when your ability to live it on your terms gets taken away from you.

"Sir.

So long, Jared.

I bring my arms down, look at the agent, and resign myself for the worst.

"You're all set."

I almost don't register what he said to me, but some primal self-preservation part of me gets it perfectly well and walks me out to the other end of the conveyor to collect my things. While I'm putting on my belt, I transfer the vial into my pocket and vow not to think about this in any fashion until we land in Florida. Yet I can't escape that overarching feeling of being watched again and that commanding voice rings through my head loud enough to make my ears hurt.

That's two, kid.

***

At 12:02pm Eastern Standard Time, American Airlines flight 1536 touches down at Palm Beach International airport, fifteen minutes ahead of schedule. The pilot tells us the weather is 85 degrees and sunny with a lazy westerly breeze and clear skies. He thanks us for flying American and hopes we enjoy our stay at the Palm beaches. My dad punches me in the arm.

"See? Safe as a kangaroo pouch. Didn't I tell you?"

"You did," I say, joining in his enthusiasm and once again unable to tell him just how safe we really are.

(*That's two, kid.*)

We disembark from the plane and follow the other travelers down to baggage claim. I watch the other passengers collect around the carousel, each with their own destinations and itineraries. They check their watches and chatter into cell-phones and huddle together, reaching eagerly for their bags like questing baby birds reaching for sustenance. As if those bags contain who they are? As if the mish-mash of things in their luggage define their lives? I want to tell them that they are so much more, that Harriet had it wrong – second chances happen all the time. You just have to be present enough to see them. But they won't hear me. They can't. It's not my place to tell them. I am only myself.

And it's good to be home.

Chapter Twelve

Sanctuary

Waiting for a pickup on the curb outside the airport, Jared's father teases him mercilessly about who his new paramour could be. He points to a bleached blonde woman in her forties with enormous fake breasts and botox lips so puckered they look in danger of bursting open. Covered in chunky jewelry, she clanks when she walks, perilous on six-inch-high yellow stilettos that look more like weapons than shoes.

"Oh, there she is," he jokes. "My one and only."

His eyes fall on a hennish Jewish grandmother with bright dyed-red hair and thick-framed oversized glasses that cover most of her face. She wears a headscarf and a Chanel pant-suit and carries an obnoxiously large handbag. She is trying to marshal three sour-faced pre-teens into a Bentley while barking commands at a blithe driver.

"I didn't tell you, she has kids, so be nice."

Barely able to contain his laughter, he directs Jared's gaze towards a tiny, chesty twenty-something in a middy blouse and tight hot-pink velour shorts with *Juicy* written across the back. She is gabbing loudly into a cellphone, followed by an entourage of three enormous men who look like they could be linebackers for a professional sports team, each carrying a piece of her luggage.

"She's a little young, I grant you," he smiles. "But what Juicy wants, Juicy gets."

The game continues in this fashion for another twenty minutes as the cast of characters outside the airport becomes increasingly more oddball and ostentatious. After a while, struck with the heat and overwhelming brightness of the day, Jared tunes him out and tries to adjust to just how much life has changed in the last three days. He begins to see glimmers of potential and the first stirrings of exhilaration wake inside him, but he is still too raw and unsure to allow them to surface.

A little green Saab convertible pulls up to the pickup zone and a curly-headed blonde woman starts waving to them. But Jared does not see her right away. He watches in amazement as his father transforms before his eyes. The man's face brightens, softens, and fills with adoring. His eyes change from teasing to tenderness and, almost imperceptibly, his entire body strains toward the car. The years on his face are wiped away and he appears boyish, devilish. He is a younger man, larger, emboldened by the unyielding force of his connection to another. There is a surety and a calm vigilance in his gaze that Jared is intimately familiar with, but has never fully appreciated until this moment. It is a look reserved for family.

It is not that Jared did not believe his father's devotion when he was told of the impending wedding, nor does he dismiss the change that came over the man during their conversation. It is more that he never really saw how much his father *could be* in the years since Lillian November died. How much more. For all the hard years, for all that was lost, to see his father instilled with so much vigor and peace, it reaches down into that stirring center and moves him. He knows that no matter what she looks like or what she does or what her personality embodies – for Stuart, she is ideally suited. This moment is pivotal for Jared and it will drive all that follows.

"Jared, this is Olivia."

And of course, she is perfectly lovely.

***

That first night, just after sunset, he makes his first pilgrimage down to the beach. It will be the first of many. His father lives a mile from the shore, in a modest one-story house with a mermaid mailbox and a lawn dotted with faded pink flamingos. From the house, the walk winds him through a quiet retirement community and past the outskirts of a golf course. Out on the main road, he follows the breeze down the boulevards and over a drawbridge to the state road that runs up the Atlantic coast. Across the highway and down a wood slatted path, the beach stretches as far as the eye can see in both directions.

The waves crest and roll in, rhythmically pounding the shore with a frothy spray. Small seabirds motor across the sand, picking through seaweed for tasty morsels. Hotels, poised like black dominos in the dying light, overlook the surf. Down the stretch, a pier rises up from the beach and leans out into the water. Overhead, the sky is fading to purple and the first sliver of a moon peeks out from behind the clouds.

He removes his shoes and socks and walks down to the shore. He rolls up his pants at the water's edge and wades into the sea. As his feet disappear into the lapping waves, his heartbeat slows and he feels some of the tension of the last few days leach out from between his toes and out into the ocean. He closes his eyes and breathes in the salt air, ripe with the tang of high summer and humid, verdant growth. Faced with a choice, more important than he will ever know, he feels for that inner tone and lets his compass guide him right to walk south down the beach.

He walks slowly, relishing the wet, crumbling sand between his toes and the spray that peppers his face with cool droplets. He walks for a mile or two until he comes up next to the jutting pylons of the pier. There, he follows the compass to a spot in the sand and sits down to contemplate the waves.

Out, over the water, he finds a woman surfing. She cuts through the waves with an easy grace that impresses him. Not for her technique, which is flawless, but for her seeming oneness with her board. Without knowing anything about her, he knows that the board is beaten and familiar, worn with the grooves of hard travel and hours of time logged on the water. She moves with a fluidity that fills him with longing. He longs to embody that, to embody her freedom and the instinctual way she anticipates the whimsy of the ocean. She glides on the water with a single-minded pursuit of play, like a kid at the end of summer vacation who only turns regretfully for home as the day dies and first of the streetlights blink on.

He waves to her, but she is absorbed with her craft and does not see him. He feels oddly self-conscious that she did not wave back, like he has been excluded from something he yearns to take part in. This is just as well. He is still too absorbed in his own drama to make a proper connection. The frenetic air of Boston still clings to him, entrenched and unyielding, and he still does not see the part of himself that is every bit as free and fluid as she is. But he watches her for a long time, and the exhilaration that is waking inside him begins to move and stretch.

When he gets up and finally turns back for home, she is still surfing.

***

Out past the kitchen, Olivia has converted an unused storage room into a makeshift art studio. The room is fanciful and alive with activity, lined with shelves of oversized art books, canvases of varying sizes, easels with unfinished works, and all manner of supplies. It is dominated by a huge plank of wood laid over two sawhorses, cluttered with sheaves of sketches and tackle boxes brimming with tubes of oil paint and charcoals. Brush ends poke out of jars and palettes lie strewn about the table, swirls of mixed color drying on the wood.

She tours Jared through the studio and he is thoroughly enamored. Excited, thrilled to have a new patron in her midst, she pulls out her favorite canvases to show him. He peruses through her mix of impressionism and surrealism with increasing wonder and admiration. Finally, when he has pored over them all, his eyes settle on a large canvas in the corner of the room with a dropcloth tossed over it.

"It's not finished yet."

With a showman's flourish, she pulls the cloth away and Jared stares, marveling at the image. It is the interior of a museum gallery with paintings on the wall. To the right, a very proper looking French family is gathered around an impressionist painting, staring intently. The mother and father stand at the center, with three girls dressed in the cloaks and outré bows of the 1930s to their right and a little dapper boy in a short-pant suit to their left. All of their backs are to the viewer and they are fully absorbed in their inspection, except the youngest boy, who is looking agog at the painting to his left.

A man in a suit and bowler hat is crawling out of the unattended painting. He already has one leg out, dangling three feet over the side. The other is perched on the ledge and he grips the top of the frame with his hand to give himself leverage. He is leaned toward the boy with a mischievous grin on his face. His other hand is raised, a finger to his lips. The boy's eyes are wide, a lollipop suspended just short of his gaping mouth.

"I love it. This is incredible."

She flushes with pride and recovers the painting. He wanders among her things, fingering them, lingering over the odds and ends, trying to absorb some of her creative flair and bring it into himself.

"Have you always painted?"

She laughs and points to the edge of the work-desk. Peeking out from a collection of sketches, is a brass nameplate set into a heavy triangular holder: Olivia Lipinski, Vice President.

"A relic, from my old days at Goldman Sachs in New York."

Jared stares at this buoyant, vibrant woman in her bright sundress with paint under her fingernails. With her wild blonde curls pinned on the top of her head, and her Birkenstocks, he can't believe she ever came from the corporate world, much less a sharktank like Goldman Sachs. She catches his look and smiles sardonically.

"Hard to believe, isn't it?"

He nods.

"I was a super bitch, make no mistake. Mergers and acquisitions for twenty-five years. I climbed the ladder and fought tooth and nail to break into the old-boy's club. You ready for this? My nickname was The 'Liviscerator."

Jared laughs, but she only gives him a tight smile and it does not reach her eyes.

"What happened?"

She runs a finger across the nameplate and sighs.

"I hit the wall. That lifestyle is a tough one. Late nights, early mornings, you're always running a game. I hated what I was doing and who I was. I got very sick and they fired me. It forced me to stop everything and focus on getting well again. I had to completely die out of my old life and re-evaluate what I wanted out of a new one."

"I'm sorry."

She shrugs and brightens.

"Don't be. I'm not. If it all hadn't happened, I never would have started painting."

She smiles.

"And I never would have met your father."

She taps the nameplate and nods her head.

"Sometimes death is liberating, Jared. Even when it's your own."

***

Out on the golf course, Jared struggles to keep up with his father. They are nine holes in and Stuart is clearly dominating the afternoon. His swings are easy and powerful and he has been peppering his son with pointers all morning like a pro. Jared poises over the ball, face scrunched up in concentration, the golf club like a complex alien contraption in his hands.

"God kid, you gotta relax. This is a finesse game."

Jared winds back, pivoting his hips like he was shown, and lets the club fly. It chips the ball on the side and it slices out and sideways into a grove of palms. He curses and shakes his club at the trees. Stuart smiles at him with infinite patience.

"It's okay, just try it again."

Jared pulls another ball from his pocket and sets it onto the tee. He wiggles himself over the ball and winds up again. Stuart stops him and comes around behind him, adjusting his arms and moving up his grip on the club.

"Jesus Jared, for all that time you're spending at the beach, go swimming. You need to loosen up."

Adjusted to his satisfaction, Stuart releases him and steps back.

"Okay, now don't try and swing. Just swing."

Jared breathes deeply in through his nose and imagines the ball sailing over the fairway. He exhales and drives the club through the ball with a satisfying *THOCK* that launches it off the tee, high and clear for 200 yards. Stuart claps his hands and laughs.

"There you go! Nice shot. I think there's hope for you yet, son."

But Jared's putting game is a comedy of errors and as they approach the eighteenth hole, he is hot, tired, and increasingly annoyed with his performance. For Jared, this day has been an exercise in frustration. For Stuart, it is flawless. Playing golf, side-by-side with his son, catching up, wasting time, and zooming around in little carts is a gift he will treasure long into old age. Coaching Jared through something with which he is not natively gifted and bringing him into his world, however awkwardly, is massively rewarding for the man. Jared could be the worst golfer in the history of the sport, but Stuart cannot imagine anyone he would rather be playing with that day.

Back at the clubhouse, they sip beers and order lunch, relaxing in the cool of the air conditioning. After the meal, Stuart grows quiet and becomes shy around Jared. He almost does not want to ask. He knows it is irrational, he can almost predict the boy's answer already, but he cannot know and he fears the ruination of a near-perfect afternoon. Jared notices the change and goads the man to speak.

Finally, in a low voice, choked with emotion, Stuart asks his son to be his best man at the wedding. Before the words are even fully out, Jared is pulling him into his arms, nodding over and over again. It is one of the greatest moments of Stuart's life.

***

He walks the beach in the late afternoon, trying to work out some of the rigidity in his body. He has no designs of becoming a pro-golfer, but he is starting to realize that he has never fully felt comfortable in his skin. He has fought for so long, forcing his body to stand and move in a precise way instead of just allowing himself to move naturally. He longs to be lithe and unencumbered in his frame. He does not yet understand that freedom in his movements comes from freedom in his heart. He is still holding on so tightly to his hurt that he has made it a part of his identity and fears he will float adrift without it. But he is making great strides and already the slower pace of life here, the salt air, and the peaceful rhythm of the ocean are working their way into him and soothing his burden.

He has been seeing the surfer off and on during his treks and reaches out fondly to her, trying to channel her easy grace. She has achieved an almost mythical status in his eyes, as each time he has spotted her, she has been out on the water. He imagines that she must live out there, like a water elemental, swimming among the fishes when the moon rises. He is caught off-guard then when he sees her walking towards him up the beach with her surfboard tucked under one arm.

It is dreamlike and somehow incongruent to see her out on dry land and he feels acutely that he needs to make contact with her, if only to acknowledge that her presence here has affected him. He struggles with something to say as she approaches.

"Hey, you look really good."

She plants her surfboard into the sand and stares at him, impassive. Standing in front of him in her bikini, dirty blonde hair dripping water on her skin, watching him calmly with startling blue eyes, he sees that she is very pretty and that he must sound like every other puffed-up single guy on the beach. He is not telling her anything she has not heard before. He struggles to correct himself, pointing emphatically towards the waves.

"Out there, I mean. I've been watching you."

She passes him a sidelong glance.

"You've been watching me, have you?"

He gives her a daffy grin.

"Yeah. You know, not in a weird way. Just admiring your form-"

He puts his arms out to his sides and rocks from side-to-side.

"-very graceful."

She says nothing, merely considers him with that calm blue gaze, the very faintest trace of a smile on her lips. Embarrassed, he makes a thumbs-up gesture.

"Okay then."

He steps widely around her and begins to march up the beach. She lets him get about ten good paces before she fires.

"Hey!"

He turns. She has her arms out to her sides, mocking his surfer impression.

"Thank you."

They share a good laugh and, though he is flustered by how foolish he thinks he appeared, he is smitten with thoughts of her for the rest of the day. And the next time he sees her out over the water, she waves to him.

***

Jared and Stuart are getting fitted for tuxedos at a bridal shop across town. Stuart made an appointment the week prior, but did not expect to do much more than get some measurements taken for a traditional black tuxedo. The process turns out to be far more labor intensive and they have spent most of the appointment in the consultation phase, flipping through style books on a hunt for something simple. Everything from vests, coat lengths, collars, and ties to English and American cuts have turned a simple search into a quest.

"This rapper crap is terrible. Who wears stuff like this? Haven't these people heard of Humphrey Bogart?"

"Hey, here's a cummerbund with parrots on it. At least they've heard of Jimmy Buffet."

They are punchy by the time they get to the fittings and the tailor is fussy and gruff with them, almost to the point of being insulting. He speaks with a thick French accent that the two have been mocking since they came in.

"Old steel! I can do notheeng weeth you two shatting about."

"I think he means chatting."

While picking out shoes – oxford, wingtip, lace-up, slip-on, round or square toe-box – Jared asks his father for advice.

"What the fuck am I doing?"

"What do you mean?"

"With my life, Dad. I'm thirty-five years old and I have nothing to show for it."

Stuart stops rifling through shoes and looks at him.

"I wouldn't go that far. You're healthy. You're smart. And you have people who love you. I wouldn't say you have nothing."

He reaches down and holds out a pair of Robin's egg blue wingtips to Jared.

"And you could be roaming around South Florida in these puppies."

But Jared is not diverted.

"I'm serious. I don't know where I'm going. All I know is I'm sick of waiting tables and living like I'm still in college."

Stuart returns the wingtips to the array, patting them with amusement.

"Don't sell yourself short, son. Knowing what you don't want is sometimes more important than knowing what you do want."

Jared catches himself in the three-way dressing mirror and stares into a face that is changing more and more with each passing day.

"I feel like I'm supposed to do something now. Something, I don't know…grand."

Stuart comes up alongside him and smiles at him through the mirror.

"Jared, as long as I've known you, you've always wanted more. Now it seems like you have a decision to make."

"And what's that?"

"You have to decide that if you want more, what that more actually is."

"Or?"

Stuart puts a hand on his shoulder.

"Or if what you have is already enough."

***

He sits on a towel, arms over his knees, staring out at the waves. He went in the water today, but only up to his waist. He kept looking back, fearful someone would walk away with his backpack and his wallet, his phone and his keys. He has not left that jittery, pensive state of vigilance, the concept that he needs to be alert, to be *on*. He is sleeping better, he is easier with his smile, and has begun waving to people on the beach during his walks. But an underlying distrust remains, in himself most of all.

His is not a religious personality, but ritual is hugely important for him. There is sanctity akin to baptism attached to throwing himself fully into the ocean. He wishes for absolution, to be cleansed of his burden and the ache in his heart, to swim and lose himself in the waves and emerge, reborn to his life. But he won't allow it. He denies himself the ritual because he feels he is not deserving of absolution. He feels like he has cheated somehow, like he has cut a corner and pulled down a lucky break instead of a genuine lesson. He does not believe he has earned his life.

He seeks a reason to jump in, a deed or an action other than surviving a suicide attempt to justify such a sweet reward. He cannot know that he has manifested this ocean before him. He chose to come here and sit at the foot of the surf. This ocean is here for him to experience and the only barriers to its enjoyment are his own self-imposed limitations. He cannot know that this is true for all experiences in life. There are no barriers. There is no separation. There is only the stretching, infinite now and how we choose to embody it.

Jared seeks what all of us seek and in more ways than we can know, his struggle is also our own. He seeks acceptance, approval, to be told that he is worthy – that he is good enough. And above all things, loved. But, as is the case with most of humanity, he seeks these things outside himself. He fixes his gaze outward, in a constant, disparaging search for the thing, the person, or the experience that will make him emerge into the light. What he does not know is that there is no division. The barriers are illusory and transient. Love is already here, shining on him, shining through him, and illuminating every tentative step he takes. He is already free. What happens here in the coming hours and days will affect all of us. For if he succeeds in opening himself, other barriers will follow, and the effects will ripple across time.

Our race is a young race and still has much to learn. We are here to experience the fusion of spirit into flesh, a cooperative venture that will prepare us for the higher realms of existence. We are not a spirit encased in flesh, nor a spirit outside or removed from flesh, we are an amalgam of the physical and the ethereal, a fusion, with equal footing in both worlds. Our work here is to experience the manifestation of our beliefs and emotions into matter. We are consciousness, always changing, never stagnant, thrust forever forward into a state of becoming. Our creativity and our desires form the world as we know it, far more literally than we realize.

Though we may feel abandoned here in a world that we do not understand, for a purpose we do not yet comprehend, we are never alone. We are protected, couched in loving kindness, and always free. He is all of us. And all of us are him. Just as I watch him sit on a beach, on the trembling verge of walking out of his prison, so I watch all of us with the same hopes and dreams. I am always here.

I am love. And I cannot be contained.

***

Shopping with his father and Olivia at the Fresh Market by their house, Jared spies the surfer by the deli. He weaves his way around the carts and the grazing patrons, but when he reaches the deli counter she is gone. He checks the nearest aisles, but she is nowhere to be found. Starting to believe he may have imagined the whole thing, he drifts over to the snack aisle. After sampling a bunch of them, he busies himself with scooping cherry yogurt-covered pretzels out of a jar and into a plastic baggie. When he looks up, she is standing next to him. He is effusive.

"I love these. I can't find them anywhere else."

She leans across him to take the scoop and opens the jar of yogurt pretzels.

"Do you remember me? From out on the beach?"

She puts a scoop into her bag and grins at him.

"The stiff guy, I remember."

He deflates.

"I'm working on it."

The grin widens.

"You're almost there. You just need to, you know-"

She puts her arms out to her sides and leans back and forth.

"-work on your form."

He shakes his head.

"Wow. Two digs in under a minute. We'll always have the pretzels at least."

She puts another scoop in her bag and says nothing.

"I'm-"

His father comes barreling gracelessly down the aisle, calling to him.

"-Jared, we're going. Come on. Liv's already checking out."

He looks at her.

"Jared, I got it."

Stuart stops in front of them and nods his head over to the surfer.

"And who's this?"

Jared opens his mouth.

"I'm Mira."

She extends a hand and Stuart takes it, ostentatiously winking at his son.

"Stuart. It's a pleasure."

The moment stretches.

"Well Jared, aren't you going to ask Mira to dinner?"

He looks agape at his father and then to Mira, who smiles and looks down at her feet. At once without words, Jared struggles, but she saves him.

"I have to work tonight. But thank you for the invitation."

She wags her bag of pretzels at him playfully.

"See you around, Jared."

Out in the parking lot, he is moodily chastising his father for embarrassing him. Stuart is undaunted.

"What? I threw you a perfect pitch. It's not my fault you couldn't close the deal."

"Dad, Jesus."

Olivia is stuffing groceries into the trunk of the Saab when she hears them approach.

"What are you two fighting about?"

"Jared's new lady friend."

"Dad, seriously, cut the shit."

She is delighted.

"You should bring her to the wedding."

"Can we drop it?"

But the two of them are just gearing up. They heckle him all the way home and through dinner until he feels like he is fourteen again, pimply and uncertain. It is only late that night, when they've finally gone to bed and the house falls quiet, that he allows her to freely enter his thoughts. Munching on pretzels at the kitchen table, he replays the encounter in his mind and wonders when he will see her again.

***

As one of the bachelor party activities, he decides to take his father parasailing. Stuart made it clear he did not want an evening of exotic dancers and drinks that were set on fire. Grudgingly respectful of his wishes, Jared set up a day with an appointment for haircuts and hot shaves at a barber, a visit to a cigar bar, a quick nine holes at the club, and an evening on the waterfront.

Six tourists stand on the launch pad of the boat, watching Stuart with blissful expectation. He is the last parasailer of the day. He scowls at his son as one of the parachute guides helps him step into an X-harness and secures the buckle around his chest.

"You could have had strippers doing the ping-pong ball trick, but no, you wanted something low key."

"You call this low key?"

Jared shrugs.

"I thought it was actually very relaxing. Just remember: don't try and float, just float."

The scowl deepens. Stuart looks anything but relaxed.

"Jared?"

"Yeah, Dad?"

"What's the ping-pong ball trick?"

In the aftermath, Jared will recall that the harnesses looked threadbare and worn and that the winch to feed the parasailers out over the water seemed outdated and clunky. He will remember that even the boat seemed shoddy and the guides lax. The whole operation hearkened back to the thrown-together carelessness of carnival rides at the county fair. All of this will be recollected with eerie detail, replayed in slow motion on an endless loop in his mind. But in the moment when Stuart's tether snaps over the water, Jared can only think that his father is going to die.

The winch catches, once, twice, and then makes a sickening groan. Almost 300 feet in the air, Stuart is oblivious of impending danger and waves ecstatically to the people below. Jared hears the winch straining and looks back in time to see the catch snap off and the flywheel spinning freely. He runs and dives to catch the rope, but Stuart is already out at nearly the end of the line and there is nothing to catch by the time he reaches the winch.

The guides panic and he screams at them to turn the boat around. Unanchored by the winch, the wind catches the chute and whips it to the side, dragging Stuart like a ragdoll. Now aware that something is wrong, he pulls at the harness, trying to guide his descent. The chute starts to fall towards the water on a sideward trajectory, fast enough to make Jared's breath catch in his throat. It catches an updraft fifty feet from the surface, buoys out, flips over, and Stuart is thrown screaming into the heart of the parachute. Tangled up in the heavy canvas, he drops like a stone and slams into the water.

The boat races up alongside him and the deckhands prepare long poles with loops on the end, but Jared has already grabbed a fishing knife out of the wheel-room and kicked off his shoes. Before anyone can stop him, he is diving off the boat and into the sea.

"Dad!"

He swims out to the tangled chute and spots a flailing lump under the canvas, struggling to free himself. Jared grabs at the chute and cuts it apart, peeling back layers until he finds his father, gasping for breath with a cord wrapped tight enough around his neck to turn his face a hectic purple. In one deft movement, he slides the knife under the nearest cord and slices up with all his strength. It splits and Jared scrabbles at it, pulling the loops free from the man's throat. Stuart breathes in great whooping gasps and clings to him.

"I got you. We're okay. I got you."

Stuart sits on the back of an ambulance, wrapped in a blue wool emergency blanket while some EMTs check the raised red welts along his neck. Two officers from the Palm Beach County Sheriff's Office take their statements. One of them points to Jared.

"That was quick thinking. You probably saved his life."

He looks at his father, shrugging off the blanket and angrily waving away the flock of emergency personnel.

"I owed him one."

In the car on the drive home, Stuart puts a hand on his leg and pats him.

"Jared?"

"Yeah, Dad."

"No more water sports for this family."

What he really means to say is *thank you*, but Jared knows. As they drive and the moon rises over the ocean, a ripple reaches back across the miles of time, and a shell-shocked little boy stops crying.

***

Four days before the wedding, after the drama with Stuart has wound down and the incident has mellowed into teasing and jokes, he sits on a towel in the late afternoon and watches the sea. He has dropped about ten pounds since he has been here, his face has leaned out, and he is moving easier and more freely in his frame. He is no longer consumed with the echoing thunder of a shotgun or the esoteric meaning behind it all. He has shaken off the electric aggression of the city and become quietly centered in the hot, humid laziness of the days.

He stands, looking up and down the shore, and smiles to himself. He peels off his shirt and casts it aside. He wheels his arms in great, spinning circles and shakes his head. He jumps in place, brimming with boyish exuberance. He lets out a great war cry from deep in his belly and charges the surf. Sprinting over the whitecaps, he reaches out his arms and dives into the waves.

The water envelops him, wrapping around him in a warm embrace. He cuts through it and all that he has been holding, the last of his burden, seeps out from his pores like steam. He surfaces, laughing, and turns his face to the sun.

Thank you. For this. Thank you.

Heedless of the other beachgoers, he cries out again in unrestrained ecstasy, slapping the top of the water with his hands. He dives to the side, and then the other side, wriggling through the sea like an otter, splashing and kicking with relish. He swims out to where the waves are cresting, waits for a big one to form, and dives into its swell. The wave catches him, lifts him up, and carries him in an exhilarating rush to the beach. As he did when he was a child, Jared feels like he is flying. He crashes down, pummeled by the wave, sand and gravel slammed into his shorts and the folds of his ears. He emerges with a mighty grin on his face and wades back out for more.

After so many long years, he has finally forgotten. He is not obsessed with who he is or where he is going. He is unconcerned with how he is perceived or how he should act. He does not feel like he has to perform or manage the threads of his life. He simply exists. In this shining moment, he exists for the sake of simple pleasure. He has forgotten himself and allowed himself to only be. He has opened to a greater joy that is only fully realized and expressed by the act of being. He is ready now, and somewhere, deep down, he knows it. Swelling with joy, barriers as fluid and permeable as the water that surrounds him, Jared November dies to his old life and becomes wholly and irrevocably new.

He plays in the ocean for hours, and Mira watches him from the shore with a knowing smile on her face.

Chapter Thirteen

E Pluribus Unum

I head down to the beach around 2pm. Those hours between three and six are perfect for the water. The overbearing heat of the day has died down and the tide always seems to be coming in. The beach has cleared out; most of the tourists have been there all morning. They're burned out and sun-soaked, retreating to hotel showers and air conditioning. High cumulus clouds, puffy and enormous, move across the sky and the light has changed, throwing a golden hue over the afternoon.

I find Mira sitting on a towel, munching on a sandwich. She waves to me and I walk over.

"What's this lying around stuff? Shouldn't you be out there shredding waves?"

"Girl's gotta eat," she says through a mouthful of chicken salad.

She is so serene, so at ease with herself, sturdy in her frame, steadfast in her gaze. I want to be around her, just an observer in her space, but her surety is strangely intimidating to me. She is beautiful, certainly, but I can handle the physical attraction – that somehow makes sense. It is her Zen knowing, an unshakeable serenity that is somehow more adult, more sage than I know how to deal with. I see my own shakiness and nervous energy in stark contrast. She bounces back my own remaining uncertainty over who I am. She makes me feel unfinished. Words, conversation, always effortless for me, die at my lips.

"Okay, I'll let you eat then. Take it easy."

I resume walking up the beach, but she stops me.

"You know you don't have to run off all the time."

I wander back up to her and set my bag down next to her things. I spread out a towel and plop down on the sand. I don't want to watch her eat, but I don't know what to say, so I look out over the water. It always amazes me how the simple shift between knowing someone, being familiar with them, and not knowing them makes all the difference in the world. How many people do I see that I just don't know yet? At one point, all my closest friends were people I didn't know. How and when do people choose to cross the gulf? That first barrier between strangers is always the hardest. Thankfully, she rescues me from the silence.

"You're moving better."

I turn and look at her.

"Thank you. I've been swimming."

She nods.

"I know. I've been watching you."

I laugh and some of that nervousness drops away.

"Been watching me, have you?"

She grins and takes an exaggerated bite of her sandwich. The silence that passes between us is much more comfortable. I don't know where it comes from, but it comes, and so I ask her.

"How do I seem to you?"

She looks me up and down.

"You want to ask someone you barely know that question?"

"Who better?"

She shakes her head.

"I don't know if I want to play this game with you. Are you messing with me?"

I look at her, incredulous.

"No. I'm serious."

"I don't play games, Jared. That's the first thing you should know about me. And I don't like it when people play games with me."

She stares at me. Behind the unruffled blue of her eyes, I see deep steel, and I understand that whatever serenity Mira has earned for herself, it has been hard won.

"I'm not playing games with you."

"Then tell me what's really on your mind."

I sigh and dig my feet into the sand.

"I can't believe I'm telling you this."

She is impassive, but wholly open, inviting me to do the same.

"I brought some acid down here with me. It was an accident, although I'm starting to think more and more that it wasn't an accident at all. It was a gift-"

(*Go get right in your head.*)

"-from a friend. I know how it sounds, but I feel like I'm meant to take it. But I'm afraid I'm just going to flip out. I wanted to know how I seemed to you."

"Have you ever tripped before?"

I shake my head.

"Never?"

"No. I don't even know much about it, aside from reading some Huxley and Leary and what people have told me. Do you know anything?"

"I know a thing or two about psychedelics," she says with a wry smile. "Enough to know they're definitely not for everyone."

"So you're telling me I shouldn't do it."

She looks me over again.

"You're a little unsure of yourself. You're not really comfortable in your own skin. That's how you seem to me. But it looks like you've turned a corner. I actually think a trip would give you some perspective."

"Really?"

She nods.

"Yes, but I don't think you should do it alone. And you're going to have to let go and not fight the experience."

I laugh and kick at the sand.

"I knew there was a catch. How do I do that exactly?"

She fixes me another wry smile.

"Well, there is one way, but we'll have to talk about it. And go over some rules."

I stop kicking.

"Wait, what are you saying?"

"You're asking me if I'll trip with you, aren't you?"

Her gaze is unflappable.

"I…guess I am."

She stands up and brushes herself off.

"Okay then, we'll have to talk about it. And go over some rules. But first, let's go swimming, yeah?"

I stand up beside her.

"You're serious?"

She points to the surf.

"Of course I am, the water is gorgeous."

Before I can say anything else, she is running to the shoreline. I chase her into the sea and, laughing, we dive headlong into the waves.

***

She has a cozy bungalow about two miles from the ocean, tucked in among a copse of thickly rooted banyan trees. It is essentially one big room, cut into a small bedroom, an open kitchen, and a bathroom with a standup shower and doors that lead outside to the garden. The house is littered with books on Buddhism, Taoism, mythology, and anthropology. The living room is bordered by comfy, padded sofas and in place of a television she has set up an altar in the corner with incense, a meditation mat, and a serene stone statue of the Buddha.

We're sitting at a picnic table in her backyard. Two strips of paper are between us.

"We need to go over a few ground rules. But first, you need to be completely honest with me."

"Okay."

"Are you dangerous?"

(*Cha-Chunk-*)

"No," I say. "But I may be a little crazy."

She laughs.

"Crazy I can handle. Violent is another story. Trips are unpredictable and they can be genuinely scary. I need to know you can control yourself if things get weird."

"I'm not violent."

She scans my face, blue eyes searching for truth. Satisfied, she settles back and holds up three fingers.

"There are three rules for tripping."

"Hit me."

(*Tempting...*)

"You can't fly."

I grin at her.

"You won't die."

(*It's just a fluke, Jared.*)

"And the third?"

"Don't be a dick in public."

"Roger."

She picks at the edge of her strip with her fingernail.

"These are applicable lessons in many areas of life. So don't forget them. Although I think we'll keep you away from the public for your first time."

"Anything else?"

She leans forward over the table, bores into me with her eyes, and the steel behind them glints.

"Why do you really want to do this, Jared? And don't tell me 'just 'cause' or our little deal here is off."

I look off into the garden, at the winding roots of the banyan trees, and to the purple dusk gathering around us.

"Something happened to me, Mira. I can't explain it and I don't really understand it. I don't even really remember it, but I've been having these flashes, like another life is being superimposed over this one. It's like I'm two me-s. I know it seems nuts, but I was-"

(*floating*)

"-somewhere else. I need to try and get back there and I know this stuff bends reality. I need to see behind the curtain."

The answer seems to ease her, but we are not finished.

"When did this happen?"

I don't want to say, but her eyes tell me that nothing short of perfect transparency will do here.

"The night I tried to kill myself."

I expect revulsion, derision, even fear. I expect her to get up, pack up the drugs, and throw me out of her house. But instead she extends her arms across the table to me. I think she's going to grasp my hands, but she rotates them over to expose the underside of her forearms. There are thick ropes of scar tissue puckered in vertical lines down the length of her wrists and lower arms. She says nothing, but all at once, we are no longer strangers.

***

"Have you ever taken Molly before?"

I shake my head.

"Outside of your comfort zone a bit," she laughs. "This is going to be interesting."

"I don't even know what it is," I confess.

"MDMA," she says. "A pleasure drug. People usually take it at raves because it makes just about everything feel good."

She smiles mysteriously.

"But it has expansive properties too – it breaks down emotional barriers."

"So how do we do this?"

She pushes my strip forward.

"It's called a candyflip. We're going to take the acid first. In a couple of hours, when we feel like we're peaking, we're going to take the Molly."

"How do you know all this?"

"I know a lot of things," she says. "Now, are you listening?"

I nod.

"They're synergistic chemicals. Combined, they accelerate the whole experience and make everything feel okay. I think, with a little luck, that you should be able to get back to where you were before."

I take the strip and hold it between my fingers. I look at her.

"My only advice to you is this," she says. "Embrace the feminine."

"What does that mean?"

"It means just trust it, Jared. Trust *her*."

"I don't get you."

She pops her strip in her mouth and winks at me.

"You will."

I look down at my strip a final time and think of-

(*It's just a fluke, Jared. Get that through your head.*)

-where I want to go. I put the acid in my mouth and swallow.

***

It's like the contrast dial of my vision has been jacked up. Everything around me, from my skin to the flowers in the garden and the mottled gray bark of the trees is saturated with color. Things are somehow *more* real, more concrete, shimmering with detail and extraordinarily vivid. The clouds above us are monstrous and alive, blooming out of themselves into ever-evolving shapes. The grass is a living, seething carpet of electric green. It is like I can see more deeply into whatever I look at. Even the simplest of objects burst with intricate detail and sparkling beauty. I am blown away.

Mira is lying on her stomach in the grass, watching something intently.

"Come here and check this out."

I get up off the picnic table and I feel gravity. It is not an abstract thing. I feel the weight of my body and its exact position in space. I know where I can pivot and bend and how each movement will align with gravity. My steps are heavier, but my body is more in my control than it has ever been. I join her on the grass and marvel at how the scratchy blades feel underneath me. She points about a foot away to a lizard on a rock in the garden.

"He's out late. They're usually all sleeping by now."

The creature is a wonder. Leathery skin a piebald mix of green and brown, a sloped, saurian head with keen slitted eyes, and a curly-cue tail poking out behind him. He pivots his head in strange jerks and twists, eyes blinking in the fading light. He pants and the sides of his flank move in and out like a tiny bellows. I cannot believe this thing is alive. It is animated, moving under its own power, possessed of a distinct and personalized life force. Its design is perfect.

She rolls over onto her arm and looks me over.

"You don't like being dirty, do you?"

I grin at her.

"What do you mean?"

"I mean dirt, grit, mud – not you."

I feel oddly self-conscious.

"I like to be neat, yes."

She laughs hard and points down at my shoes.

"Take them off. Socks too. Right now."

I balk at her.

"This is why hippies are hippies, man. Take 'em off. Do it."

I take my shoes off. She grabs them and throws them off into the garden and they are lost among the flowers.

"Now," she says. "Feel the grass under your toes, squeeze it."

I do as she instructs and the splendor of naked feet in lush grass is overwhelming. I squeeze the earth and let it slide between my toes and it is a revelation. I look at her with wide, boyish eyes.

"Shoes are stupid," I say.

She smiles and points to my chest.

"How attached are you to that shirt?"

I look down at it.

"Not very, why?"

She points to the banyan trees.

"Keep it on or take it off, but we're going to go climb trees. Come on."

We play in the garden with abandon and, for a night, I am a child again.

***

As soon as I swallow the water, there is a change. I sweep clumped crystals of MDMA out of the bottom of the glass and suck my fingers. Something shifts. The trip has changed direction and a new channel has been added to it. I am able to pick up more signals, like radio waves, but bigger, more like rays. I stand over the open fridge door and look out her window. The night is teeming with unseen activity. I feel it stirring, the trees, the creatures, the air itself. I hear a chorus of things moving on the earth. I am through the window and scampering among them, slipping through each blade of grass.

I reach into the fridge and pour more water into the glass. It sparkles and I lose myself in the luminescence for a while. I shake the glass and slosh water around. I down it and shut the door. The room is homey, lit with strings of red Mexican pepper lights. There is a glass vase with orange flowers on the table and I can see the striations in the petals and the honey brown lushness doming out of the center.

I decide to sit down on the floor. The clock ticks and a small single engine airplane passes by overhead. I am reminded of sitting at the kitchen table as a boy, building models over sheets of newspaper on summer nights. The windows were always open and I'd be so focused on building, I would tune everything else out and the background noises would rise to the surface. I would hear the farm planes flying over the backyard and-

The clock ticks. The plane drones.

There is a doubling, larger than any prior, and then a dam breaks open in my mind. The feeling of déjà vu collides with the vastness of the moment and I snap into the present as one. I realize that this instant of hearing the airplane over Mira's kitchen lies on top of, not ahead of those moments I heard planes as a boy. The *now*, the swollen space in which those flyovers took place, is the same. The huge, sprawling template that everything – all of reality –is built out of is always *here*. It is always *now*. I feel like I did when my parents took me to the play – I see the kitchen as a set, the decorations as props, and the whole bungalow as a theater. And what does that make me? Am I just an actor?

There is no more doubling, but my sanity overloads with new information. The concept of linear time dissolves, or rather, I step out of it. I feel insane. In an instant, everything I have done in my life is rendered insignificant. But where there would be longing, even sadness, there are instead mighty questions: *What is this? What's happening to me? Where am I?* If I am not this personality, this identity, then: *what am I?* It is no longer a question of *who*, the ego has collapsed in dumbstruck awe.

I have been here before, building models as a boy, here in this great, spanning now. The silence of it has always been around me, I just couldn't hear it. Those moments of focus, fragments of pure concentration, put me right up alongside the now, put my perception right up against the barrier. What would have happened if I'd gleaned it then? Would I have gone insane? Would I have thought myself possessed? Undone? Stupefied? Shrieking for comfortable barriers? Am I insane now?

There are trails along the strings of pepper lights. The flowers and the corners and edges of things shake like flags in a storm, so rapidly that it feels like the room itself is going to peel off and whip away in the grip of a hellish cyclone. My mind, punchdrunk, crashes into itself, trying to absorb how it can always be now and there can still be a past and a future. In the trembling box of the kitchen, I am here in the present moment. But in a little while, that moment will be behind me and it will still be now. And eventually the now that exists in the future will rush up to meet me and I will step into it is as cleanly as tearing a paper towel from the rack.

The backdrop is constant. We don't slide across the now in a line, we move through it, stacking our years on top of each other. The past and the future are each accessible because they are happening simultaneously. All of creation is happening at once. Time is meaningless. It exists as a cushion for the mind, a sorting mechanism, but it is not reality. Whether I live or I die, I will always be *here*. Here is always.

Yes, I have been here before. I haven't snapped into something new, I have remembered something very old. The difference is acutely known. How many times have I done this before? How many countless lives? How many times have I seen the trick and jolted awake? I have woken up. I have woken into. I want to come down from this feeling of being so immense, but I can't. My mother was right. It is one long day. Forever.

How many times have I forgotten this? Has it been eons of this? Waking to the present, catching up with time, only to die and forget and fall back into the illusion of linear life?

I feel paranoia take hold in my gut. How can no one know? How can the truth hide in plain sight like that? Is this a prison? How do I get out of this? My mind reels.

She pads into the room, the soft lime acrylic on her toenails shimmers. She has small, sturdy feet, strong like a gymnast. She looks alien without a board under her. But then the world is her board, she is so solid, so perfectly rooted. She sits down across from me, tucking her feet under her legs.

"How you doing, space cadet? Anybody still home in there?"

"I feel like I'm in the Matrix."

She wipes my brow with her hand, the feel of her fingertips lingering.

"You're sweating."

"It's like I've woken up inside the Matrix. I can see it's all fake, constructed somehow, but I'm not sloshing around in my little cocoon yet."

She puts a hand to my brow and holds it there.

"I can't get out, can I?"

"There is no out, Jared," she says. "There just is. Congratulations, you've just experienced non-duality."

I want to scream, but there's no reason for it. I will eventually stop and it will still be now and nothing will have changed. But-

"Everything's changed."

She stands and draws me to my feet.

"Come in the other room with me. It's time to go inward now."

I let her lead me back across the bungalow to her room. Through the beaded curtain, her space is warm and inviting.

She's thrown blankets out across the floor, with pillows scattered across the spread. She's drawn the curtains to the outside and turned off all the lamps but one, the shade covered with a gauzy red headscarf. Tealights flicker from inside tiny globes, flames dancing and licking the air around their black wicks. She's drawn down the canopy over her bed and the flaps hang slightly open, revealing an alluring featherpuff inside. The room is cast into a dim, flickering, pinkish glow that relaxes away the massiveness.

"We can do anything you want," she says. "We can draw or color. We can lounge out on the floor and talk. Or we can lie down. Whatever you feel like you most want to do right now."

She sits at her desk and fiddles with her computer.

"How are you feeling?"

I am fingering the gauzy cloth of the scarf over the shade, marveling at the texture and the intricacy of the weave.

"Better."

She smiles contentedly.

"Good. I've got a Pandora station here just for you. It's jazzy, electronic. Definitely chill. I think you'll like it."

Hooverphonic comes on, and from the speakers on the corner of her desk, notes march out and dance into the room. The music is just as alive as we are. Palpable. Vibrant. Breathing with a life of its own. I feel my insides wanting to leap out of my skin to join the procession of dancing notes.

"I think I wanna lie down. I'm feeling kind of drifty."

She hands me a packed bowl and a Bic lighter.

"That Molly should be kicking in pretty soon. Smoke some of that for the transition."

We share the bowl in companionable silence. It takes some of the jaggedness and buzziness away and makes me feel smoother, more mellow around the edges. I push through the slit in the canopy and roll onto the featherpuff with a sigh of delight. I sprawl out on my back and stare up at the wooden ring suspended from the ceiling. The billowing curtains rise up in a cone to the ring, giving the bed the look of a teepee or a sheet fort from some half-remembered childhood. Candlelight flickers outside and Mira's furniture appears as hazy blobs and half-seen shapes through the fabric. The bed is like a spaceship in a sea of stars.

She crawls inside with me and puts a hand on my forehead.

"What happens now is different for everyone," she says. "But I'm right here. I'm going to lie down with you and we can drift. Okay?"

"Okay," I say, lazily, eyelids heavy, breathing already slowing.

She cuddles up next to me and slips her hands into mine, fingers interlocking. I close my eyes. And flip.

***

It starts out slinky. Stiletto sexual. An invitation. It's not like being turned on, where you want to zero in on someone and possess them. It's bigger than that. The scope is wider. There is no force here, no pressing urgency. All is permitted. All appetites delivered. You don't need to seek it out, or pursue it; it's already here for your perusal. In fact, it has always been here. There is pride here, a clear and resounding showmanship. A table is being pulled up for you. You *will* be entertained.

There is no ego here, as there are no restrictions. This place is fueled by desire. Not your baser preferences, but Desire itself. Relax, this is all for you. Smiling at me, vulvas open and close, pulsating past me in a dance. Legs, perhaps thousands, swirl in kaleidoscopic patterns. Breasts bubble into the scene, nipples cutting through the air like hard candy gumdrops. It is a march of erotica.

They are, it is, leading me through the corridors of my deepest sexuality, rejoicing in my lusty excitement, conveying to me through my richest cravings that Desire is the very foundation for life. It is a parade of skin, an orgy of fleshy delights, drawing me onward. I get the sense that I have full permission to stay here as long as I want, to indulge in heaving sex, and explore the slipperiest crevices of what gets me off. But as tantalizing as that offer is, I know it's not what I came here for, and so the parade leads me onward.

Finally, I come to a great red curtain with women writhing through all the folds, the whole surface crawling with nameless contorted bodies. The curtain fans open, seemingly with regret, and I move deeper into a new, far vaster place.

***

It's a factory. Amazing. Enormous. It buzzes with activity, each area moving with joyous synchronization, like people in a grand stage musical. In every corner, there is exuberant dancing and each cog and wheel in this titanic machine beams with pride. Even the smallest piece is ecstatic to BE that piece, and they shiver with joy at their own perfect, individual place in this undulating foundry. Multicolored blobs like starfish and sea anemones shuffle supplies across the expanse, sliding along on iridescent gossamer lines and spirals, all moving together in harmony. They dance, they all dance, and I wonder if they are the spirits of the notes in the music, the sprites that inhabit the places between chords and melodies – the secret life inside the radio.

I am suspended, and even though my physical body is far above me, my ethereal body is being moved. It is a strange schism, to be aware of two bodies at once, to be in two places at once. One of me is dim, distant, and heavy, oceans away, lying in Mira's bed, her hand slipped into mine, warm and wonderful. The other me is behind him, behind his eyes, below him, deep in another realm of reality that is separated from all I know only by the meaty shields of my eyelids and yet farther away than I could have ever imagined.

A massive feminine presence descends and envelops me, cocooning me in a silk of kindness that I have never known. I am stretched out and still, like a car up on a hydraulic lift, and yet drifting, floating along the slipstream and through the various parts of this incredible factory. As I drift, the blobs surround me, tickling me, nuzzling into me with affection. Seemingly from everywhere, her voice booms out, and yet it is so soft and so adoring. It is not a booming in volume, but a strength of vibration that penetrates all the way through me and touches a place so old and so total, that I can only obey.

REST.

A sigh passes through me. Not a physical exhalation, but a sigh from the spaces between my atoms, a release from within the very orbits of my electrons. It is not a physical release, nor even a release of my psyche –it is a letting go within my soul. I yield and heaviness begins to collapse out of me in dark clumps like paper-mache in rain.

REST NOW.

The blobs collect the pieces and ferret them off to the unseen corners of the factory. Hundreds of them, millions, in trains like a great assembly line carry my pain away. Each piece is a memory, a moment in time. Each clump of dark, damp, sticky tar is a place where I have forgotten this Grace that surrounds me. In this surging, cosmic gyre, drifting through the mechanism that spins the universe, I surrender.

YOU HAVE BEEN SO TIRED.

My soul hitches, fills, and cries out, wailing out a dirge of suffering and accumulated hurt that I have carried for so long. Eddies ripple through me, and then waves, and then the whole of me is shaking and crying and I am deafened by it. There is no shame here. No derision. There is nothing here to tell me to stop, to keep it together, to just stifle it. There is only this cocoon of gentle kindness and the sweet, blinding totality of complete release. Busy blobs lovingly catch every tear, cradling them as if they were giant pearls, and carry them away. Far above me, tears slip out from behind closed eyes and roll down my cheeks in rivulets.

LET GO.

I sense areas of my ethereal body, concentrations of darkness, where I have been physically holding on to pain in black knots. The blobs center on these spots and with spines and tendrils, they work to untangle the knots like an army of diligent surgeons. Above me, lying on the bed, my muscles ripple with activity and my body contorts. Sinew resets itself, joints crack, vertebrae separate and my entire spine elongates. With a glorious snap, my hips open and my sacrum breathes for the first time in fifteen years. My neck unravels and opens. My shoulders free themselves from fused sockets. My ribcage spreads apart in a series of short pops.

THIS IS THE REVIEW OF YOUR LIFE.

I realize as each knot is diligently picked apart that we are examining a memory or an emotional snapshot of my travels. This dark template is the collected events and imprints of a lifetime of experience on Earth. It is a map, a library of each moment of my life, faithfully transcribed and archived, indelibly stamped into the catalog of my being. We are moving through the course of my life, not through time, not in a linear fashion, but through impact. The events that moved me, for better or worse, are the hubs from which all other activity has spread. My existence is not realized here in time, but in size.

SHE IS HERE.

There is a surge in the great knot at the base of my ethereal back and a crushing wave of loss pours through all of me like an explosion. A flurry of snapshots pass in front of me, each a frozen moment in time, but somehow alive, vibrant and moving – they are living pictures. She is helping me into my winter coat so we can build snowmen. She is cleaning the house with her kerchief around her head and oldies music blasting out of the stereo. She is sipping cocoa, nestled into my father's shoulder, watching me tear open Christmas presents with abandon.

I miss you.

She is taking off her wig to show me the hectic scar along the side of her head. She is groggy from surgery and doesn't remember who I am. She is throwing a speech therapy book across the room in a frustrated rage while her therapist patiently waits and coaxes her back. She is holding the side of her head and collapsing onto the kitchen floor. She is in the coat room, bags packed for the hospital, holding me to her, telling me through tears to mind my father – that she won't be here forever. She is dying alone in a hospital bed. I am a twelve year old boy in a somber black suit. It is a perfect day in June. She is slowly, reverently lowered into the ground.

I miss you so much.

I heave and sob and let it happen. I let myself see it, relive it, experience it without reservation, and I grieve in a way I have never allowed for myself since those first dim days when it all began. I let go of it and I open, stretching out in all directions. A lifetime of repression and stifled anguish shakes through me and the last knot lets go. Floating in the dark wonder of it all, I finally put my mother to rest. I find peace. Above me, increasingly distant and dimming, my lower spine unwinds and a tingling, returning feeling like warm water cascades across my whole back and I release a heady sigh of towering ecstasy.

YOU ARE NOT ALONE.

I look around and see, floating along with me, countless ethereal beings in mismatched rows and columns. Each of the myriad is being cared for by colorful attendants, diligently carrying away sticky chunks of tarry darkness. My vision, my understanding expands, and I can see an unknowable number of those living pictures flash across the ether. Lifetimes, billions upon billions of lifetimes sparkle across my eyes like a night sky thick with stars. When I cry, millions of others cry with me. When I laugh, the multitude laughs with me. When we sing, we all sing together. When we strive, when we seek, when we *are*, we are together.

YOU ARE ALL.

It is a march, a glorious march. A procession of interconnectedness. We are all marching forward. Forever forward. We are all in the slipstream. The factory, the voice, all of it, all of *us*, every single atom, are being pulled along by a universal current, a titanic, pulsing rhythm that is forever tugging us upward. It is not a river, nor a sea. It is a much bigger tide. It is the only tide, big enough to hold all of creation. It is all-that-is.

THIS IS LIFE.

As each part is removed and carried away by my unknowable attendants, I am lighter, more buoyant, and more attuned to the greater current that is carrying all of us along. I am moving faster, spiraling farther outward. The blobs fall away and the mighty factory floor recedes. Another great curtain sweeps open and I pass through.

***

I am in a blank place, a halfway point, suspended between worlds. My ethereal body has vanished and I exist now only as pure consciousness, filling all space, expanded without limits. Millions of miles away, far above on the bed, my heartbeat slows and my breathing becomes shallow. I feel that I am hanging here, perched between two distinct states, on the very crest of becoming something else entirely. Somewhere out there, I am resting in the luxuriant comfort of Mira's featherpuff. But beyond me is a foggy, undulating whiteness that appears impenetrable. I know, with the deepest instinct, that I am on the precipice. This layer of reality is the last.

YOU ARE IN BETWEEN.

I've been here before.

MANY MANY TIMES.

What happens now?

THIS IS WHERE YOU MAKE THE CHOICE.

Live or die.

NO. THERE IS NO ALIVE OR DEAD. THERE IS ONLY STAY OR GO.

But I can't make the choice until I'm dead.

YOU ARE FREE TO LEAVE AT ANY POINT.

What happens if I choose to go into the white?

YOU CANNOT KNOW. THAT IS THE MYSTERY. TO GO PAST THE BARRIER, YOU CANNOT KNOW WHAT LIES ON THE OTHER SIDE.

And what happens to me?

WHEN YOU ARE READY, YOU WILL LET GO. YOU WILL FORGET. TO GO IS TO LEAVE AND RETURN, NAKED, FREE OF ATTACHMENT, INTO ALL THAT IS.

I'll forget it all, won't I?

WHAT YOU HAVE EXPERIENCED WILL BE LEFT BEHIND LIKE A DREAM.

What kind of a choice is that?

IT IS THE NATURE OF TIME IN FLESH. YOUR LIFETIMES EXIST MERELY TO LAY DOWN A SERIES OF EXPERIENCES THAT PREPARE YOU TO LEAVE THEM. YOU WILL CONTINUE TO INCORPORATE UNTIL YOU CHOOSE TO GO.

That's not fair.

The voice laughs, rich and bellowing.

IS IT NOT? KNOWING THAT YOU ARE LOVED, THAT JOY IS YOUR BIRTHRIGHT? TO FIND THAT AGAIN AT THE END OF YOUR TRAVELS? THE SUBLIME REMEMBERING OF GRACE? IS THAT NOT WORTH ALL THAT YOU SUFFER IN SEEMING SEPARATION?

Then I choose to stay?

YES. WHY?

I think of the body, the life, lying above me on a bed.

He's tried so hard.

WHY DO YOU STAY?

He has so much potential, so much to give.

The voice booms, unparalleled, thundering across space.

WHY DO YOU STAY?

Because I love him!

And in a smaller voice:

I love all of them.

YOU PICKED HIM. OUT OF MORE NUMBERS THAN YOU CAN FATHOM, YOU CHOSE HIM.

I love him.

OUT OF MANY, ONE. OUT OF MANY, A UNIQUE, LOVED INDIVIDUAL THROUGH WHICH YOU CHOOSE TO EXPERIENCE THE UNIVERSE.

OUT OF MANY INDIVIDUALS, ONE CONSCIOUSNESS. THIS IS WHAT IT MEANS TO BE.

What am I?

YOU ARE A YOUNG SOUL. THAT IS WHY YOU STAY.

***

I'm tired.

ARE YOU READY TO GO?

I feel him, on the verge of seeing YOU in himself. I have to stay with him until he does.

WHAT WILL IT TAKE?

A grid appears before me, rising miles high and stretched out across the expanse. Within the panes, potential unfolds, the possible skeins of all of his futures. The directions he can take, the choices he can make, the many-layered paths of his timeline are all available. I see him in other countries. I see him teaching in a classroom. I see him giving a great speech at a podium. I see him reaching out to shake a dignitary's hand. I see him running around with a house full of children. I see the deadly vomit of a shotgun.

WHAT WILL IT TAKE FOR YOU TO LET HIM GO?

The panels in the grid change and I see a boy wanting to reach out to a falling man, but unable and unwilling. I see a boy standing against a wall during a junior high school formal, wanting to dance, but fearful of looking foolish. I see a young man, taking insults from someone who intimidates him and hating himself furiously for censoring his feelings. I see a man caught in a web of lies and shame, self-loathing bright on his face. I see a man staring at the shore, looking pensively out over the waves. I see a litany of constraint. I see a cascade of self-correction and denial.

I want him to feel free.

I see him, sullen and alone as a child, reading a book under a tree. I see him, scribbling at his writing desk as a boy, penning fervent teenage love letters to a girl who will never read them. I see him staring longingly at a young girl in a high school science lab, knowing she will reject him. I see him drunk at a bar, making passes at a woman who feels badly for him. I see him at a friend's wedding, sitting in a chair, glumly watching other people dance. I see his awkward, fumbling first attempts at sex. I see him embittered, the walls around his heart growing with every picture.

I want him to let love in.

The grid changes and now there are women. Old, young, middle-aged, at the altar, cooking dinners in kitchens, wrangling children out in a backyard. There is a woman in a ski lodge, putting logs on a fire. A woman in the passenger seat, hand over his on the gear shift. Another in a long gold dress with her hair up, her back turned to him, sipping champagne. And off in one of the other panels, surfing by herself in the brilliant orange of a fading afternoon, is Mira.

YOU HAVE KNOWN HER BEFORE.

From far outside, I feel her hand squeeze mine, and I know. Wondrous, booming laughter rings out in the blank space.

YOU ARE NOT FINISHED YET.

I feel the space around me begin to move, pounding in and out around me, like the beating of a tremendous drum.

Buoyancy fills me and from outside, Mira's music seems louder, calling me back. The space disintegrates and a bright light eclipses everything. The drum beats faster, harder, rallying me to action. Readying me for launch. I feel it ramping up, pure excitement, an infusion of purpose that makes even the molecules in the air ring with intent.

YES.

I am gathering speed, accelerating towards the grid at impossible velocity. The music gets even louder and now I can see the bedroom and the canopy and Mira coming closer. I am shooting through a tunnel of light, and far behind me, the factory is cheering for me. The laughter is all around me and the benevolence drives me forward like a rocket. Faster and faster, I thrust forward. The grid looms in front of me and I am racing up the distance, closing in on it. I am in thrilling ecstasy. Tunneling up the channel, I soar and fly and laugh and a white hole opens.

The light is blinding and the drums thunder me through the pane and up. There is a glorious merging, a fusion, and I crash through the barrier and back *into* myself. There is a flash of white and I open my eyes.

***

I see the top of the bed canopy, seeing it for what feels like the first time. I draw my eyes down the drapes, marveling at the folds in the material and the shimmers of light in the fabric. I sit up in a rush and *feel* myself – the weight of my body, the seamless workings of my musculature, the visceral perfection of my flesh. I look at my hands in amazement and squeeze them. I breathe in air and smell the candles, the gathering dawn outside the windows, and the spicy musk of her perfume.

Mira.

I turn and look at her. She is lying on her side, hand propped under her head, watching me with that calm blue gaze. With fresh eyes, I marvel at her and I am overwhelmed with affection. She smiles and nods, passing me a knowing look that I can never repay. She is simply the most beautiful woman I have ever seen and now I'm laughing, superbly tickled and moved by the wonder and the beauty of all of it.

Thank you.

She reaches out and takes my hand. The feel of her skin is marvelous. I look at her and her smile widens. I reach down into the mane of her hair with both hands and touch her forehead with my own. Our noses bump and she giggles. I press into her head and close my eyes, trying to pass my immeasurable gratitude into her. I kiss her cheek, once, twice, and again. I pull away and our lips brush. I kiss her lips, once, twice, and again. They are big and soft and slightly open. She leans her head up. With her face in my hands, I kiss her again and linger. Her tongue slips out and over mine. We breathe, embrace, and tumble into a kiss that, in so many ways, has never ended.

***

She sits beside me on the beach and we watch the sunrise over the ocean. I have never seen its equal. She leans into me and sighs, resting her head on my shoulders.

"Can I ask you something crazy?" I ask.

"I don't know if it can get any crazier than what just happened," she says, amused.

I hug her to me.

"Okay, not crazy – forward."

She pulls away so she can look at me and nods. I think of all I want, the last of what remains unfinished.

"Do you want to go to a wedding with me tomorrow?"

She answers me with a kiss. And the day flips.

Chapter Fourteen

Be Sweet

I sneak in the back door just after sunrise. Olivia has gone for her morning walk, while Stuart lounges across the couch in the living room, thumbing through his paper. He regards me over the top of the sports section.

"Someone didn't come home last night."

I fix him a pert grin.

"Am I grounded?"

He lowers his paper so he can get a good look at me.

"Not grounded, but guilty."

"It just happened. I should have called. I'm sorry."

He tosses the sports section onto the floor amongst the rest of the paper and puts his hands behind his head. He waggles his toes at me.

"Forgiven. Still guilty."

I try to suppress a smile, but my eyes betray the truth of me.

"I made a friend."

He frowns in pretend consideration.

"A lady friend? Perhaps from the food store?"

I smile and it is sunny and new on my face and he is right, I am guilty.

"Perhaps."

He sits upright, the ruse is past.

"Olivia already included Mira on the guest list."

I am powerless to do anything but smile.

"You're welcome."

I have to escape his satisfaction and the shining tease in his voice.

"Thank you, Stuart."

He beams.

"For everything."

I put my hands up, prayer-style alongside one cheek and rest into them. He nods and waves me away, reaching down among his stacks to pluck a new section free.

"Dad?"

He looks up.

"For everything."

***

Mira calls me a little after eleven.

"How you doing?"

I grip the phone and stare up at the ceiling plaster, kicking at my tangled sheets. I want to throw up my soul, but I can't. And it is far too bright in my room.

"God, I just want to sleep."

She laughs with real sympathy.

"You will," she says. "But listen. I want you to know something, while you're still sort of there."

I groan.

"Don't be a dick in public. I know, I keep telling myself that."

I feel that sage grin spread across the phone connection and some of that steel, and I stop making light.

"I'm here."

"These drugs, they're a key of sorts. But you had to open the door. You did that, Jared. You allowed yourself to do that. Don't forget."

She pauses.

"Don't forget how special you are..."

(*OUT OF MANY, ONE.*)

There is more, but I get the feeling that she either can't or won't say it, and I am too universed out to push.

"See you tomorrow then?"

"I bet you'd like to think so," she says.

And hangs up.

***

I abandon the prospect of sleep around noon and trudge out into the kitchen to find some water. I hear the Steve Miller Band banging out from Olivia's studio and I poke my head inside.

Billie Jo shot a man while robbing his castle.

She is perched on a stool, paintbrush hovering inches from the canvas. She is singing along, bobbing her head, big curls unfurled and spilling around her shoulders.

"Knock-knock."

She swivels on her stool.

"Well look what the cat dragged in," she says. "Your timing is perfect."

She turns and dabs one more line across the little boy's nose.

"Finished."

She strikes her initials into the bottom right hand corner of the painting, and sits back to look at it.

"What do you think?"

"The boy is different," I say.

She points to him with the tip of her paintbrush.

"I think he looks like you. I wasn't sure whether to make you the boy or the prankster in the painting, so I sort of did them both."

I stare at the two of them, doubled, and I feel a mix of elation and vertigo.

"It's beautiful," I say. "It's perfect."

She claps her hands together and swivels back to face me.

"Good, it's yours."

I am lost for words.

"It's a wedding present. From me to you. I can pack and ship to Boston, but I do have a lovely spot picked out for it to the left of the television."

"So…"

She laughs and her curls shake.

"It's yours, but we're keeping it."

I notice she has signed the painting: O.N. She follows my gaze and puts a hand over her mouth.

"Too soon?"

I make a circle with my thumb and forefinger.

"Just right."

She reaches out to hug me, stops, and looks into my face.

"Well now," she says, rotating me from side-to-side by my shoulders. "I may have to paint these boys again, you look different. Where did *you* come from?"

I am honest.

"That's hard to explain."

She nods.

"We girls tend to do that."

"Can I ask you something in confidence?"

She zips her lips.

"Mum's the word."

"Have you ever taken acid?"

She leans back in her stool and studies me as if I were a painting.

"You're talking to a starchild of the sixties, my young friend. How was it?"

"It was pretty heavy stuff."

She frowns.

"Not the drug, Jared, the experience."

I frown back.

"Same answer."

She cocks her head.

"Did you take anything back with you?"

I did, more than I can possibly surmise, but I give her what's left.

"Be sweet."

She raises her eyebrows, brings her hands up to cup my face and kisses me on the forehead.

"Good souvenir from the great beyond. You're a brave one. Said stuff is not for the feint-of-heart. Have you slept?"

I shake my head.

"A hot shower will fix you right up."

"I swam in the ocean," I try.

She rolls her eyes and gets up off the stool.

"Boys," she says. "Always dirty boys. Go take a proper shower. Soap, scrub, hot water, get all the pixie dust off you and start fresh. I'll make you some warm milk and you can sleep like a sane person."

I mind her dutifully and turn to leave her studio. She stops me.

"Jared, can I ask *you* something in confidence?"

I zip my lip.

"What was your mother like?"

I tell her, only what matters.

"She was sweet. And very kind. And I think she would have liked you."

Her eyes fill up, but the vice-president won't allow tears.

"Go take a shower, Jared."

She means to say *thank you*. I think, in the end, that's all any of us means to say.

***

Olivia is right on the money. After scrubbing and breathing in the hot steam, I am heady and heavy and finally drowsy. The warm milk coats my stomach and my belly gurgles with appreciation. When it's finished, I feel myself indulging a series of long blinks.

"It means a lot to us that you're here."

I blink.

"Go to sleep now. We have a big day tomorrow."

I blink and rise, moving on autopilot and shuffle back to my bedroom. There, I sleep for fourteen hours.

And I do not dream.

***

The morning of the wedding, my dad tosses me a letter across the kitchen table from the stack of mail in his hand.

"What's this?"

He shrugs and leaves the room.

"I don't know, but you better read it quick. We gotta get a move on."

I flip the envelope over and I know the handwriting at once. This letter is from Gayle.

Dear Jared,

I didn't know where to send this, I know you've moved a lot. But I knew your Dad would still be in Florida and he'd know how to find you. I'm writing to you because I had a dream about you. I know it sounds funny after all these years, but you were really there! It was a powerful connection and you've been on my mind ever since.

I want to tell you something you need to hear more than I need to say. I know how you hold onto things and I don't want you to hold onto me anymore. I've made peace with what happened and I forgive you. I know how you torture yourself and how you never really let go of hurting me. But I think, for both of us, that it's time. I release you.

I'm married now, and I'm pregnant with my third! Can you believe it? It's been a wild ride and honestly if I hadn't met you, I wouldn't be where I am now. Thank you for that and for a thousand other things I can't say without wanting to punch you a little bit. I hope this letter finds you well and being something incredible. I always knew you would. Say hello to Stuart for me and know that both of you are still in my prayers at night.

With love,
G.

I love you, Gayle.

Stuart is bellowing at me from the other end of the house.

"Let's suit up, kid. The bus is leaving in fifteen. Let's go go go."

I leave the letter on the table and get up to go put on my tuxedo, but what was said, I reverently carry with me.

***

In the car, fumbling with his cufflinks and the steering wheel, Stuart passes me two sheets of paper.

"I want you to take a look at that for me. Let me know if I need to change anything."

He nearly careens into a dusty VW convertible, driven by a little old lady in an oversized sunhat.

"Dad, the road."

He's trying to look at me and drive, pointing to the paper.

"Come on, I need you for this."

"Dad. Road," I command.

He snaps alert again and returns his eyes to the lanes ahead. He places his hands back at ten and two and I breathe a little easier. I look down at the sheets and see his handwriting, stroked in his small, precise script.

"What is this?"

"We wrote our own vows."

I look at the perfect care in his writing, the formative determination of the letters.

"What can you possibly want me to do with this?"

He passes me a sidelong look, half annoyed, half loving.

"You've always had a way with words, Jared. It would really be something if you could just take a look and tell me if I'm on the right track."

I am touched.

"Really?"

He nods.

"No one tells a story like you do, kiddo. No one," he says. "Hey, maybe you should be a writer."

In the weight of his nervous silence, I read. When I am finished, I point to the sheets.

"Do you mean everything you say here?"

He grips the wheel and nods.

"Then I wouldn't change a thing."

He hesitates.

"You really think so?"

I pass the papers carefully back to him.

"I'm sure of it."

He chuckles, and then he's laughing, banging on the steering wheel like a kid wailing on the drums.

"Well all right," he says. "Let's have some music."

He reaches down and starts fiddling with the radio and the car drifts.

"Dad," I snap. "Road. I got the radio."

The car corrects itself and I turn on the radio to find Norman Greenbaum riffing on a big guitar.

Prepare yourself, you know it's a must.

"Gotta have a friend in Jeeeezus," my dad belts.

His voice is horrible, but Stuart is a lion on the march, and I let him belt it out.

***

The wedding is intimate and moving. It is an honor for me to witness this. We weren't around for the courtship of our parents. Those first nervous glances. Those first moments of trust. Those first days when you miss them when they are gone. Instants when you realize the first person you need to call is them. We come into the world seeing something that has already taken place, an established union. As small children we simply assume that our parents have always been our parents and they've always been together. It never occurs to us that they are just like we are.

They face the same struggles, the same questions, the same decisions that we face. And like us, they reach out to find someone at their side to help them move through it. We are all looking for the same thing and we are grateful when it finds us. To see my father and Olivia experience that love, that connection, is a crowning triumph.

When they speak their vows, when they let love in, they are speaking only to each other. And yet the entire church resounds with their declaration.

***

Mira saves me from a rambling toast with decisive action.

"Give it to me."

I am already nervous, and I don't know what she means. She flaps her hand: *gimme.*

"The speech, let me have it."

I have no idea what she's up to until I hand it to her and she tears it violently in two pieces.

"Mira, what the f-"

"Gimme the backup."

"How did you-"

The hand again, urgent, undeniable. I give it to her and watch her rip it neatly apart. She wrinkles her nose, fixes my tie, and plants one on me.

"Now you're ready."

Forks clink on glasses and a hush falls over the banquet hall.

"Knock 'em dead, sugar."

I panic, but she only smiles at me. And in that knowing smile, something shifts inside me, and with a mix of adoration and sweet regret, I finally understand what that smile means. In the peaceful security of her gaze, I am no longer afraid. I feel my own gaze become calm like hers, and I know exactly what I am going to say.

***

"It is the great gravity of being that makes us human. Each of us, alone, must shoulder the burden of our hopes and our dreams and our responsibilities. If we are steadfast, and a little lucky, we meet someone out there who chooses us, out of all the leaves on the tree. This person will help us be excellent, even when we fear we cannot. They will harbor us during storms and shine a light for us into the darkness. If we are steadfast, and a little lucky, we will always try our hardest to show them the best of us. And of themselves.

"We are all here, suspended in an unknowable gyre of existence, moving forever forward into the unknown. We are the many, and yet we are all one. I cannot tell you what it means, or how it came to be, but I can tell you this, with perfect surety: be sweet. To yourselves. To each other. Open up your doors, and love will find its way in."

Mira rises from her chair. My father follows. Then they all stand, and I am almost finished.

***

I sit at the head table, nursing a Scotch, watching the others on the parquet dancefloor. The DJ is rocking some seventies boogie and the guests are living it up. Mira is dancing with my father and Olivia. Stuart is pointing to the sky and shaking his hips like John Travolta, having a time of it and I can't help but smile.

She's mighty mighty, just lettin' it all hang out.

I wonder if all this would have happened if I wasn't here. If it had been another time, after black suits and a funeral, would Stuart and Olivia still be foolishly losing themselves on the dancefloor, caught up in the gaiety of their wedding reception? Would their vows still be as touching and as heartfelt? Would he still be captivated by her, seeing her each time as if it was the first? There is no ego in these questions, and with great certainty, I know somehow that this would still happen, no matter what I did. Something tells me that love always finds a way. That life goes on, regardless of who is there to see it. The privilege, I am coming to understand, is that we *do* get to see it.

I am still deep in thought when the DJ changes to a slow song and Mira comes over to the table to collect me. I try to fight her, hating that I've never felt even slightly comfortable with dancing, but she won't take no for an answer. She takes my hand and leads me to the center of the floor. Surrounded by other couples, feeling them spinning around us, I feel the old hesitation rise and I stiffen. But she puts my arms around her waist and presses her body into mine and my hesitation subsides. She rests into me. And we dance.

I catch Stuart's eye as we sway and he winks at me. His tie is loosened and his cheeks are red from dancing. He is supremely content, carefully leading his wife in perfect, easy steps around the floor. Again I find myself wondering if all this would have happened without me. But Mira is looking up at me and her lips are full and inviting and the time for thought has passed. I kiss her and, for a song, we are the only people in the hall.

The song ends and the music changes to something fast. I instinctively start to pull away, but she holds me.

"Oh no," she says. "You're all mine."

"Mira, I-"

"Loosen up," she says, shaking her hips at me, grinning devilishly. "You know you want to."

Something in her eyes shows me I have nothing to fear and that the only thing stopping me from throwing myself into the music is some distant, dismal terror that has no power over who I've become. I grin back, feeling my feet start to move of their own accord. My hips catch the beat like a wave on the ocean and now my arms come up to match them. The last of the stiffness in my body breaks away and I feel a rush climb up my spine. I start laughing uncontrollably and let go, trusting the music to carry me. I close my eyes, throw my head back, and for the first time in perhaps my entire life, I am utterly and deliriously free.

Seven songs in and I'm unstoppable, ten songs in and I'm a superstar, the crowd forming a circle around me, clapping and cheering while I bust out moves I didn't even know I had. I'm giddy with the music, the feel of a body without reservation, letting the rhythm guide my movements, warm in the glow of Stuart's exuberance, Olivia's welcoming delight, and Mira's easy grin. We dance well into the night and I feel myself swell and grow, embodying a love that is, at last, large enough to contain all of me.

***

She finally finds me, rocking back and forth on a white, rickety lawn swing in the field behind the reception hall. I am smoking a cigarette, staring off into the busy night, listening to the DJ stir up the crowd. Clapping. Cheering.

Stuart's great laugh. Olivia's wicked cackle. A grand party to celebrate love.

"What are you doing out here all by yourself?" she asks.

"Hi," I say. "I just needed to get some air. Join me?"

The swing squeaks and groans. She looks at it, unsure. I rock it back and forth against its frame.

"Tougher than it looks. Hop up."

I extend a hand and help her up beside me. She plants her feet next to mine and we gently pump the swing. Squeak. Groan. She is wearing a sleeveless evening dress in a soft powder blue. I play with her hem, rubbing it between my fingers.

"You look like the sky."

She turns on me.

"I don't know how to take that. Is that a compliment? Are you saying I look huge in this dress? Do better."

"It's a compliment. And I can't do any better."

She eyes my cigarette, reaches for it, and takes a drag. She holds it, considers, and then takes another puff.

"Don't tell."

I zip my lip.

"Mum's the word."

She snuggles into me and the smell of her is all I want right now.

"I need to ask you something, Mira. But I'm afraid of the answer."

She leans her head back to look at me and her eyes are huge with blue adoring.

"You can ask me anything."

I sigh and I am terrifically tired.

"You're not really here, are you?"

She leans away and puts her hands on my knee. She watches me with great sadness and a look that has no words.

"No," she says at last. "It's just you. It's always been just you."

I try to speak, but my voice is choked by a withering sob. She holds me and we swing.

"His story has ended," she says. "But you needed to see what could have been. What you'd hoped for him."

The swing stops and I cling to her. With wonder, fear, and perhaps a touch of madness, I ask her the question that contains all of me.

"Why did he do it?"

She reaches for me and kisses my lips.

"He did it because he didn't believe."

I squeeze my fists together and I shake. When the words form, I fear I will scream them, but they only come out as a furious whisper.

"Believe *what*?"

She pulls me up and out of the swing and stands before me on solid ground. In the darkness, the space around her shoulders shimmers.

"That I chose him. That out of all the leaves on the tree, I picked him to *be*."

Her wings bloom, expand, and stretch out across the night. She kisses me and her lips are sweet.

"But I did. And I will do it over and over again until he sees. Until the last of the stars go out."

I linger on the threshold.

"Why?"

"Because I love him too."

She takes my hand and music grows louder.

"One more dance with me."

I play for more time. It is not a question.

"I don't think I have much left tonight."

I'm afraid.

"I think you have one more."

I've got you.

She squeezes my hand and now I see countless others, streaming across the field, drifting out across the meadow. One by one, they line up and press up against the windows, peering into the revelry inside. My mother is with them. There is the sound of wings. The music becomes clearer and I feel it start to move through me.

A moment. A love. A dream aloud.

She leads me towards the reception and the others part to let us pass. I hear Stuart's stalwart bellow from inside and I know everything is going to be okay. The doorway fills with light and I feel myself lift. And rise.

***

In another when, a shaking finger squeezes the tempered metal of a shotgun trigger. A catch releases and a bolt shoots forward. The hammer slams down, striking the firing pin and driving it forward with a definitive snap. In milliseconds, the firing pin travels a quarter of an inch and launches out of its sheath, punching into the primer at the center of the shotgun shell with perfect killing efficiency.

***

There is a trumpeting *BOOM!* And I am gone.